Figurehead

Figurehead
Short Stories

George Conklin

George S Conklin

Contents

Dedication

This book is dedicated to my family. They have been supportive of me taking the time away from them to play around. There are no words enough to express my love for all of them.

I especially want to dedicate this to my granddaughter, Meghan, who supplied the artwork for the cover. What a talent!

Cover artwork by Meghan Reeves, 2021

Figurehead

The bow went down into the raging sea, and I was submerged in it. If I could have blinked or gagged, I would have, but I'm made from wood and can't. Here we go again, up and down and up and down. This used to scare me, but now, I live with it. Every day, hundreds of times a day.

I wasn't always this way...

I once was Alicia Arias—well, I guess I still am somehow—and I was a reporter in our city's major newspaper. Because I had a reputation for aggressive reporting and not taking any B.S., my editor assigned me to do an investigative piece on a group of people called the Razers, who'd been growing in popularity, a cult seemingly.

Led by a charismatic former preacher named Luis Cuvier, the Razers had attracted many people, especially the young and many professionals. They believed Cuvier had connected with ancient spirits that offered enormous power and safety from the growing insecurities of our world. The Razers said they believed in taking an aggressive stance against prejudice, racism, anti-feminism and supporting an array of other supposedly progressive goals. As a result, they'd attracted the very liberal to their organization.

Something was just not right about Cuvier, though.

He came across on TV like an old-time snake oil salesman. He had a slicked-down appearance that gave me the creeps. So, I jumped at doing the story. After doing some deep research on Cuvier and the cult, one of the first things I did was to reach out to the Razer PR office. They were charming and open to me interviewing Cuvier if they could review what I had written before going to press. I told them I'd be happy to allow them a look at it but would not permit any changes to my writing. They said they were okay with that. That should have been a red flag, the first of many it turned out that I was oblivious to in my eagerness to get a story that might get me national recognition.

So, I met with Cuvier at the Razer offices, a place they called the Bastion. I thought that was an odd choice for a name; it should have been another red flag. I asked Cuvier about it when we met.

He smiled graciously. "Look around this world, Ms. Arias. See all kinds of shootings every day. We killed hundreds. Robberies, corporate corruption, xenophobia, slavery, the humiliation of women, debasement of our environment. More violence here than anywhere else in the world outside of those countries at active war with someone or themselves or us. It's like we're under siege. So, we think Bastion is a noble name. Because we stand against all of this. The powers that I've connected with have told me they see us imploding and want my help in stopping that," said Cuvier.

The Messianic and egotistical gleam in his eyes was blinding, intense, and unsettling. All I heard, though was, yet another loud voice adding to the dissonance in our society. Rather than a message of working together, this was another one of those "My way or the highway" messages. Just what we didn't need. I confronted him about that. He shrugged and said there were a lot of voices, but only his was the voice everyone should listen to. Screwball, I thought.

Beyond this, though, he was not awfully specific. When I pressed him on his ancient powers connections, he wouldn't talk about them unless I agreed to join them, which I told him I could not and remain a reporter in good conscience anyway. He smiled and wished me well.

My story was straight and factual and caused a firestorm in town and nationally—he had a lot of heavy-duty backing around the country. Cuvier's supporters called me a hatchet woman, and his detractors latched on to some things I'd said and used them to confirm their own, usually extreme, biases. Cuvier himself called to say that his PR people had told him that he'd be disappointed in the story, and he was when he read it. I told him I wrote what I thought based on what I saw and what he had told me contained too many gaps, which made what he talked about sound like some New Age gobbledygook. Nothing seemed to hang together. He said, again, that it disappointed him as I had appeared to be open-minded and not one of the Destroyers as he called his opponents. I had the creeps with him before and now got them even worse. He invited me back for a "deeper dive" as he put it at one of their roundtables. Looking back on that now, I see the double entendre of those words, "deeper dive." He invited me to attend a Razer worldwide leadership roundtable that weekend being held at the Bastion. He said to pack a bag because I wouldn't be able to leave until Monday morning once I got there. That should have been another red flag.

With my bag packed, I waited outside my apartment building for the car that Cuvier said he'd send for me. I told him he didn't need to do that, but he insisted, saying that parking at the Bastion would be at a premium. I should've been thinking more; the red flags were piling up. Everything he was doing was separating me from my friends and the world that I knew. The car was an older but very well-maintained Lincoln. The driver was a charming young woman. She said her name was Tina.

When we arrived at the Bastion, she told me to go in and that she'd bring in my bags. I tried to get her to let me carry them, but she was stubborn. She also told me that phones and other recording devices were not allowed in the meeting areas, so she asked me to give her any I might have. I was taught, "have pad and pencil will travel" at an old school journalism program, so this was just a minor inconvenience.

Cuvier's head of PR met me; she smiled sweetly and took me in to see him. He'd just finished a meeting and seemed a little out of sorts. I asked if he needed time to relax before seeing me. "No, I'm fine. Thanks for thinking of me, though. I enjoyed our last conversation, even though it looks like I left you with a lot of terrible impressions. I think we'll set them straight this weekend. Can I offer you a drink? By the way, we're not teetotalers." He walked over to a credenza in the office, pushed a button, and raised the top, and a small bar appeared.

"Do you have a Diet Coke?" I asked.

"Sure." He put ice in two glasses and opened a can of Diet Coke and put it in one and put two fingers of a nice Scotch in the other. He handed the Diet Coke to me.

"Last chance. Want to change your mind?" he asked with a smile.

"I'll stick with the soda, Sir. Maybe later," I said.

"The Razers," he said, "Came together based on work done in the latter part of the 20th century by some scientists working together on the Large Hadron Collider near Geneva, Switzerland. As they worked on the exceedingly small particles they were studying, the scientists saw that something else was going on with them to cause the kinds of movements they were seeing. What they saw was that sometimes these things were there, and then they were not. Pop!" and he gave a popping gesture with his hands. "Just like that, they would disappear. And then they'd reappear somewhere else. They based their original observations on Quantum Mechanics, and they made sense until they didn't because the scientists found something else."

"Now, I'm not an expert in that discipline by any stretch of the imagination, so a lot of what they were working on was what you called in your article 'gobbledygook' to me," he said with a droll smile.

I flushed a little with embarrassment.

"At that time, and you mention this in your article, I was a mega-church pastor in Arizona but frankly had begun to have second thoughts about where we were headed. I'm responsible for that, I know, but I felt at the time that the direction in which we were going would not end well. So, I left the church. You know what happened about five years after I did. A stand-off with the ATF and the FBI culminated in a conflagration for the people who stayed on. I have to live with that."

"Another drink?" he asked.

I was feeling a little thirsty, so I said yes.

"Could I talk you into something a little stronger?" he asked again.

I said yes, and he brought out a fresh glass and put some ice into it. "This is from the Island of Islay. It's called Lagavulin. I love it. Warms me right to the cockles of my heart."

"Anyway," he said, "I had gone into semi-retirement, a retreat, trying to figure out where I went wrong in Arizona and if there was anything else for me to do. I had moved to Albuquerque, New Mexico, to get out of the Arizona limelight, especially after the bloodbath.... Down the street from me were two scientists who worked at Sandia National Laboratories. They were engaged in the Collider work and talked to me some about it. During one dinner conversation, I mentioned how there might be a greater spirit at work. They laughed at me. I was used to that, so I wasn't bothered."

"One day, though," Cuvier continued, "one of the scientists said that there might be some truth in what I'd said, though maybe not what I'd thought. He talked to me about quantum physics and how particles can have multiple, simultaneous existences in different states, like as both energy and a physical particle."

"They'd apparently been looking at these really tiny Hadron Collider particles and found they could see those multiple planes. Believed, though, that they had seen something else and wanted me to look with him. I asked him why and he said that I wasn't a scientist and didn't have their biases. So, an innocent, at least of all of that."

"I did and was astounded at what I saw. I called what I saw 'the Ancients' because they had to have been around forever, well, at least from the start of time. They aren't beings like we know, you and me, but composed of non-corporeal energy."

I sat back with, I'm sure, a look of disbelief on my face. "Mr. Cuvier...."

"Call me Luis," he said.

I shouldn't have, but "Luis, this sounds crazy. I'm sorry. I can't believe any of this."

"I knew you'd said that," he said with a small smile. "Come with me."

We walked out of a back door to his office and to an elevator. We went down many floors below ground level. I got a little nervous, though the Lagavulin warmed me to the cockles of my heart as well. Maybe it was the alcohol, but I missed, totally, the cascade of red flags that had fallen around me. In a reassessment of the events, I also reasoned that it was by then likely too late for me. I cast my die the second the door to his office shut.

"When I saw these beings, I decided we needed to explore them more. My scientist friends thought so too. Working with some others with bottomless pockets, we built what you're going to see here in a few minutes. It's all for one purpose: to house one of the Ancients we contained in the Collider. When you see him, you'll see why we think like we do."

"Still sounds crazy to me, Luis."

"By the end of the night, you'll feel differently. We'll transform you; I know it," he said. His self-assurance at my upcoming transformation was overpowering.

We stepped out of the elevator, and we walked down a featureless hall into a dressing room. "Now, rightfully, I shouldn't be showing you this given that you're an uninitiated, but I think you need to see this so you can better appreciate and defend us." Defend them; what did he think I was going to do? "Put on one of these robes. Silly, maybe, but a part of our ritual." He picked one off a rack, held it up to me, shook his head no, and then grabbed another one for me. I slipped it on over my clothes, and we walked out of the room into a much larger space.

"So, how did you come up with the name Razer, Luis? I know it as a gaming company based in the Far East but could find nothing else on it in my research," I asked.

Figurehead

He smiled. "I'm a gamer myself and have liked what the Razer folks developed. I'd even named my dog Razer, so why not this religion? Pretty dumb, huh?"

I smiled back at him. "I'd say so, but I kind of like it." Also, said a lot about his ego. I was now a little scared about being many floors underground with him and no one else around.

"What do you know about figureheads in the maritime world, Alicia?" he asked, abruptly changing the direction of the conversation.

My head was spinning with this turn in the conversation, I thought. "Not much, Luis. I know they were popular in the 1800s on the bows of ships, but nothing else."

"Well, you're right. Emblems that were welded to the side of big metal ships replaced them in the last century. They signified special things to mariners. Initially, they were thought to protect ships, and the figurehead would lead sailors to heaven should they ever sink. Later, they became symbolic of important events or locations. For instance, the British made over forty of them for each of the counties in the country. They welded them to the sides of their big metal ships. Figureheads were popular when there were wooden ships. Not so much now, but they're coming back a little. See, we have a bunch of them around the room here. I've collected them from all around the world."

I looked around at the room walls and saw many hanging there—all different shapes and styles. Again, I thought about the weirdness of this man and got more apprehensive. He led me toward the center of the room, where there were two things I could see next to each other. First, a large glass tank filled with what looked like swirling smoke, and second, a figurehead of a woman sitting on a pedestal. "This is Bertha Marion Coghill. She was the figurehead on her ship at one time. She was the owner's daughter, and he named the ship a year after she was born. So, this full-grown woman is who-knows-who. Probably someone like you," said Cuvier.

"Huh?" I asked.

"Her daddy's lover. A whore," he responded. His smile had turned into something nasty.

Two men appeared out of nowhere and grabbed me. I was feeling a little woozy anyway, I thought from the Scotch. Their support felt good. "What's happening, Luis? I thought we were getting on."

"Well, we are, Alicia. We're getting on very well. Are you feeling a little weak?"

"Yes, a little."

"Good. I put a little something in your glass to relax you for what's coming up," Cuvier said.

"I'm sorry, Alicia, but my leadership and I have talked this through carefully and agree that it would be good for us to have a devotee in the media outside of the Bastion. We were talking about that before you came in. That's why I looked out of sorts to you. I didn't want to do this to you but see the rationale for it. Hence, I'm going to introduce you to our Ancient, and we're going to use his good offices to transform you into our media devotee. I wish this could have ended in another way. I liked you," he said with what looked like a sad smile.

He pointed over at the tank. A shape had resolved itself in the clouds there. It was giant, not human or even humanoid. It seemed to shift between body types, first vaguely human, then down on all fours, then floating on wings, then swimming like a fish or a lizard. I felt sick watching it make these shifts. "Good, good, Alicia. Keep watching the Ancient. Hypnotizing, isn't he?" Cuvier said. The men brought me over to the side of the tank, and I reached my hand up to the side of it. Sparks flew from the interior of the tank toward my hand.

"Like one of those plasma globe things," I said. As I withdrew my hand, a large spark erupted from the tank to my hand, and I stepped back, and the men pushed me into the figurehead. When I came to, I couldn't move. My hands, eyes, mouth, arms, legs all felt like they were paralyzed. Cuvier stepped in front of me.

"There you are. Remember, before I said we'd transform you tonight?" he asked.

I tried to talk but couldn't. He smiled and held up a mirror. All I could see was Bertha Marion Coghill. "Yes, that's you, Alicia. The Ancient transferred your consciousness into the figurehead, and that is where you will live from now on. Forever, basically," He rotated me, and I saw myself standing next to the tank, gently caressing the glass. Sparks followed my fingertips as I did. I, the being, turned and looked at Bertha and smiled. In place of my green eyes were now black voids that spark as the Ancient had in the tank.

I was removed from the room and secured to the bow of a tall ship used for training midshipmen. Here I'm fixed and will permanently be fixed, I guess. I'm still human, I think. It drives me mad I can't speak or do anything like I used to do. But the Ancient keeps me right on the edge of sanity....

The bow went down into the raging sea, and I was submerged in it. If I could have blinked my eyes or gagged, I would have, but I'm made from wood and can't. Here we go again, up and down and up and down.

The End

{ **2** }

Miel

Here I am, sitting at the mouth of my cave with my mate, Joe, and our best friends. I've been around here long as I've lived. It's Year 19 for me, now, in the forest, we call the Zone. I wouldn't be anywhere else. I'm a creature of this place. Mom, Emmeline, and Dad, Aard, used to worry about me when I was alone here, but the truth is, I've never really been alone. I've got the forest, my friends, the surrogates, and the knowledge I carry in my head.

Before I came around, it was mom and dad. Then they added me and, after that, Joe's family. And I added Jak and all his friends. I don't mean to make it sound like mom, dad, and others are dead 'cause they're not. They're just away. For a few years, they've been away on a "long walk," as my dad called it. It would be nice if they came back sometime soon, but we're okay here on our own 'til they do.

I'm here now because I'm too much like my dad. I'll tell you more about that, but basically, it's because I'm my own person: Independent, a loner, rebellious, and tough. I'm no one's little girl. Right from the beginning, mom and dad told me I was fierce in my independence. That independence has got me into a lot of trouble. So, I'm here now because of that and to learn about consequences. Well, I have to say that I'm not learning much. This has been a good few years out here with my best buddies. We're doing very well.

My dad and mom used to tell me stories. Dad called them Miel stories for what their land used to be called. Now we call it nothing, just home.

When I was very young, dad would sit with me in the woods, on the riverside, or here at the cave and tell me his stories about growing up. He said that was partly to teach me about those days and the mistakes people made and somewhat to get me to know him and mom better.

I liked his stories as they gave me a look into another world and let me learn why we are here, and we are the way we are.

Miel Stories

Mom and dad lived in a land called Miel. They'd always lived there and thought they always would. Their country wasn't large, but everything they needed was always there. Food and drink were available everywhere. Mielians, and what we call surrogates they had built to help with that, cared for each other in the society they'd made. When mom and dad were kids, many surrogates cared for them. At birth, they got their surrogates; they've been with them their whole lives. I've got dad's now. It's part parent, part teacher, and part disciplinarian. Well, a major part disciplinarian.

Miel was what's called a utopia when it started out. I'm not sure what that meant, but it was supposedly something good. Dad told me that people were happy, they worked together, and everyone had all that they needed—at the beginning, anyway. Community, food, work, many friends, and the things they needed to survive, like homes, clothing, furniture, and stuff like that. Because they lived in community, they didn't have envy, greed, pride, jealousy, all things that came from a world where people lived apart and could look out their windows and see "what other people had" and then lust after it. Again, at least in the beginning, anyway.

A surrogate was a substitute, in our cases a substitute parent and eventually a life assistant. They specially trained the first ones, humans who had decided not to have children of their own or couldn't. There weren't enough of them to go around, so some smart Mielians built self-regulating ones.

The first of these automated surrogates were highly primitive, as the scientists didn't have the technology to do anything more sophisticated. They weren't much better than listeners and speakers that sat by cribs or in play areas. Over time, though, Miel scientists learned how to make the surrogates more intelligent and more independent. They gave them legs, arms, heads, the best of brains, and the responsibility of caring for us all. They made the surrogates wiser and wiser.

The first surrogates were, again, stupid compared to what we have now. As old ones aged, Mielians recycled them. After some time passed, the surrogates "decided" to think through their existence and development and created a path so they didn't need to be recycled and could just be, what they called, upgraded. A new model might come out now and then, but, mostly, existing models—that looked a lot like us—were all we needed with periodic upgrades of what dad called their software. When an upgrade was available, it was downloaded directly to the surrogates, usually late at night, most of the time. We also had these things called "firmware" upgrades that would require surrogates to go back to the plant to have that update made. That didn't happen too often.

Surrogates operated within a large network that connected them and all of us eventually to the outside world. This network was critical because it allowed individual surrogates to learn from many people's experiences and other surrogates. Ultimately, the surrogates designed into each surrogate the ability autonomously to generate and join networks. This became very important for us here in the Zone.

I was something new for Miel: I knew my mom and dad. Aard and Emmeline never knew who their mothers or fathers were. The rule back then was children came to be in the usual way but were raised in a communal facility, called a kindergarden, from birth, and were organized into what they called "cohorts" by age with other kids.

You stayed with your cohort through your junior years and then afterward when they trained you for work. Dad was behind his cohort because he'd been what they called "Isolated" in a place called the Zone where we live now. You got sent there when you didn't fit in. Dad was a rebel—and we're happy that he was. So, when he was a little over three years, he was Isolated in the Zone with his surrogate, which he eventually named Vark. So, Aard Vark. A funny man, Vark, told me and showed me a picture of an aardvark. From the beginning, dad was something of an outlier, being five years older than the cohort he eventually joined.

Dad struggled with being Isolated and dearly missed his friends when he was. So, he suppressed his rebelliousness, in the end, and conformed. He made that decision when he was about 7.99 years old, almost five years after being Isolated. Dad's surrogate knew he'd had no epiphany or changed himself, but it also wanted to get out of Isolation. He said nothing negative when quizzed about dad's readiness to join a cohort and return to Miel society. So, dad reintegrated into the same cohort as mom, who was about five years younger than him. "Divine Intervention," he called it later. We all agree about that.

Mom didn't have the same rebelliousness problems but says that she wouldn't have survived what came if she hadn't paired with dad. Having been imprisoned in the Isolation Zone for five years until the community felt he was ready to rejoin gave him the tools to live in the wild. I was lucky also, as he taught me everything that I know.

All Mielians were trained for a job of some kind. Matching a person to a job was not complex. You tried everything and landed where you showed some aptitude. Dad didn't like the sit-down jobs that required talking, working with others, and much mental activity. He was an action sort of guy. So was mom. They fell in love with the police. (I was always tempted to ask if things were so great, why did Miel need cops? I never did, though.)

Over time, they found they enjoyed walking a beat together, Emmeline and Aard, and talking with people they met. They'd get asked questions they'd answer or try to, anyway. Crime was rare, so they never used their clubs or guns, but they always carried them. Dad and mom were so good with the kids that their bosses asked them to go back to kindergarden and talk to the older kids there about the job. They also helped with the training of trainees when they were coming in for their cohort rotations.

Mom-to-be reached her 18th summer when dad-to-be was in his 23rd; she was passed into adulthood by the community and became a full-time police officer and paired with dad. They agreed to mate about a year after becoming beat officers, even though Emmeline was younger than dad. It pleased his sergeant they'd decided to do that, and he put in the request for the relationship to consummate and for them to get a home together. Miel didn't have the same concerns about "robbing the cradle" that some societies did. When you were ready, you just moved on to whatever was to come next. This encouraged people to be flexible.

When they received their appointments as police officers, mom and dad's surrogates were upgraded to newer, law-support models. That gave them added capabilities: advanced access to the law and legislative databases; more advanced first aid knowledge even up to birthing a child; and, as it turned out advantageously for us, advanced weaponry and offensive and defensive capabilities, even though we rarely used them on Mielians—initially in any case.

Turns out the most activity police saw was with visitors who acted out when they were in town. Some young guys would come to town from outside of Miel from farmlands that were part of a bordering country. They would be looking for fun that they couldn't find in their cities. The beat officers had to make sure that these people didn't cause problems and, when they did, saw that we escorted them out of town.

Those were their golden years. Mom and dad were happy and healthy. They came to work every day energized with whatever they had to do and left it each night, exhausted but ready to take on and learn more the next day. They planned to have children but decided to wait a bit on that to become established. Dad also wanted to make sure that mom was ready for that as her getting pregnant would put a crimp into her work.

Nothing separated Mielians; at first, anyway.

Dad said when he looked back on those days, he should've seen what was coming: Should've seen that visitors would infect Miel with their ideas and eventually cause our downfall. Of course, he also says, hindsight is 20:20, whatever the hell that means. He has all these cute little phrases he uses.

The viruses brought in from the outside by people who saw Mielians as stupid and boring took hold. Dad said his best friend said that someone found wishing; another said that someone started matching up. Envy crept in. The government tried to fix this but only made things worse as they stumbled around trying to fix human behavior.

One day Mielians were all the same as they always had been, and the next day someone started hoarding things, seeds, and plants for growing and corn and wheat for making flour and bread. The hoarders began building walls around their homes and turning on their surrogates' defensive measures when someone bartered the knowledge to do that to protect their hoards. Hoarders became increasingly nervous about protecting what they were hoarding; some allied in what they called "neighborhood preservation groups" to ensure that "others" wouldn't take what they were hoarding. To protect their properties, some would attack and absorb bordering hoarders to increase their land and gain new resources, like weapons, food, and even people.

As police officers, mom and dad saw increasing instances of hoarding of the strangest things. Forget food; you could even understand that. But they found one guy hoarding ribbons. He said he did it because he wanted to ensure that he always had enough for his kites' tails. He also built an electrified fence around his property. His house was one of the last to fall because no one cared about his ribbons other than him. But his electric fence turned out to be another thing. Others ended up wanting it and so killed him and took it.

Hoarding spread to the fields and farms as the hoarders moved closer to the sources of food. So, there were your fields and my fields. The environment suffered because they weren't working communally, and everyone was trying to extract as much as they could from the land. One example: Rather than plowing the plants back into the ground for fertilizer for the next generations, people began burning the fields to clear them so that they could plant right away. Soon, what they had thought might happen happened. Our food sources began drying up, and the hoarders felt vindicated for the path that they'd taken. Dad said, "Oh, how fragile we were."

The surrogates tried to step in, but hoarders fought against them and eventually destroyed many of them. Because mom and dad were police officers, Vark and my mom's surrogate, Godolphin (named for an old fairy tale she loved), were spared. As officer surrogates, their advanced capabilities made them more difficult to attack, and they could respond independently when attacked. They called it adaptive defense measures; a feature other surrogates did not have turned on.

My dad said that once the whirlpool started swirling, it didn't stop, and all Miel went down with it. So sad. Mom and dad lost many friends in the collapse. Mom's and dad's police officer groups got whittled down through killings, desertion, and resignations. Officers found it wiser to ally with one or another of the hoarders rather than to stick with their jobs. Two of dad's best friends had quite different ends. Jim and his partner, Elaine, had just decided to become mates. Cary, and his mate Louise, had been coupled for as long as my mom and dad. Jim was very concerned about what he saw, and he wanted to make sure that Elaine was protected. Cary and Louise, like mom and dad, stuck with their mission. One day, when they were out on patrol, they saw Jim up ahead and hailed him.

Jim turned and smiled at them, giving them a hearty hello, according to my dad. He walked toward them. Cary's and Louise's surrogates gave them a warning, but it was too late. When Jim reached them, he pulled out his service weapon and shot them both, dead. The hoarders he and Elaine had enlisted with shot an E.M.P. grenade into the air, and the two surrogates collapsed to the ground, knocked out. According to Vark, one of them awoke when he was being dismembered and executed a destruct protocol. The explosion killed Jim, Elaine, and their hoarder friends.

The decision to move came right after those friends of dad died. Mom and dad moved out of the city to a cave in the Isolation Zone as Miel collapsed. They'd already packed a little, expecting that they might have to move out quick at some point, but now they rapidly loaded their weapons, ammunition, food supplies, some tools, and clothing. They moved it out to the Zone over a month, quietly at night.

When they'd gotten out all of the stuff they thought they'd need, dad, set their old house on fire when he was on patrol. He then acted insane with grief over mom's death in the fire and wandered off into the Zone to "die" on his own. Thankfully, no one came out to check on him. In part, that was because they thought dad was armed and crazy and didn't want to be anywhere near him, and in part, all thought that there was only danger in the Zone. Not having been raised there as dad had been and more accustomed to the programmed existence of old Miel, city dwellers thought they could never survive the Zone.

In the Zone

Mom and dad stayed out here in the Zone, living off the land, with the help of the surrogates. The first months were tough, but then they developed a "rhythm" for living outdoors. They got up early, made something to eat, then went out foraging, all the time keeping their eyes open for anyone—or anything—else. Late in the day, they'd return to the cave and prepare their nighttime meal. They ate it, watching the glow of fires from Miel below them. Sometimes they saw larger fires, as it looked like one or another band of hoarders had attacked or been attacked. After that, they returned to the cave, shut the door, and made love. After about five years in the Zone, that's where they made me.

The ending of society hurt mom, but the act of creating a new life and all of that entailed gave her strength. She worked with Godolphin to be prepared to be the best mom. And that she was. The two of them built all kinds of furniture and toys and created clothing out of scraps of cloth, bits of animal fur and reeds, and other things they found while foraging. Godolphin was a great help because she had all of the kindergarden databases she could look at, and she used to teach mom to be a mom. The first in Miel in a very long time.

Mom also prepared and dried tremendous amounts of food that Vark taught her to make for me to eat once I was able. Mom adapted her clothes so she could breastfeed me easily when we were out in the woods. Just like the original pioneers did, said mom once. She and the surrogates also made a backpack so that either mom or dad could carry me when we were out. We still have some of the stuff they made for me. Dad said, you never knew when it might be of use again. He usually looked at mom and smiled when he said something like that. She usually just shook her head. And turned bright red.

Miel was flawed, dad had come to believe, always he thought. Vark says that he may have been right to be rebellious. After the fall of Miel, they sat and watched the fighting going on from the hilltop above the cave. They knew they were the lucky ones and kept to themselves mostly. Vark and dad foraged. Mom and Godolphin stayed at the cave while she created me.

Dad enjoyed being out in the Zone, foraging. There's much to eat if you know where to look. It isn't that hard to survive if you're smart and focus on what you need. Truth be told, though, if dad and mom hadn't had Vark and Godolphin, we probably would have starved to death in those first years. When dad went into Isolation, while they had widespread access to networks and corporate intelligence, Vark had downloaded all the information on survival he could. And it was still there inside his head. Plus, remember that dad was only three when he went in and eight when he returned home. So, the surrogates were critical for our survival in those early years.

Figurehead

Miel had a temperate climate, thankfully. But, even with that, temperate meant that mom and dad had to survive through cold times and hot ones. The cave was not the place to be in the summer's heat but the only place to be in the winter. They slept outside the cave during the summer, even though they had to watch out for wild animals, some of which were dangerous. For the winter when I was born, their sixth in the cave, dad had been collecting wood and building a new doorway to the cave so they wouldn't lose as much heat as they did in those early winters. Plus, he knew that he needed to make our home as safe as possible, given that not all animals in the Zone were friendly, especially the Zone wolves. Big brutes that skulked through the woods. They mainly kept away from us, except when they were having trouble getting food. Dad was no-nonsense with them, killing a few of them; that seemed to give them a message and they stayed away from us.

When they retreated to the Zone, mom and dad made sure that they took their service weapons and an ample supply of ammunition. Dad knew that for them to survive, maybe for years or forever, all the ammunition in the world wouldn't be enough if they weren't conservative. So, they hid their weapons and ammunition in a nook in the cave, and they made and used bows and arrows they assembled for hunting and day-to-day survival. Dad eventually taught me to make bows and arrows, and I make them today for all of my friends.

Dad told me a story about a time when, with Vark's and Godolphin's help, they snuck back into Miel and took some old arms and ammunition and several long knives, axes, and a few other things they'd find helpful in the woods. Good news was that the surrogates could light fires, so they wouldn't have to monkey around with flint and steel or a fireboard and a spindle.

Mom was maybe four months pregnant with me at the time they made this foray into town. She hid up at ground level with Godolphin to keep watch while Vark and dad worked their way into the basement of their old, burned-out police station to see what they could find. From up the street, mom heard a noise and saw several men working their way down it toward their hiding place in their old station. One of them carried what looked like an RPG. About a block away from them, he hefted the weapon to his shoulder and fired it. There was an explosion overhead, and Emmeline heard Godolphin say, "An E.M..." and then go silent. She looked over her shoulder at the surrogate and saw that the E.M.P. had crumpled it to the ground. Mom called out to dad and Vark, but they never heard her.

Mom was so focused on the men down the street, and her ears were still ringing from the E.M.P. explosion, she didn't hear the other men behind her until a voice spoke, "Well, well, if it isn't, Officer Emmeline. I thought you were supposed to be dead."

Figurehead

When dad and Vark got back up to the surface, mom was kneeling in the street. Godolphin was lying next to her, and several men surrounded them.

"Hello, Officer Aard. It's been a long time," said a bearded man in the group's front. He held onto mom's long, red hair and pulled her head up as he talked. "Emmeline looks good. Knocked up, huh? Congratulations to you both.... Look, we don't want to hurt either of you unless you make us. If you come out here right now and leave us everything you found and your surrogates, you can go back to whatever hole you're hiding in."

Dad lifted the automatic weapon they'd found in a vault and pointed it at the man. He hadn't loaded it, but what did they know? "Well, I'm not happy to see any of you, Blunt. I've another proposal. You let Emmeline go. We'll pick up her surrogate and leave, and I'll let you all live. You'll not get a better deal than that." He racked a shell into the gun.

The show of force had its desired effect as several of Blunt's group began edging away. Blunt looked around and saw that he'd lost the advantage. "You won't risk her getting hit," he said.

"Right," dad said, "But the only one I have to shoot that you should care about is you. Trust me; you'll be the very first to go."

He smiled at dad. Let mom's hair go, and put his hands in the air. "You sure you wouldn't want to come back with us? We could use people like you," he said.

"Nope. We're safe out in the Zone, Blunt. I'd say come visit, but if I see any of you out there, I'll shoot you dead. Get out of here."

They did, but dad wasn't naïve enough to believe that would be the last they'd see of him or his men.

And he was right. He loves to tell this story, even acting out the parts he remembers of the people using different voices:

"A week later, we were sitting on top of the hill, your mom and me, watching the old city when we saw two parties of men leave it and head into the Zone. I asked your mom if she was up for a 'hide and seek' game with the men. Sure, she said, and we left the cave to lead them around in the forest down and to the river. The men were unaccustomed to being in the woods, and so as time wore on, you could see them getting more and more frustrated and scared. They were freaking out as the sun set, and they thought that they might have to spend the night in the woods," said dad.

"We set a trap for Blunt and his people. The river was about as far as you could get from our cave and still be in the Zone. What we liked most about it was that it was deceptive: What you thought was the shoreline wasn't, and so you ran down to what you're thinking is still dry land and plunk, you find yourself underwater quick. Swimming wasn't a big thing for Mielians; once in the water, most of these guys would be in big trouble. Mom and me knew of a little sandbar that cut the river right opposite the false beach, and we made a trail a blind man could follow and set up a little camp on the sandbar to wait for Blunt and his buddies," said dad.

"It didn't take long for them to show up," he continued. "The two parties converged on the campsite, and mom and I stood up to meet them."

"As Blunt came out of the woods, he said, 'So you thought you wouldn't see us again, huh?'"

Dad told him he wasn't surprised. He said that he knew Blunt couldn't resist coming after us but that he should remember that he was now on their turf and what he had said to him in town. "Remember that I warned you." Mom and dad hefted their rifles.

"What do you plan to do? Looks like you've backed yourselves against a wall. You're the ones that's in trouble," said Blunt, grinning like he was the cat about to eat the canary. Another saying of dad's.

Smiling, dad said, "Not exactly, Blunt. We've been out here so long we taught ourselves to swim. So, all we need to do is to jump into the water like this and float away. Just leave you guys standing there." That was it for Blunt and was the provocation that mom and dad hoped it would be.

Blunt'd promised his friends that they'd have fun with mom and dad and for us to float away was not in his dreamed of end games. He rallied his boys and then charged right into the water. A couple of them never got to the fake beach, being slower than their compadres. When they saw what was happening, they ran off.

The others floundered around in the water, and one or two went under and then didn't come up. That was when mom and dad rescued them. Dad jumped in, rescued Blunt and a few of his men; mom jumped in and rescued a couple more. The surrogates saved the guys that had almost drowned and a few more: no fatalities, but a lot of water spit-up.

Blunt and his buddies left us alone after that. Partly because they were glad to be alive and partly because they were ashamed. If they'd ever come back, they thought, mom and dad might not be as generous and rescue them. Maybe they were wrong; more likely, they were right.

Mom and dad decided not to push their luck, though, so they moved further into the Zone.

Dad told me they'd found a better cave several miles away and higher in the hills, with a beautiful view of the city and only one path up to it they could easily protect. That's where we live now and where I'm sitting.

Vark and Godolphin had been experimenting with their regenerative abilities and were now turning out smaller surrogate-like machines. Some of these machines flew, and a bunch didn't. The ones that flew looked like bats, but they flew day and night. The others were smaller, and the surrogates let them out on the trails in the forest so we could get early warning of anyone approaching. They were kind of cute. Squirrels, groundhogs, muskrats, and a few newts. Maybe twenty or so of them.

After I was born, mom and dad told me I had thought these machines were cute too. A few of them were always around the cave and kept me busy and laughing. One of my best friends turned out to be one groundhog.

I was named Arwen because I was honestly a noble maiden—and would always be for them, as far as mom and dad were concerned. I'd also be the only Mielian baby, up to that point, to know her parents and to grow up in an actual family. I had hair that, as I grew, became thick and the same auburn color as my mom's—a bunch of firsts.

Our first winter in the new cave was rough. Between mom being unable to help with a lot of the provisioning, the new cave being a lot larger than the last one, and we couldn't move a lot of what we'd collected for the coming winter except the food, almost all the work fell to dad and the surrogates. They, of course, were unflagging, working day and night to make sure that we had enough wood for fires while dad worked to make the cave livable. The first thing they did was build a large doorway that we could close to keep the heat in. Once they finished it, dad and the surrogates moved it out of the way so they wouldn't wreck it by carrying in our belongings, wood, and the food we needed for survival.

Vark and Godolphin adapted a few of the little bots they built to help cut wood for construction and firewood. That helped a lot to make sure that we didn't freeze once the winter weather came. And the winter came, earlier than usual, unfortunately, and with a vengeance, dad told me.

Snow came by the end of 10 Month, which was not usual for us. It was usually 11 Month or 12 before the snow came. Not this year—our bad luck. Not a small amount either—more bad luck. Dad was reluctant to leave the cave because mom was almost due with me, and he didn't want to leave tracks that someone or something could follow to us. Not that dad didn't trust Blunt, but.... So, he stayed at or near the cave.

Many a night, dad spent just outside of the cave looking at the night skies. Where we are, they're glorious. With no lights now from the nearly dark city, or anywhere for that matter, all you could see were black skies, some clouds, and millions of stars. Vark sat with dad many nights and taught him about the constellations and how you could use them for wayfinding. He learned a lot. Vark also told dad a lot about the larger world that he had learned from the databases he could access. Vark could read news feeds from outside of Miel as most of his brother and sister surrogates could; they'd hacked those networks years ago. That was how we knew that our problems had spread from Miel to the other kingdoms around us. Dad and Vark passed all of this on to me years later as I traveled more widely in the Zone and encountered people from the surrounding nations.

While Miel was a failed land, the rest of the world was little better than us. The pictures Vark drew showed how people treated each other and how they survived were gruesome. Women, he told dad, were treated like property. They trained male children from birth to treat their female family members and female friends as slaves. Men and boys, he called it, felt entitled to their favored positions and positions in their societies. Dad wondered what its appeal to those audiences was. He could think of none, except that it was natural for men to do this.

Mom was the most important thing in dad's life, and I was the second right after her, almost a tie. Dad couldn't see how he would treat us as anything other than that. We felt the same way about him. We were partners in survival.

As he was sitting at the mouth of the cave with Vark, the surrogate perked up one night. "Our lookouts see something approaching us. It's huge, but they feel it isn't a danger to us." A few minutes later, they saw a large shape walking up the trail toward them. "A bear," Vark said, "Maybe this was one of his caves."

The creature stopped down the trail from them, sniffed, grunted, and turned to walk away. "Wait!" dad yelled, thinking that he might talk to it somehow. It stopped and turned. This time, it growled. But it just stood there for a few minutes before taking a cautious step toward dad and Vark, watching them. Vark said that he had kept his defensive weaponry at the ready, but like his and Godolphin's children, he felt no danger from the creature.

When it was about a bear length away from them, the bear rolled over on its back in the snow and showed them its enormous belly. "An offer of peace," said Vark.

Dad walked over to the bear, mumbling what he hoped were calming words to it. He reached out and rubbed its belly. What he thought were pleased sounds rumbled from its vast chest. After a few minutes, he stopped stroking, and the bear got up on all fours and stood there with its head canted slightly, looking at Vark and him. He shook the snow off, giving dad and Vark a shower in the flakes. Dad laughed, and the bear snorted.

"Will he fit through the cave door, do you think, Vark?" dad asked.

"Yes, but I wonder what Emmeline will have to say," he said.

Mom was excited about our new roommate. We had more than enough space, and he turned out to be a most excellent lodger and a friend for me. Finding a place at the cave's back, he circled a few times and then laid down. That was the last we saw of him until Spring when I was about three months old.

My first meeting with the bear surprised my mom and dad, they told me. I was out on the lip of the cave with them, looking at the sunrise, when the bear came out, plopping down next to us with a massive grunt and a sigh. I thought that was funny, according to mom, and started clapping and laughing. The bear looked over at me and then at us. Dad took me from mom and held me up to the bear. He snuffed at me a few times and then stuck his huge, pink tongue out and licked me. I thought that was even funnier and reached out to grab him by his nose. We stayed like that for a few minutes until the bear stood up and walked down toward the river a few miles away.

Dad told me he and Vark followed him. The bear lumbered down the trail, and when they reached the river, he walked straight in, submerging himself so you could only see his nose above the water. He stayed like that for a long time and then suddenly rose and threw a large fish up on the shore. He did that several more times and finally came up and ate them. You could hear his stomach growling, dad said.

He did this almost every day. And we followed him. Sometimes, mom told me, she'd bring me along in the special backpack they'd built. The bear often went to the river to fish, but he also searched the woods for other foods. His favorite was honey from one of several beehives that had just come back to life. He'd come back to the cave with honey dripping from his snout and then would nuzzle me; I loved the sweetness and getting sticky. No one loved the mess that the honey made or the clean-up afterward.

Being practical and down-to-earth people like we were, we named the bear, "Bear" and he stayed with us, living in the back of our cave. It scared my parents that I'd sleep with him nights as I grew up. He was gentle with me but not overly patient. If I were doing something stupid, he'd bat me with one of his great paws, but with claws retracted.

Bear enjoyed immersing himself in the river to fish and swim. He'd also taken to leaving several of his catch for us when he went into the water. Dad and mom didn't expect him to "share," that being more of a human trait and something they'd only expect from a higher being. Then again, the people of mom's and dad's home had almost killed themselves off; so, who were the higher beings here? Anyway, maybe, mom said, he was paying us rent for his space in our house.

We continued to live like this for the following years, and I grew into a thing of the forest. Mom made me more clothes from fragments of hers and Dad's and skins of animals that we caught. She told me I looked like a wild child, a wood nymph. Also, it didn't help at all that I hated baths. So, after a while, they were fine with me sleeping with Bear, I think.

I did like to swim, though. Just below the section of the river nearest our cave, there were rapids. I loved floating them. I'd often meet Bear fishing at the bottom of them, and we'd share a meal before we went home. One time when we were walking home, he stopped, kneeled in front of me, and waited until I figured out that he wanted me to climb on his back. That made the walks go a lot faster. All this scared the poop out of mom and dad. Also, it told them what I was going to be like as I got older.

My Year 10 came, and we celebrated it, a party with my favorite foods and friends around me. I learned later, from Joe, about birthday cakes and things like that. We didn't have that, but mom ensured I had everything I liked for my Year 10 recognition. My parents gave me a new adult-size bow, a real one, and real arrows. Probably one of my greatest treasures. Every time I go into the woods, I take it with me, even today, almost ten years later.

Increasingly, mom and dad let me hunt alone in the woods if I brought Bear and one of the surrogate's surrogates along with me. My favorite surrogate was a groundhog I named Candlemas for the time between winter and spring. He always came with me into the woods, shadowing me a few feet ahead or behind. Unlike real groundhogs, he could move fast and keep up with me. Like I said already, I was like a nymph in the woods.

I was about as far away from my home as I'd ever been when Bear sensed a presence and stopped walking. He made a slight huffing sound, which I took to mean something was ahead. I signaled for him to stay put and moved into the woods. In a clearing down a short hill from us stood a boy about my age. He looked lost and scared. I started toward him, but two men came out of the woods on either side of him. "No," he screamed and ran. One man threw a large net and caught him before he got more than a few feet. He struggled until the other man clubbed him.

The men took him out of the net, tied him up, and then one man said, "We should take him back to the camp and put him with the others."

"Okay, but what about the other one, the girl?" asked the other man.

"She'll keep. Let's get him back to the camp and then come out to look for her. We'll put some food out and set a trap," said the first man.

The men left, and Bear, Candlemas, and I searched for the girl. After a few minutes, Candlemas said that he'd found her. A girl about the boy's age. So maybe a twin. And he told me where she was. I snuck up and stepped out of the woods a few feet from her. "I'm a friend," I said, "don't be scared."

She was startled, but when she got over that and my wild appearance, we talked. She told me her name was Glory and that she and her family were migrant laborers, moving to pick fruits and vegetables at a community a few days away from here. "These men," she said, "hit us yesterday and took the rest of my family, except for my brother and me. I think they may be slavers."

"How many of them are there, Glory?" I asked.

"Maybe five or six, but they all have guns," she answered.

"How many people in your family?" I asked.

"Well, there's mom and dad, my big brother and sister and their families, and me and my twin brother. Maybe fifteen of us."

"Well, they just caught your brother, and they're going to set a trap to catch you," I said.

Candlemas reached out to Vark and Godolphin through their network, and they said mom and dad said to hang tight, that they'd be to us shortly. Bear came over, scaring Glory a lot, but I showed her he was friendly. "Like a big Teddy Bear," she said.

"Whatever that is," I said. I explained I'd always lived in the woods and didn't know about Teddy Bears or anything like that. Just my family and friends like Bear and Candlemas.

A bit later, Bear grunted, and my parents and the surrogates appeared, along with several of the flying and ground-based surrogates. I didn't need to explain anything to them because they'd been listening to Glory's story. "Mom and Dad, why don't we find where these guys' trap is and then see if we can spring it?" I was excited about getting some action.

Figurehead

The aerial surrogates went out to search for the men and the trap. They reported they found it a short distance away and showed us a disguised net hanging a few feet up in the air above some food left on the ground. The men were hiding on either side of the spot. We split up, half going toward one man, half to the other. When we were in position, Bear walked into the clearing and sniffed the food. The men were startled and looked at each other across the clearing, not knowing what to do.

We stood up behind them, and the surrogates clubbed them to the ground. They woke up later, tied up and wrapped in their net. "Hi, boys," said dad, "Are you going to be a problem for us? If you are, our friend...," and Bear walked over to them and sniffed a few times and then growled, "... likes his meat."

Bear pawed them a few times and then sat down next to them. They stayed still, except for the trickle of what looked like water coming from the net. It smelled funny, so I knew it wasn't water, exactly.

With them tied up, we moved on to the rest of the group. They were a distance away at the edge of the forest, butted up on a swamp. They'd built a few large fires around their camp, it looked like to keep animals away. From our perspective, all it did was make them stand out. We could easily see three men with weapons and all the prisoners, tied together on the ground, with ropes around their hands, knees, and necks.

Because I was small and slippery, mom and dad sent me and Candlemas around behind the men. We worked our way through the swamp and came up behind the prisoners. When I was in position, dad stepped out into the firelight and said, "Hello, the camp! I'm here to talk. We have your other two men, and right now, you're surrounded. We want your prisoners... We'll trade. Your friends for your prisoners." My mom shot into the camp at the feet of one man, and from another position, one surrogate, Vark possibly, took a shot with his defensive lasers.

As they talked and occupied the men, I slipped into the camp and cut the ropes tying the prisoners together. We slipped away into the swamp with the slavers, pretty much unaware that the tables had turned on them—another one of dad's favorite phrases. This one I got, though.

"Come any closer, and we'll kill these people," said one man. He gestured over his shoulder, thankfully not looking back. Well, for him anyway; I had an arrow knocked and was ready to shoot if he'd looked back.

"We don't want this to get messy," said my dad. "You're not in a good position backed up to a swamp there. Like I said, all we want are your prisoners."

"You slavers? Why don't we just work together?" asked the man.

"No. We're not. We're not like you guys. We *do* have automatic rifles like these or attack lasers. Just let them go, and we'll let you go. You guys don't stand a chance."

It was then that one of the other men looked toward their prisoners and saw they were gone. "Boss, the prisoners are gone. We got nothing to bargain with anymore."

So, that was the end of the confrontation. The men dropped their weapons, and we reunited them with their friends. Dad and Vark led them all out of the forest toward where they'd been heading, with Bear taking up the rear and making it very apparent they might be a meal at any moment. When dad, Vark, and Bear left them, they gave them their weapons back and told them they shouldn't come back into the forest if they wanted to live. They must have believed us because we never saw them again.

Glory's twin brother, Joe, and I hit it off right away. The rest of the family did as well. We took them back to our cave and let them rest for a few days. At the end of that, finding that we liked them, dad offered to let them stay with us. There were two other caves in the hillside and plenty of time for us to work together to outfit them for the winter. They talked about it, and a few of them said they wanted to stay, and a few wanted to move on and catch up to the other migrants. So, they left with an invitation to return when or if they wanted to settle down.

Fortunately, Glory's and Joe's parents decided they wanted to settle down. There were now 12 of us, not counting the surrogates or Bear. A lot of new people. We were becoming a town.

Glory and Joe were a year older than me but didn't know how to live and survive in the woods. With me serving as their teacher, the three of us connected. Mom and dad them each a surrogate like Candlemas, and we imprinted them on these new friends. Glory took a squirrel, and Joe surprised me by taking a groundhog in the same generation as Candlemas. I should have known that would mean something.

We all turned Year 18 about the same time a few years later. Well, they turned it a year ahead of me. My mom and dad told me that was an important day in the old Miel community. It was the day that a child became independent, well independent in how the old Miel community saw independence. In ours, my father said that I was now ready to make my own decisions. Not that I hadn't been doing that since a bit after I'd hit Year 10, but now it was official, I guess. He also said, like he and mom, I could take a mate if I wanted to. I was inclined toward Joe but decided not to let him know that right away.

I was nervous about asking him. What if he said no? I wasn't the most presentable person. I envied Glory's looks and thought Joe would want to find someone like her. Glory was far prettier than me and more intelligent too. At least that's what I thought. But she was his sister. I didn't know how all this love thing was supposed to work. I couldn't think of how he'd want to be with someone like me. Boy, was I wrong.

Bear disappeared for a few days as he would occasionally do—more often over the last three or four months—when I was wrestling with this. Usually, he returned alone. This time, though, he returned with another big black bear, but a female. Now we had a problem. What do you call her? Girl Bear, Momma Bear, Bear 2? An answer to that question became clear a few months later.

Figurehead

We spent the rest of the summer doing what we did every other summer: preparing for the winter. Parties of us hunted and fished, foraged, cut wood, and otherwise winterized our caves. By Month 9, we were ready for the winter, which, as things would have it, didn't happen very early. In fact, the first snow didn't occur until Month 1, and it wasn't very much. The rest of the winter was pretty much the same. Very mild ...

Except that Momma Bear gave birth to four cubs that winter. We were all excited.

Joe and I spent increasing amounts of time together in the woods, hunting and patrolling our borders. I went with him, not totally because I expected we'd find anything. More and more, I just wanted to be with him. I still struggled with my feelings about him and tried to get up the courage to say something.

One of our patrols took us toward the old city. From what my dad later told me, we were on the hill above their first home. We could look down into the town. That night, Joe and I could see a few fires in the town, but not much else. During the day, we couldn't see anything at all.

"Why don't we go down and take a look?" asked Joe.

"My mom and dad say it's very dangerous, and we should only get this close to monitor them. If we go down there and scare anything up that follows us home, mom and dad would be upset with me. And they'd be right to be."

"Let's wait until dark and slip in and out. I've never seen the old city but heard a lot about it from my parents," said Joe.

"Okay, but only for a few minutes, and if we see anybody else, we get out. Are you all right with that?" I asked.

"Sure," he said.

We waited until dark and then slipped into town. There was not a lot to see. We found an old walled-in building that was vacant and burned out and foraged around it. I found an old book and stuck it in my pack. We walked around for a while before we saw signs of other people. A fire ahead.

"Let's check it out," said Joe.

"That's not what we agreed to. We need to get out of here," I said.

"Too late for that, kids," said a voice from behind us in the dark. Several shapes materialized, surrounding us. I took few baths or thought a lot about them, but it looked like these kids, who may or may not have been the same age as us—and still called us kids, had never, ever bathed. But they were all armed, two with guns, a few with bows, with arrows, knocked, and a few with clubs. One kid walked up and hit Joe on the head, knocking him to the ground. He grabbed Joe's pistol and howled, sounding like some sort of crazy wolf.

I knew Candlemas and Joe's groundhog were in the dark behind us. They'd armed their defenses and reached out back to Vark and Godolphin. We could get away from these guys. I wasn't worried about that, but all I could think about was the lecture I would get from my parents. So it goes, my father told me he had once said; I broke a rule and deserved what I'd get for that. Anyway, I didn't feel too scared. I put my hands in the air. "You guys don't want to do anything stupid. Why don't we just go our different ways? I'll take my friend and our weapon, and we'll just go back into the woods."

"Not going to happen, sweetie. Right away, anyway. We want to take you two back to our camp over there and branch out our gene pool," said the speaker.

Huh? What did these guys know about that? I'd thought they were feral, not learned types. "What did you say?" I asked.

"You heard me, sweetie. We've been here since the city fell. My granddad was a scientist working in the factory here on new types of surrogates. Not just machines, but part human. He taught me a lot before those damn hoarders with Blunt killed him. Well, we fixed them. Blunt and his boys ain't with us anymore." He gestured to the burned-out hulk behind us.

"But what I learned," he said, "was that the same group of people, like us, repeatedly breeding together we're going to create some sick things at some point. Well, that's happening to us, and I think adding you and your buddy there into the gene pool will help fix that."

"Well, I'm not as educated as you are," I said, "but it seems to me that just two of us will not do much for you. You need more people."

"Probably, but the two of you would be a start. Plus, you're kind of cute. What's your name?" he asked.

"Arwen, and again I ask that you just let us go. Better yet, why don't you come with us and join our community? I don't want to have to hurt you," I said.

"That's pretty funny. We're the ones with all the guns. Go out there? You crazy? We barely survive here. We'd be dead in a few weeks out there. Let's stop talking and get moving to our camp," the leader-boy said.

Just then, a huge shape bound into the group of kids, pitching them over. Bear. He looked around and growled at them. They started to scatter but ran into mom and dad and Joe's parents, all armed with automatic weapons. The surrogates strode into their midst, disarming them all.

"What is that thing?" the guy I'd been speaking to said as he picked himself up off the ground.

"My friend Bear. All right, let's settle down before someone gets hurt—or eaten—looking at Bear," I said with a smile.

The kids all did, and we marched into their campsite. There were about twenty of them, all of them malnourished and some looking diseased. We sat down to talk, and, in the end, they agreed to accompany Joe and me back to our camp to become part of my dad's new community.

Dad had a little surprise for me when we got back. "Arwen, you know I'm not happy with you and Joe right now, but what I'm going to tell you has nothing to do with that. Before you nitwits did your excursion, mom and I and Joe's parents decided we wanted to get out and see some more of the world. So, we're going to do a long walk. I can't say how long we'll be gone, but it will be a few years. We're going to take some of the new surrogates and Godolphin along as well.

"Now, it looks like you'll get your turn at Isolation as I did, but the good news is that you won't be alone. You have your new friends, Bear and Momma Bear and their cubs, and we're going to leave Vark with you. Joe will be with you, and Glory wants to stay, along with some other family members. Vark volunteered to stay when we talked a little earlier."

"This isn't exactly punishment. I didn't look at it that way when it happened to me. Actually, I was only three, so I barely remember going into Isolation. Besides, you invited those kids to join us; you can't just leave them now," said dad.

I was sad, mostly because being with him and mom meant so much to me, and they were heading off for an adventure that I wouldn't experience.

"Plus, I promise you we'll have a surprise for you when we return," said mom.

"What would that be, mom?" I asked.

"Wouldn't be a surprise if I told you," she replied.

So, here I sit at the mouth of our cave with my mate Joe, his sister Glory, and her mate, Jak, the intelligent guy I spoke to in the old city, and my oldest friends Bear and Vark, looking at the sunset—waiting for my surprise.

The End

{ 3 }

Archangel

Doesn't take a genius to figure out I was in a pile of trouble; S.O.L. I was thinking.

I am because this gang called the Grus is tracking me. They didn't name themselves for that guy in those Disney movies; he was a nice guy when you came down to it. Nah, their name was a shortened form of The Gruesomes because they were, well, gruesome. Intentionally gruesome. They cut themselves to make scars, a few of them had cut off body parts, and they loved big, ugly tattoos, brands, and piercings. Otherwise, they dressed and looked like Goths and only mixed with themselves. Hideous, nasty people. Not stupid, though. Just the opposite, as I was finding out.

They're after me 'cause I saw them do terrible things to some animals. When their leader caught me watching, he told me he'd give me a fifteen-minute head start, and then they were coming after me. He didn't say, "If," he said, "When we catch you, we'll make you a member of the gang. We've been looking for a babe to join us, and you're going to be it." They let me go next to this big old manufacturing plant that I've been getting lost in for the last few hours. I mean, really lost. I don't know where the hell I am. Hopefully, that means they don't either.

I'm 17 years old, about to be 18, and live with my grandparents. I've been with them since a car crash killed my parents when I was a baby. A head-on collision with a drunk blew their car to pieces, and then the parts of it fell into the Intracoastal Waterway. By the time divers got to what remained of the car, neither of my parents were there. The police told my grandparents with whom I'd been that it was likely that the tide had washed them out to Oyster Bay. Naturally, the drunk was thrown clear and survived the accident.

My name's Margaret Lane, but I'm called Penny by most, because of my grandparents' love of the Beatles and my coppery-colored hair. I go by Penny 'cause I kind of like it. I'm told that I'm pretty, but I don't know about that. I know I'm tall for my age, nearly 5'10", athletic, skinny, fair-skinned but tan rather than burn, and I love the surf. Have always loved the surf and am pretty good at riding it. I've been doing this since I was a kid, hah, and thought I might like to try it out competitively at some point. Who knows? Maybe I could get an Olympic Gold Medal like Carissa Moore. I idolize her.

I attend a private school here in Alabama and spend every spare moment on the beaches. Until this moment, I was planning to get a job at a friend's beach tee-shirt shop this summer, but I'm not sure if that's going to happen now. Or, if anything will, especially if I get caught by these guys.

I'd come down to Orange Beach earlier today with some friends. I told my grandparents that I was going to spend the weekend with another friend. So, mistakes number 1 and 2. When you came down to it, no one knew where I was. If my grandparents checked on me before Sunday night when I didn't show up, all they would know was that my friend didn't know where I was. Mistake 1. When we got to the beach earlier today, I put on my wetsuit and paddled out into the water. Rip currents are strong on these beaches, and though I wasn't worried about getting out of them, by the time I did, I was miles away from where my friends had dropped me off; I didn't know until much later that I'd made it into Florida. I'd taken my cell phone with me in a waterproof go-bag, along with my clothes, but I left it with my stuff on the beach with my board when I called it a day and went to relax near where I saw the Grus a few minutes later. Mistake 2. Now, when I needed it, I had no way to communicate with anyone, and no one would start looking for me for hours, maybe days.

I was hiding behind a big old machine in the manufacturing plant. It was crusted with rust and may have been blue at one point. At least there were flakes of blue paint all over the ground.... I heard voices. "She's hiding real good. Also, not leaving any tracks. At least we found her board and ditty bag." My heart sank.

Another voice said, "I hope the fishies like the pieces of her phone we fed them." I heard several people chuckling. My heart skipped a few beats. I had to stay hidden until night and then slip away. If I didn't, I wasn't sure what they would do to me, but it wouldn't be pretty—no way I wanted to look like them. Be like them. Or have anything to do with them.

"Anyway," the first guy said, "She's somewhere in here. I'm pretty sure of that. Let's start up a search line and move room by room. This old plant has a lot of nooks and crannies, but we should be able to find her before dark if we move along. Let's line up and walk through here, shoulder-width apart, just like they tried to teach us in Boy Scouts." Again, laughter and someone saying, "Yeah, Scouts, right."

I tiptoed out of the room into an even larger one, full of huge derelict machines. This room had windows high in the ceiling. Most broken; so, there was a lot of glass on the floor. I had to be careful that I didn't cut my booties or make noise. A flight of stairs at the back of the room went up to what looked like some offices. Up there, I also saw a doorway in the back wall I thought might lead to stairs out of the building. I climbed up very quietly as the Grus hunted in the next room. They entered the big machine room about the time I got to the top of the stairs; I dashed down the walkway to the back door. It had a simple push bar, and I slowly and quietly pushed it down. The door felt rusty, and so I had to push pretty hard. I was lucky, though; it made little noise. When I saw the bolt had retracted, I slowly pushed the door. It didn't want to move. "Dang," I thought. I didn't want to try hard on the door, but soon I'd have no choice. I heard the Grus finish their search of the room below me.

"Okay. Why don't you guys head outside, and Jimmie and I'll check upstairs," said the first guy, who I had figured out was their leader. I heard them begin walking up the stairs and the others go out through a backdoor I'd not seen. "Dang," I thought again.

I looked around and found a metal bar next to the door and figured I could use it to brace the door from the other side so they couldn't come out. I grabbed it and pushed the door hard. It squealed, and I heard the guys coming up the stairs start to run and yell to their buddies. I slipped out the door, slammed it shut, locking it behind me. Then I saw two things: First, there was no handle on the outside of the door. Only a lock and, of course, I had no key—not that I would've wanted to go back in that way, anyway. The bar must have been there to brace the door open when someone stepped out on what appeared to be a balcony for a smoke or some fresh air. Second, there had been one of those retractable ladders up there at one time, but it was long gone. I had trapped myself about 30 feet above the ground, covered by old machine parts and a bunch of other broken stuff. It wouldn't have been a great landing place, even if I was stupid enough to jump from that height.

I jammed the bar into a space under the door, hoping it would hold against them, and then looked over the side at four of the Grus looking up at me. One of them waved at me with a badly deformed right hand and a great big smile. "Tag, you're it," he said. I gave him the finger.

Figurehead

A few minutes later, the two guys that had been inside the building came out, and the six of them whispered. Finally, the leader, who had only one hand and a pile of gross, ugly tattoos and piercings on his body, looked up at me. "Well, Penny Lane." How did these guys know my name? "Looks like we caught you. Want to come down and join us?" One guy had searched the Internet for the song and began playing it on his phone. At the end of it, they all laughed, and the leader said, "I know how we initiate you. You know what fish and finger pie means, little girl?"

I looked down and said, "Look, my parents are coming to pick me up. You guys are going to get in real trouble if you don't let me go."

"Oh, they come here to this steelyard to pick you up? I kinda doubt it," he said. "I bet they think you're somewhere else, and you think you're up a creek without a paddle because your phone is in the Perdido Bay. Right? ... For something to look forward to, a fish and finger pie is when a guy plays with a girl's private parts, and you get wet. Some guys say it smells like fish. I don't know, but that's what that means. What I was thinking was that we cut off a few of your fingers for your initiation and make them up into a pie for you to eat. What you think of that?"

"Not much," I said to myself and looked around for another way off the balcony. The backside of the building was steel sheeting and looked very slick. The roof was maybe 10 feet over my head, so no way up there without a rope and a hook. Two of the guys had disappeared and returned a few minutes later with a ladder they must have found in the building. I was definitely up a creek now, I knew.

"Look," I said, "I'll come down, but I want nothing cut off. Okay?" I said.

"You're not in a position to wrangle, Penny," said the leader. "We know what we're doing. Two fingers from each hand will leave you plenty of fingers to use for other things." They all laughed. "We'll just wait here until you agree to become a Gru. The longer you wait, the more we pierce and color. If we have to wait all night, we may decide to color your face. Only another Gru would have you then." They all laughed.

Four of them settled down to wait. Two left, and the leader told her they'd be back with food and drink—for them. Only Grus would be fed. He also told them to bring back their cutting tools, tattoo guns, and piercing tools. I liked the sound of this less and less, but here I sat, in the fading hours of the day in bright sunlight, parboiling in my wetsuit.

"Bet you're wondering how we know your name, huh, Penny? Well, we're top-notch hackers. Busted your phone and got your personal information. The guys that make these phones think they have this seriously good security. Poo on them. Their security sucks," said the leader guy. More evidence that these guys were smart.

Maybe an hour later, according to my watch, the two other guys came back with pizzas, and it looked like sodas. They sat down to eat and chatted amiably. One guy had brought several tools and laid them out on a piece of cloth as a sort of display for me. I saw a pair of heavy meat shears, a bit of wood with a large rubber band strung through holes in it, a blow torch, some alcohol, and some bandages. He unrolled another piece of cloth, and I saw several other tools. I didn't know what they were but could only guess. I shivered despite the heat.

"Cutting off parts of the body, even if you're committed as we are and I'm pretty sure you're not, really hurts. So, that," and he pointed to the piece of wood, "is a bit. We put it in your mouth to muffle the screams, so you don't bite your tongue off. The torch is to cauterize the wounds, so you don't bleed to death, and the other stuff is to make sure the wounds don't get infected. I figured we would take off your pinky and ring fingers on both hands. Leaves you the rest of them to write with. Me," and he gestured with his right arm, "I had to teach myself to write lefty."

"These things here," and he gestured to the other cloth, "are for piercing and tattooing. While you're out, because you'll surely pass out when we cut off your fingers, we're going to pull your tongue out and put it in a clamp. When you wake back up, we'll pierce it. Then we move down to your nipples and pierce them with this gun. It shoots this metal thing called a receiving tube through your nipple so we can put different kinds of stuff through it. You know, like weights, bells, and things like that. Next, if your navel isn't pierced, we go there. You're not pierced down there, are you? Lots of kids are nowadays. Sounds like quite a night, huh?"

"You won't be fully a Gru, though, until you get branded like the rest of us. These last things are branding irons. We all get them, so we're not singling you out. When you're done, you'll be a fully baked member of the club.... Why don't you come down so we can get started?" he asked.

"You gotta be kidding me. I'll die up here before I let you touch me with that crap," I yelled at him, now scared to death.

He shrugged and sat back down, and we all waited.

The sun set, and the skies darkened. I was sure that, by now, my friends were frantic and maybe had called my parents. Yes, I called my grandfather and grandmother my parents. They had been there for me for nearly seventeen years. I sat down against the side of the building, which was still warm from the sun. I bet it would not stay that way much longer, and me, still inside my wetsuit, would start getting cold.

"Any time you decide to change your mind and join us, just let me know, and we'll swing the ladder up there," said the Gru leader.

"Bite me," I replied.

Near 11 PM, I dozed off. Sometime later, according to my dive watch, the guys below awakened me yelling. "What the hell was that?" "No idea." "It was like the stars turned off for a few seconds." "Damn, that was cool."

I wondered what I'd missed. I wasn't about to ask, though.

"Hey, Penny. You still up there? Did you see that?" asked one of the Grus.

"Nope. Maybe it's the end of the world," I said.

"Damn, maybe she's right," said one of them.

"Don't be a jackass. It's probably some experimental aircraft from the naval air station. They're flying that stuff all the time over the Gulf. Remember that report that they issued a few months back on U.F.O.s? Still sayin' they're not from out there somewhere and makin' fake explanations for them. You know, like 'fake news.'" They all thought that was pretty funny.

Things quieted down after that. I settled down back against the wall of the building, and they sat around below, talking. One by one, they fell asleep, and I began looking for a way to get away. The balcony was right in the middle of the building's wall, so there weren't many options, and I didn't have any rope. So, I settled down for the rest of the night, praying that cops made a circuit through the grounds now and then to make sure there weren't any vandals.

Near dawn, the Grus started to move around. I saw the leader of the group and one of the other guys standing a ways away from where I was. They looked at me and gestured toward the balcony several times. The second guy shook his head yes and then left.

He was back in a few minutes with a crowbar and a probe that he must have found in the building, or they had in a car. They woke the other guys and then pulled the ladder up and balanced it against the wall a few feet below the balcony and right below me. The only guy with two hands climbed up the ladder and disappeared under the balcony. Why couldn't he have not had a foot or a leg or something, I thought. I

GEORGE CONKLIN

tried to lean over to see what he was up to but couldn't see. Then I didn't need to see because I heard him begin tearing away at the struts holding the balcony up. I heard something clang as it hit the ground—and I hoped it was the guy—but the noise started up again. The balcony shook, and the side he was working on slipped down a few inches. Dang, Dang, Dang, I thought.

"Look, Penny," the leader said, "We want to injure you, anyway. So, a broken leg or arm would be fine with us. Maybe even an amputation beyond what we're planning. This is your last chance. If we have to cut you down, I won't be happy with you."

"And you don't want that," said the guy beneath me. Another piece of the strut work fell away, and the balcony sank even further. I moved to the opposite side and held onto the guard rail as the balcony slid down. The Gru climbed down and then repositioned the ladder so that he was right underneath me. He began working, seriously hard, on the struts and first one and then a second fell away. The balcony folded inward toward the building. I wrapped my legs around the guardrail but knew I had only a few minutes before the whole thing came down. Maybe on the guy cutting it away was all I could think.

But no luck on that. He pulled the ladder away, and they watched the balcony collapse in toward the building. I had one foot on one railing and was holding on to the top guardrail for dear life. The rest of the balcony just hung onto the building. It was a question of time before it fell completely, but they wanted to move that along as quickly as they could.

"Do we have any rope?" asked the leader. One guy ran back to their cars and came back a few minutes later with a length of rope. They tied the pry bar to it and then threw it over the balcony guardrail, and it caught solidly there. They pulled, and the balcony fell away from the wall opposite from where I was holding on. I heard the metal break, and the balcony slid down toward the Grus. One of them grabbed it, and another scampered up the surface and caught me. He reached into his pocket and pulled out what looked like one of those tech flashlights. I thought he was going to club me with it, so I tried to fight him off. He caught my hand and pressed the light into my hand, and the next thing I knew, I was convulsing.

I found myself on the ground, still groggy, and with the bit gag in my mouth. "Good, you're awake. We want you to start off this with you with us at least a little." He turned to one of his buddies, "Light up the torch."

He reached down, grabbed my right hand, and I saw him bring the meat shear down to my pinky. I howled as I felt the blades cutting into my finger. Then it was gone. Just like that. Gone. The finger, I mean. The next thing I felt was the searing pain from the blowtorch as it scorched my finger. I passed out from the pain.

I awoke God knows how much later when they splashed cold water on my face. Then the Gru leader cut off my ring finger. My vision went gray, but before I passed out, I saw what looked like a giant of a man walk up behind the Grus and do something.

Everything was black for me until I awoke in what looked to be a hospital, but not like any I'd ever seen.

I was looking up at what I thought was a window, but it couldn't have been that because I saw the Moon like it was only a hundred feet away. The rest of the room wasn't like anything I'd seen before, either. The walls glowed a very soft white and curved up to the ceiling window. I had a few I.V.s stuck in me, but I didn't see any needles when I lifted my arm. I expected my right hand to be hurting like hell, but when I looked at it, there were five fingers there. Two of them looked metallic, for sure, but when I opened and closed my hand, they worked just like the rest of my fingers.

A door opened, and a tall person rolled through it. Okay, what I thought was a person wasn't. It was some kind of robot, I thought, but with a distinctly human face. Otherwise, it had hands that looked like my new fingers.

"Good. You're awake. Let me raise your bed so we can talk face to face. You're not quite ready to walk around yet, but we can start that tomorrow when we go to Grav-1," he said (I was pretty sure it was a male). It was then that I noticed I was strapped to the bed. My hands were free to release the straps; this wasn't me being imprisoned or anything. "Right. You're being restrained on the bed until we return to Earth-neutral gravity, not imprisoned. Right now, if we were to release you, you'd just float away." As he said that, he moved his hands through the air in a remarkably graceful movement. "Yes. Your fingers are as graceful, Penny. Try them."

I did and was surprised at how naturally they moved and felt. "Who are you? Where am I?" I asked.

"Good questions. You're on the Stephen Hawking, and I'm Dr. Immanuel Kroner. I run the sickbay here, though I have to say that most of what we do is automated. But you still can't beat the human mind for diagnosis." He tapped the top of his head, and a door slid open. I could see what looked like a brain through a glass plate. "I just love doing that. It freaks people out. Did it freak you out?"

"Uh... no. It's a little weird, yeah, but I'm studying to be a forensic scientist, so I get to see a lot of strange things," I said.

"Wonderful!" he said and seemed delighted. "A fellow scientist. We'll have a lot we can teach each other, I bet. Right now, though, please get some more sleep. When you wake up, we will be back at Grav-1, and we can talk more." He tapped something on my arm, and I went right to sleep.

I woke up when I heard a bell ringing in the room. "Hello? Is someone there?"

"You have a caller at your door," said a soft, female voice. "Simply say 'open,' and the door will open."

"Thanks," I said, "Uh... who are you?"

"I'm Ariel. I'm the Hawking's Archangel," she said. "We will have plenty of time to talk, Penny. Remember you have a visitor."

"Oh yeah. Okay. Please open the door," I said.

In walked the man who I thought I'd imagined when the Grus were cutting me up. He was at least seven feet tall and bulked out like a linebacker. He stopped at the end of the bed and looked down at me with a smile. "I'm Michael," he said, pulled up a chair, and sat down. After him, Dr. Kroner rolled in along with three other, well, I'll call them people. One of them was a gorgeous, very dark, almost purple-skinned woman with long hair that seemed to change colors as she moved. The second was a robot creature like Kroner but similar to Michael, and he walked on mechanical legs. The last was a tiny man if you could call him that. He was green-skinned, and his eyes looked like a reptile's. He even had the tongue. It flicked in and out of his mouth, scenting what I understood from biology class.

"The man you're staring at, Penny, is our captain. His language is full of sibilants, and we can't speak it easily. The name we use for him," and he gestured at the rest of the group, "is Chuck."

Not sure of what to say, I tried to be polite, "Nice to meet you, Captain Chuck."

"No, just Chuck. In his language, that's as close as we can get to saying, Captain. The big guy is my right-hand man, Loren, and the magnificent babe over here is Nazym," said Michael.

Nazym turned a radiant smile on me, and I warmed to her immediately. She was easily six and a half feet tall and very muscular. "It's very nice to meet you all. I'm just not sure where I am or why I'm here. The last thing I remember was a gang of guys called the Grus had just cut off my pinky and ring fingers." I held them up and wiggled them in the air. "I'd expected to wake up missing four fingers and who knows what else. I guess I have you to thank, Michael, for rescuing me."

"Well, yes, but there's a lot more you need to know. Right now, we're back at Grav-1, so you should be able to walk. Nazym will help you get dressed, and then we can meet for dinner. Food here isn't too bad," he said.

"When will I be going home? My grandparents are probably crazy by now," I said.

"Let's talk," Michael said, and they all got up and walked out of the room.

Nazym walked over to the wall and pressed a panel I hadn't seen before, and a clothing rack slid out of the wall. There was a uniform hanging there that looked like Nazym's, though possibly a little more ornate. I got up from the bed, which simply slipped into the wall as I got off it. In five seconds, it slipped back out, entirely made with fresh sheets. "Wow, I wish I had that at home," I said. Nazym laughed a wonderful little trill. Not at all human.

A reflective panel slipped up on the wall at another gesture from Nazym. She helped me out of my gown. The first thing I noticed was that I looked different. I looked older, looked more fit, and had this metal disk embedded in the side of my head. "What's this?" I asked, pointing at the disk.

Nazym pulled her hair back and showed she had one as well. She said in heavily accented English, "It's what we call an amplifier. It puts us in direct communication with each other and with Archangel Ariel. She's our ship's brain and our protector. She was the one who told us about you and how important you are. We like to talk like we are right now, but we don't have to. The amplifier makes it easier for us to talk over long distances and when we need to be silent. It takes some getting used to. I don't speak a word of English. You're hearing me through the amplifier right now." she said. "One thing you need to know. The amplifier connects us mind-to-mind, which means we can hear each other's thoughts unless you direct Ariel to keep your thoughts private. Amazing, isn't it?"

"Absolutely," I said. My head was spinning. "I was wondering how the doctor seemed to know what I was saying before I said it."

Nazym held up the uniform. I've always been a little shy about my body, but I saw nothing there that resembled underwear. Nazym laughed and said, "This is an extraordinary suit. Not strictly clothing. If you were to fall out there right now," and she gestured out the window, "the suit would provide a helmet and O^2 for you to survive with. It takes a little practice, but it will become like a second skin for you." I slipped it on. Well, it actually slipped on to me. She was correct; it felt, after a couple of minutes, exactly like skin. "But way stronger than any of our skin," she said, handing me booties like those from my wetsuit. They went on like the rest of the outfit. I looked at myself in the mirror and watched the suit as it fit my body. I liked what I saw, though it was more than I usually showed, even in my wetsuit.

Figurehead

"You'll need to train it to meet your needs. It comprises billions of nano-bots that Ariel can tell what to do. If you feel too hot or too cold, just tell Ariel, and she will see that the temperature is adjusted. Once it learns your desires or needs, it will always meet them. Where I come from is a lot hotter than you're accustomed to, so the nano-bots keep my body constantly comfortable." She zipped down the front of her suit, took my hand, and put it to her chest. I pulled my hand back. It felt like I had stuck it on a hot frying pan.

"Wow. You're pretty hot, Nazym," I said and instantly thought about what I'd said. She laughed, and I did too.

"I knew the instant I met you, I was going to like you a lot, Penny," said Nazym. "Let's go find the others."

We walked out of the room and down a hallway. Every person we passed, and there were many of them, greeted us and called me Major. Also, they seemed genuinely happy that I was there.

"What's that about, Nazym? Why are they calling me Major?" I asked.

"That's your rank. The gold oak leaf says that you are a Space Force Major, ma'am," she said.

"Huh?" I was becoming increasingly confused.

"We will explain all. We're almost there," she said.

We entered a room that was the most incredible I'd ever seen. The entire opposite wall was a window to space. All I could see were stars—billions of them. I stopped dead. There were maybe ten people in the room. Chuck, Michael, Loren,

Nazym, Dr. Kroner, and five other people I was to find out were leaders of different areas of the ship.

Michael spoke first. "I know you have got a lot of questions, and we'll try to answer them all, but for right now, I'd like us just to eat and get to know each other. I will answer all your questions before you leave this room tonight."

"Pretty much what Nazym said, too. I'm all ears as soon as you want to talk." I sat down in a seat between Chuck and Michael. I didn't realize how hungry I was until the food came out. The conversation was pleasant. Everyone was very friendly. Of course, that made me suspicious. I hoped I hadn't flown from the frying pan with the Grus into the fire out here in space.

The food was excellent, as Michael had said it would be. When dinner was over, he pushed his chair back and explained what was going on. He started from the night he and Ariel had rescued me from the Grus.

"Parts of this will be hard to understand, Penny, but I hope you come to accept what I'm going to tell you. I'm pretty sure you've figured out that we're not from around here. Well, that's right and wrong. We *are* from around here. Just not around the *when* you lived in. We are from 2762, so almost 740 years into your future. We've done a lot over those centuries. The Hawking is the climax of those centuries of work. It's part spaceship and part time machine. We can move from one place in the galaxy to another in the blink of an eye because we move faster than light and can compress time."

Figurehead

"A few years from the night we rescued you, your people will start sending people to the stars. When you do, you'll put people into hibernation so they can survive the trips. Many won't survive because fate loaded these sub-light trips with many dangers. We've gone out, and where we could, rescued these brave explorers and took them to their target planets when those planets were hospitable. When they weren't, we've integrated them into our crews. You've probably seen some of your contemporaries on your walk here tonight. You'd never know that because they've integrated completely into us. They deserved that reward," he said.

He stopped and asked me, "Have you ever heard of Stephen Hawking?"

"Well, yes," I said. "Other than this ship, the British physicist. We studied his work at school. He died in 2018 from a degenerative disease, right? I read some of his daughter Lucy's stuff. She made his work very simple for us."

"Correct," said Michael. "Hawking was brilliant. We've gone back and talked to him several times. He's helped us with all of this," and he motioned around the ship, "and our sister ships. We suggested we bring him to our when with us, but he refused, though he took a brief look in 2016 because he knew that his time had come, and he was about to pass on."

He continued, "After a while, though, your people understood that interstellar travel was not in the cards for humans without significant advances in the sciences. So, they canceled those programs and did two things, one smart and the other stupid, as it turns out. The smart thing they did: they studied Stephen Hawking's work on black holes and discovered that they could cut paths through them to emerge elsewhere in the universe. The stupid thing they did: was to navigate these paths. On one of these experimental trips, they encountered a technologically advanced warlike society, called the Crech, that followed them back to Earth. And the rest is history. Bloody history. Billions have died, including the man who figured all of this out, Gru Lane."

I sat back, shocked. Lane?

"Yes, Gru Lane, Penny. More on him in a second," said Michael.

"Our Earth today is a colony of these creatures. Humans live in large pens and are farmed for food, research, and, uh, entertainment," he said. "It is a horrible existence in these camps. The Crech do everything they can to make life as difficult as possible for the poor survivors."

"We can move back and forth in time in the Hawking and have many times explored the many-worlds that Hawking hypothesized. In almost all of them, humanity becomes slaves of these creatures and eventually dies out. So, I said before that our people did smart and stupid things. I guess I overstated because as we explored the many worlds, what has happened was *mostly* inevitable. Therefore, it wasn't that trip that brought the creatures back to us. It would have happened anyway. But, that said, we've found two worlds where the creatures either never appeared or were beaten back," he said.

Figurehead

"Now, this is where you come into the picture. A year after that night with the Grus, you have a little boy with one of them. That little boy is the guy who figures out how to make Hawking's work practical. He comes up with the technique for crossing black holes. We figured if that boy were never born, then the war would never have happened, and we wouldn't exist out here. Seems it was wrong to believe that we'd have never existed if we had never developed the technology. 'Cause, here we are."

"The second path, interestingly, also keys around you and the Grus. This time you are rescued and never birth a child who creates us but are key to the insurgency on Earth to return the planet to us. This woman, you, we identified, had been injured before the rescue and went to her death many thousands of years into the future with two bionic fingers. This is the hard part. Know that I am very sorry about this, Penny."

"We had to let the Grus cut off your two fingers before rescuing you. I'm sorry you had to go through that, but we saw different worlds where you had no injuries and worlds where you had many more. The outcomes were always the same. The creatures always won. The last thing we needed to do was steal two more things from you: Ten years of your life and your family. You're now in 2762, and your grandparents are long dead. They went to their graves believing that you drowned that day. My lasting shame is that I put your board into the water so that the searchers would find it."

All of this piled on me was too much. I got up and walked out of the room. Nazym followed me into the hallway and said that she was here if I needed her. I shook my head no and waved her off as I walked back toward my room. I thought to my room, anyway.

I got lost and wandered. Outside of a room I came to, I saw the name Ariel in a beautiful script. "My home," her voice said in my head. "Care to come to visit?" The door opened.

I walked into the room and stopped. It was like I was back on old, old Earth, except for the panoramic view of space. A tall, fair, white-skinned woman walked toward me. Well, actually floated. "I'm one physical version of Ariel," she said and came over and caressed me lightly. "Please, sit," and we walked over to a setting of very comfortable chairs next to, believe it or not, a fireplace that had a real fire burning in it. She pointed to a chair, and I sat. She gestured again, and a carafe with two cups appeared next to me. "Care to pour? This is some of the finest tea imaginable."

It was. "The power of suggestion is amazing, isn't it?" she asked. "None of this is real aside from your belief in it. I poked through your head and saw some things you liked and made them for you. You can un-believe them at any time, but let's just keep things the way they are. I kind of like this. Now, let's talk."

We did for many hours. I learned about the Archangels as I processed what Michael had told me. She said that she would talk about whatever I wanted to when I wanted to. And she was true to her word.

Figurehead

There were seven Archangels—one on each of the Earth fleet cruisers. The Archangels were the last survivors of a planet called Esit that had been attacked early by the Crech and decimated. The remaining Esits, Cassiel, Gabriel, Haniel, Jegudiel, Jerameel, and Jophiel, were across the galaxy, fighting the losing war against the Crech. These survivors had wandered the galaxy until they found an early version of one of Earth's interstellar ships and helped it get back to Earth. They assisted Gru Lane in developing the now-advanced capabilities they had. The Hawking was the largest and most complex of the Earth's ships, she said proudly, likely the most advanced entity ever created anywhere or in anywhen.

The Crech were large, reptilian, and very smart and war-like. They came in monstrous spaceships and sent many thousands of their soldiers to the ground in capsules that opened as soon as they hit the ground. The Crech came out shooting. After the first wave of them came in and we learned that they were not peaceful and killed many thousands of us, we met them with stiff resistance. But that resistance was useless as the Crech seemed to have millions of soldiers they would sacrifice to subjugate us. One of the military leaders said it reminded him of stories he'd read about the Taliban in Afghanistan. They threw hundreds of their men against much better armed and trained government forces and eventually overwhelmed them with sheer numbers of fanatics. The few Crech we captured alive told us that before they took their own lives, kamikaze-style, so many more earth people were killed along with them.

As their attacks became more and more successful, they herded human survivors into large, fenced enclosures. They culled out and took men to separate camps where the Crech put them to work on building or mining projects. Most didn't survive. The women and children were placed into large camps and used for pleasure or experimentation. This was partly what you'd think, Ariel told me: sex. Most women didn't survive sex with the creatures. They put others into coliseums that the men had built for them to fight and to die. Finally, they brought others to labs where they tried out all kinds of horrendous experiments, breeding genetic monstrosities. Many of these crossbreeds between the Crech and humans became soldiers for the Crech. Others became the contenders in the coliseums, sometimes killing their mothers. The Crech had studied our history and looked at the work of Nazi scientists as guidelines for theirs.

A small group of humans had kept away from the Crech and fought a losing battle against them. The Hawking had discovered a many-world where the Crech had been counter-attacked and beaten by, well, me, leading these insurrectionists. The actions were bloody, but the ground-based insurrection and attacks from the space fleet on the mother ships eventually ended the occupation. That Earth had fewer than 5 million people left on it at the end of the battle. Ariel said they hoped that we could save more by replicating those attacks sooner.

"I'm not a warrior, Ariel. I wouldn't even know what to do with a gun," I said.

Figurehead

"You'd be surprised at what I've been filling your head with. Michael will train with you, though I bet you'll best him quickly," she said. "Why don't you spend the night by the fire? I don't sleep as you might guess." I did and woke up the next morning when she touched me. She'd had a meal brought in for me, and I found I was famished. When I finished, I got up and walked back to my apartment. Now, I knew right where it was.

Michael was waiting for me with the rest of the crew when I came in. "I hope it was all right we came in. We didn't have any idea when Ariel was going to be through with you."

"No, no. That was fine. Better than you guys hanging out in the hallway," I said.

Nazym walked over to the wall and made the mirror thing appear again. This time, when I saw myself, I was surprised again. I was even more fit looking than when I saw myself the day before. Amazing what another night with Ariel did for me. She bulked me out a lot like Nazym and I was nearly as tall as her. "All of this overnight?" I asked.

"Yes," she said. "Ariel can do miracles with a little quiet time with a subject. We're going to work out. We'd like you to come, and so we can see what you're capable of. And, well, for you to see us as well," she said.

I looked around at the group and shrugged. I thought that there was no way that I could take on even Chuck and beat him-her-it in a fight. But I was up for trying.

One thing that Ariel did to me overnight was that she helped me process being over 700 years in the future. While I was sad about losing my grandparents and being here alone, in 2762, it was not as overpowering a sadness as it had been the day before. I'd accepted my fate and moved on. She spoke to me, "You should never lose touch with those you love. You'll remember them fondly and be sad. You would not want it any other way. Nor do I. We all still remember our families and friends we lost on Esit thousands of years ago."

"Thank you," I said. Everyone looked at me. "Oops. I was talking to Ariel," I said, embarrassed.

"You'll get used to it," said Loren. "I keep slipping myself."

We left, walked down the hall, and then took a lift down several levels to a large, open room. There was a collection of equipment around the outside wall, some of which I almost recognized. The others looked like torture machines, and I was about to find out that was pretty much what they were.

"We'll show you the equipment in a bit, Penny. Right now, though, we want to get an assessment of your status. So, I'd like you to fight us," said Michael.

"All of you?" I whined. "No way am I going to take all of you on."

"That wasn't elective, Penny," he said and took a swing at me with his huge paw. I saw it coming at me and ducked. I felt a breeze from his hand and arm as it passed overhead. Reflexively, I struck out with a closed fist and caught him on the side where he was exposed. I heard an "Oof" and then was fighting for my life against the rest of them. After about fifteen minutes of blocking, sidestepping, and punching, we took a breather. I was shocked to be standing and not feeling too winded.

"Excellent," Ariel said in my head. "You still have some more work to do, but that was a great first fight."

"Are we resting?" I asked.

"Never," Michael said and threw an uppercut that caught me under my chin. I flopped back and saw stars, but I was back at him in less than a second. "You need to watch all the time. You'll never know where an attack might come from. Down on the surface, the Crech have enlisted humans to infiltrate and take out insurrection leaders. You'll never know who they are. So, stay on your toes all the time."

"Uh-huh." And I kicked out with my knee, catching him on the inside of his thigh. He grunted, stumbled, and danced away from me. I advanced to attack again. My bad. I was so focused on Michael, I lost sight and track of Nazym. She swept my legs out from underneath me, and I went down on my face. I heard a pop, and when I came up, blood was flowing out of my nose. I growled and kicked back, caught her in the gut, she went down. I then felt, rather than saw, Loren and Michael advancing on me. I rolled away, just missing a foot that would likely have knocked me out. These guys played for real. I stood up and backed away, wiping blood from my face. "Now, I'm pissed, boys."

They smiled and advanced on me. "You haven't tried your fingers yet," said Ariel.

"Huh?"

"Point at them, touch your thumb to the base of your pinky and watch what happens."

I did, and an arc of electricity shot from my fingers, finding all three of them. Down they went, flopping like fish on land, like I did with that taser days, well really, centuries ago. I smiled. I had my very own taser now. Cool.

"That wasn't fair, Ariel," kvetched Michael.

"All's fair in love and war, Michael," said Ariel on the overhead speakers. There was a little tweet of laughter from her.

Nazym walked over and slapped me on my back. "And you thought you couldn't do this. A few more days of training and you'll be better than us. Come over here." We walked over to the wall, where I saw a receptacle opening. A mirror on the rear of it showed my nose turned off to the side and still bleeding. "Put your head in the recess and close your eyes."

I felt a warm light bathe my face and then a light mist of some medicinal substance. When I stepped back and looked at the mirror, my nose was straight again, and the machine had cleaned the blood off. It still hurt a bit, but the pain disappeared over the next few minutes. The guys were also stepping away from similar receptacles.

"Well, that was fun," I said. "Now, who's going to show me the machines?"

At the end of another couple of hours, we were all sweaty. I knew I would feel it tomorrow. That is until I tried out that healing machine again. Ariel told me to step into the full-body version of it and let it warm me. I did and felt great when I left it. "After you eat, why don't you come by and re-visit me, Penny?" she asked.

"Another sleep-over?" I asked.

"Whatever you want. My place is yours," she said. I look back at that now and see that she was not just being friendly, the minx.

We ate in the mess hall again. Michael told me that they manufactured all their food. You wouldn't have known that by me. I asked for a burger and believed it was impossible for it to be anything other than real meat. After dinner, I wandered down to Ariel's apartment, and as I approached the door, it opened. This time, it looked just like my bedroom back at home 700 years ago. "Sweet," I said. "Thanks, Ariel. Now we can have a real sleep-over." It was funny. She might not have a body, but I sensed a smile.

Again, we spent hours talking. She was cramming me, she said, with the knowledge I would need to survive on the surface and for my mission. That happened best when the subject—me again—wasn't distracted and was in familiar surroundings. My stereo was playing quietly in the background music of Anderson East. My grandparents had made friends with these folks from Michigan who were summering nearby our home, and they'd turned them on to him. He played a mix of R&B and country that was smooth and easy to listen to. I was a little sad: He and that music were long gone, as were my grandparents and everyone else I knew.

Finally, I couldn't focus anymore, and I laid down on my bed and fell asleep. When I awoke, I was alone. Anyway, as alone as you could be with a computer that was always in your head. "I'm not a computer, Penny. Would you like to see me? I warn you I'm not pretty like you."

"Sure. I'd like that, Ariel," I said.

The surrounding walls disappeared, and I was in a bare room. A door opened opposite me, and I took that as an invitation to enter. I stopped at the entry, more than a little shocked. "This is me," said Ariel. In the room was a large tank, and suspended in the tank was a creature. Not a human, but a humanoid. It had female features, but it also had beautiful wings. "My brothers and sisters and I come from a planet where the atmosphere is this soup you see me floating in. I get all my nutrition from it, and it helps connect me to the others and the rest of the ship." She gestured to what looked like cables that came out of the tank. "These are not cables, like other cables here in the ship. These are connective tissue and are part of me. When I came here, we grew them. They allow me to manage the ship and to support you."

"You're beautiful, Ariel.... Don't you ever think about your world and want to be back on it, free?" I asked.

"Thanks, Penny. I do, many times a day, think about our home. The Crech, though, destroyed my world eternities ago. We are the last of our race, but as soon as we wipe them out in this many-world, my brothers and sisters and I plan to get together and make more of us and to rebuild. We all agreed, though, we do not want to bring young into a universe where those evil creatures live. Your mission is important not just to your people but to us as well, Penny."

Figurehead

"Huh. I will do my best for all of us, Ariel."

"I know you will. Now, I would like to try something. Do you trust me?" she asked.

"Why yes. Is there a reason that I shouldn't?"

Ariel turned to me, looked down, and smiled. This time, I knew she was laughing. "There is a receptacle like what you used in the gym in the wall over there. Step into it."

I did, and the wall closed around me. I felt a slight movement, and then I was in the tank with her. "Don't panic. You can breathe our atmosphere. It is far richer in O^2 than yours, so breathe slowly. I am going to come over to you and wrap you in my wings. I want to impart a little of me to you."

She floated over to me and stopped when she was inches away. She had to be ten feet tall but looked like she weighed half my weight. "That is close to correct, Penny. I'm about eleven of your feet and weigh about 70 of your pounds. This chamber is constantly at Grav-0, so why you are floating as well. When I touch you, you'll probably feel a little shock; I have that effect on people. Then I'll enfold you in my wings, and we'll stay that way for a while."

When she touched me, I felt a slight tingle all over my body, and then she wrapped me in her wings. They were covered in, I wasn't sure what, but not feathers—sort of leathery, but also incredibly soft. "You don't have a word for what I am," she said to me. "When we're done here, you will see what other worlds offer. The Hawking is a remarkable achievement. You also will be able to return home if you want to. I'm not sure you know that."

"I didn't. I'm not sure what I might want to do. I guess right now, I want to stay focused on beating the Crech. Then I can decide on what I want to do," I said.

"Good girl. Stay focused on today, I always say."

Whatever today is, I thought and smiled.

I felt a warmth spread through me as Ariel was doing whatever she was doing. It felt good, and I felt powerful. I fell asleep there.

When I woke up, I was back on the bed in my old bedroom. "How long was I asleep, Ariel?" I asked.

"Another couple hours. The others are waiting for you at the gym. You depart for the surface tomorrow, and they want to make sure that you're ready for it."

I got up and moved toward the bathroom. "Can you hold off on that?" she asked.

"Sure. Why?"

"I have got a little surprise for all of you."

I shrugged and walked out of her room and then down to the gym. As before, people I saw stopped and saluted me. I didn't like that. I was still 17, as far as I was concerned. The doors slid open, and I walked in. Michael and Loren had their backs to me, talking to Nazym, who was facing me. She did a double-take and then said something to the others. "What the hell?" asked Michael. "Penny?"

"Yes. What's the matter?" I asked.

"Look at yourself," said Nazym and gestured out one of those mirror things. The only thing about me that was still me was my hair, but even that was different. My hair had always been coppery; now, it was a bright, almost fire-engine red. My skin was now as white as Ariel's. "I've given you some of me," she said. "Not just this, but other things that you'll discover."

Nazym looked at me and then said, "Okay, Ariel." She left the room and came back a few minutes later with a different uniform. "Here, put this on," she said.

I looked around at the guys and twirled my hand around, so they knew I wanted them to look away. I peeled off the old uniform, and the instant that I did, I felt something strange happen on my back. Nazym said, "Oh my goodness." And the guys turned around, catching me completely naked. Their eyes bugged out. "Come over here," Nazym said. We walked over to the mirror thing, and I looked at myself. I had wings! Just like Ariel.

"Think about flying," Ariel said. I did, and the wings beat, and I rose from the floor. "I instructed you last night on how to fly. I can't give you confidence; you'll have to build that yourself. But you have all the knowledge you need. Now, you might want to get dressed."

I flushed a deep red all over my body. Nazym laughed and helped me to get into the uniform. Other than it being backless, it was much like my other one. "Should you end up in outer space, the suit will continue to protect you if you want it to. You have the added ability now, like my people do, to use starlight to move you. Our wings are like sails and convert starlight to power. Do you want to try it?"

"Uh, sure...."

Michael, Loren, and Nazym led me to a hatchway. Michael entered, and his suit reformed to provide him with a helmet and gloves. I stepped in and a helmet formed over my head, and I felt the suit's fabric expand over my bare back, leaving my wings on the outside. Nazym started the opening sequence, and we heard the hatch's air be removed. The outer door opened. I panicked for an instant, but Ariel said, "You'll be fine. Think about the new being you are becoming. A creature of the stars. My sister."

My anxiety evaporated, and I pushed out of the ship. Michael followed, his suit shooting jets of steam so he could move. My wings unfurled to catch the sun, and I felt warm to the core. "Let's go to the bridge," said Ariel. I turned and used slight movements of the wings to move us forward and up toward the ship's bridge. When we arrived, I stopped. Michael came up next to me, and we saw Chuck and the bridge crew standing there, staring. Chuck applauded, and the others did too. I did a little pirouette and then bowed to them all.

Ariel said, "Are you still trusting me?"

"Sure, yes. Should I not be?" I asked. I heard her little laugh in my head.

"Retract your helmet," she said.

"Huh? Won't I freeze? I remember seeing a movie where a guy went out into space, froze, and shattered. Is it a good idea?" I asked.

"Try it. Trust me," she said.

I looked over at Michael and shrugged. He hadn't heard a word of my conversation with Ariel, so was stunned when my helmet retracted. He reached out to grab me. But I asked him to stop. Other than not feeling air anymore, I didn't feel a thing. I looked over at him, and he said, "My God, Penny. Who are you?"

"Still Penny Lane, Michael. Just a new and, I guess, improved version of me. Let's go work out," I said.

He looked like he had misgivings about that, but I waved to Chuck, and we headed back down to the hatch. When we got back to the gym, everyone asked what it was like. I told them no different from being there with them, except I didn't need to breathe. Ariel told me that the new body would create what I needed, as it required energy from its surroundings. She said that there was a lot of O^2 in space if you knew where to look. My skin would find it and transform it into something useful to me. She told me it would do the same thing in water.

Exercise went differently this time. We sparred as before, but I now had a hugely unfair advantage with my wings and enhanced strength. Loren tried to disable me by holding on to me from behind, but I reflexively opened my wings and threw him across the room. It also felt like I had eyes in the back of my head. I had sense around me all 360^0 and so no one could attack me from behind. Ariel had also added several enhancements so that I could access new weapons that I carried. Beyond the taser-like ability, I also could shoot a jet of plasma at an opponent. I tried it in the gym and demolished a treadmill. "That'll come out of your pay," said Michael.

"Which is what?" I asked.

"Exactly nothing," he laughed. "Room and board, I guess. You're pretty awesome, Penny." He hesitated for a second and then added, "Pretty and awesome."

Nazym and Loren made choking sounds.

At dinner, Michael told us we'd be heading to Earth tomorrow. The Hawking would appear for a moment, fire on the giant Crech mother ship, and as they did that, we'd slip out. "We?" I asked.

"Did you think we'd leave you alone down there?" Nazym asked.

"I've been looking forward to this fun since we found you. Now, even more, when I see what you can do," said Loren. "No way I'd miss this."

"There are a group of insurrectionists that we're going to connect with," said Michael. "They've been harassing the Crech for a few years now but are getting whittled down by them. So, we four will go down first, and then later, we'll bring a larger ground force if needed. Once we get established, the plan is to bring the other Archangels and their ships back to engage the Crech starships. While they are attacking them up here, we will attack the Crech leader down there and hopefully eliminate him."

"The Crech," he said, "are hierarchically organized like many of these kinds of armies. Their supreme leader, or whatever it calls itself, runs his army and space force like it's his own. He goes, and we think they'll fall apart. Over the last few years, he's eliminated anyone down in the next leadership tier who might be a danger to him. That's pretty much everyone, except for some bootlickers. He goes, they'll all go. These guys are the same the universe over. Not a single brain between them. He lives in the large Crech base in what used to be New Orleans. That's where the insurrectionists are, and we'll go there as well. There's a huge prison facility, experimental labs, and a coliseum there along with the Crech leader home."

I spent my last night with Ariel in her suite, though it felt more and more like mine. I had learned over the previous days that the passage of time here on the ship was, well, special was the best way I could think about it. You slept when you were tired, ate when you wanted to, and exercised whenever you felt the desire. Early or late came to have no meaning. So, for leaving the ship, Michael said we would go tomorrow, not specifying whether it would be early or late.

We landed, though, in the middle of a battle. Literally, one side was over here, and the other side was over there, and we were right in the middle of it, in what looked like a bomb crater. "This'll be fun," said Loren. "Wonder who the bad guys are?"

"Look for the green slithery things. They're the villains," said Nazym. "See. Right over there." She pointed to a cluster of what I now knew to be the Crech. Ugly-looking things. She fired her pulse weapon at the group, and I watched them liquefy. Splut! Everyone except me carried several weapons. I didn't because Ariel had made me into a weapon. I saw another cluster of the Crech moving toward our position, and I gestured at them with my ring finger, and a jet of plasma shot out. Splut again. Then again and again as we fired at the clusters of the Crech warriors.

While we fired at the Crech, the automatic gunfire from the other side stopped. I guess because they realized we were on their side. When the Crech were wiped out, at least for the time being, we turned toward the other line. We weren't stupid enough to just stand up. Michael yelled to them, "Hello, the fighters. We're here to help. Can we come out?"

A voice to my immediate right, not two or three yards away, said, "You'd have been dead if we didn't think you were on our side."

Five men stepped over the mud wall of the crater from where they'd been hiding. They were holding old automatic rifles at their sides, pointing down and away from us. I was pretty sure that they realized that what they had was no match for ours. The man in the lead smiled and walked over to Michael. "I'm Gru Lane." He held out his hand, and I could see that his pinky and ring finger were missing.

Michael smiled back at the man, "I'm Michael, this is Nazym, Loren, and this is Major Lane." He let that hang for a moment. Gru Lane looked at me for a second and then at my hand.

"Huh, my great-great-grandmother was missing these fingers as well, but she didn't have replacements like those. I saw what you could do with them, and I'm impressed," Gru Lane said. "This probably not the best place to be confabbing. Why don't we move back to our camp?"

He led us away.

Figurehead

I thought that I was likely looking at my great-great-grandson in this many-world. Way weird.

We followed Gru Lane to their camp. It looked like something out of an old sci-fi movie. People lived in their vehicles, and these looked like they were patched together from chain and barbed wire. Lane lived in an old R.V. that now looked like a cyclops and a tank, right down to the single porthole/eye. The place stank inside, so we sat outside. It shocked me that the Grus, this version of them anyway, had survived. Lane explained the Grus had always been survivors, and so when the Crech showed up, they hunkered down and waited for a chance to fight back. Typical. By the time they fought back, billions had died or were imprisoned, and the chances of beating the Crech were microscopic. I, honestly, was wondering what we were going to do.

"The Hawking and the others will attack the Crech mother ship and its sisters shortly. As soon as they do, our attack will focus on the Crech headquarters and we will infiltrate the base to take out the Crech leader," said Michael.

Talking to Gru, I said, "We plan to kill the leader of the Crech in his sanctuary here, and hopefully, they will fall apart after that. Do you know if there are other groups of rebels like you around the world?"

"Uh... yeah, but there's a problem. The Crech have been herding survivors in their camps onto their ships to prepare for moving on, we bet. They're all up on the mother ship in pens there. We're still fighting, yeah, but figure that they have plans for the planet after they take all they want. I'm pretty sure they don't include us surviving," Lane said.

"I've let Chuck know," said Michael. "He had hoped to take the ships out, but now this changes things. They'll go for the engines to disable them. Then hang back and wait for us. That was kind of Plan B, anyway. He'll let us know when he's ready to attack. Are you ready, Penny?"

Gru looked up at that. "Funny, my great-great-grandma was named Penny. She was the first one of us that was a Gru."

"How old are you, anyway?" I asked.

"I don't know, really. A few hundred years, I guess. Before the Crech came, we'd figured out how to extend life. It turned out to be one of those good idea/bad idea things. We figured out how to extend life but not how to slow population growth. By the time the Crech arrived, we had nearly 15 billion people on the Earth, and it was groaning under the weight," he said.

We knew billions had died here, but not nearly that many people. I teared up a little at that surprise. Maybe I would tell Gru I was his great-great-grandmother at some point if we all survived. Maybe not. I was still leaning toward no.

"So, are you the Gru Lane that helped build the new starships?" I asked.

"No, that was my younger brother. He was the brains of the family. I was the brawn. All the others are dead, though," he said.

I unfolded my wings to prepare for the attack. My role was simple. Simple up and down, Michael called it. He, Loren, and Nazym were going to work toward the Crech base while they were dealing with the attacks on their ships and going after me. We supposed they would think they knew right away what I was and try to bring me down. I was like Ariel's people, but oh-so-much more she had told me. We would see soon.

I looked at Michael and the others, waved goodbye, and shot off into the air. Above, I could see, with the enhanced vision that Ariel had given me, that the Hawking had just appeared near the engines of the Crech mother ship that was in synchronous orbit over New Orleans. It blasted away, and there were massive secondary explosions from the ship. It heeled over but then righted itself using jets from the side of the ship. But it was wallowing. I smiled to myself. A shipping term I'd learned. It never had time to turn on any shields that it might have, as every time it tried to do something defensive, the Hawking open fired again. Eventually, they got the message and just wallowed.

I sailed directly over New Orleans and floated down over their gun batteries, making myself a target. They fired, and when the dust cleared, I was still there, encased in a plasma protection bubble I created. I gestured toward the guns and released a jet of plasma across them. This time, there were many spluts as the guns, and their crews went up in, well, not smoke, but turned to jelly. I left behind only smoking craters. More guns fired, and I replied.

"You, the bird. I thought we'd destroyed all of you eons ago," said a voice in my head. "I am Jagozk, leader of the Crech forces that have subjugated this planet. I think the predicament you thought you had me in is changing. Yes, it is."

Michael, Loren, and Nazym had been captured, it seemed. Jagozk let me see them. I couldn't hear a word from them, though, which was disturbing. "They are being shielded," said Ariel in my head. "Maybe you'll be able to talk to them when you get down into the Superdome."

"What happened?" I asked.

"No idea, but it looks like someone gave them up," she said.

Just then, my great-great-grandson walked into the image that Jagozk was sending to me. Never trusted those Grus.

"I have your friends, as you can see," said Jagozk. "Come to me, and I will see that you are all dispatched quickly and as painlessly as possible. You," and he turned to Gru, "deserve a reward for your help." He nodded to one of his men, who pulled a weapon and evaporated Gru. "Never trust a traitor, I always say. Now, are you coming?"

A version of this was what we had hoped would happen anyway, so, "All right. Where are you?" I'm glad that he'd taken care of Gru for me. I wasn't sure I could have done the same to kin.

He told me to come down to the old Superdome, to his home-away-from-home. They'd also been using the old Smoothie King Stadium to house prisoners. The rest of the city was a wreck, though there was a spaceport in the French Quarter. There was a lot of activity there, and I was tempted to give them a taste of my plasma, but I held off a little while.

Figurehead

I reached the ceiling of the Superdome. Back on my Earth many years ago, work had begun on renovating the Dome, giving it an updated 21st-century look and feel. They never got that far here. So, I simply cut myself a hole and settled through it. As soon as I was inside the Dome, there was a massive explosion, a bright light that nearly blinded me, and then I saw a large, what looked like metal net flying toward me.

The net wrapped around me and drew me to the floor. I let it for the time being. I felt it straining to squeeze me, but the plasma shield was stronger. Far below, I saw Michael and the others and several Crech surrounding what looked like a dais on the 50-yard line of the stadium. On it sat the biggest, grossest looking thing I'd ever seen. Green, of course, but this thing looked like a cross between Jabba the Hutt, some even uglier evil toad, and a turd. Its enormous eyes tracked me as the net brought me in front of him. He reached out and touched the net to draw me toward him.

"Beautiful," it said to me. "You are very impressive."

You ain't seen nothing yet, I thought.

"Come sit with me," it said, and he drew me toward him. I wondered what he was thinking. I'd already shown that I'd no problem killing his kind. There must be more to what is happening here. It turned toward my friends, "Take them to the pens and prepare to take them up to our ship when it can take us." They marched them away.

"Now to you," it said. "I thought we had wiped out the Esits centuries ago. I guess we didn't." He looked at me strangely, "But then you are not an Esit, are you? Just what are you? I'm sure my scientists will enjoy taking you apart. In the meantime, I want you to sit here at my feet."

Now, I felt like Princess Leia at the feet of Jabba the Hutt. It was not a good feeling. I expanded my plasma globe. The net shrieked, and Jagozk looked down at me, a little surprised. "What are you trying to do, my little bird? You cannot escape my net, even if you wanted to. We entrapped your friends in its mate. You destroy it, the other will destroy your friends."

"Yeah," said Michael through our links that now seemed to work. "When you just did whatever you did, the net we're in shrank around us. Loren thinks he can cut us out, and Nazym said she has a trick or two she could use, but I think we'll need to coordinate."

I felt my egg being lifted in the air and found myself inches away from the toad-face. I bet he's near-sighted, I thought. I rushed to the side of the bubble, and he gave a high-pitched, effeminate shriek and reared back, dropping me to the floor. "Whoa! The hellion is a fighter," he said, trying to regain the upper hand in the room.

He turned to a soldier and said, "Take the creature to the pit. Throw her in for a while. Maybe she'll be a little more sociable after seeing some of our failed experiments." The Crech soldier giggled insanely as it dragged me across the football field to the 20-yard line to what looked like a large hole around which were stationed several soldiers, all looking into it, weapons at the ready.

The soldier clipped me to a hook hanging from a chain near the edge of the pit and pushed me into it. The chain played out rapidly, and I dropped maybe fifty feet into a cement-lined room, stopping a few feet above its floor. Whiplash, and wow, did it stink. I thought Jagozk smelled awful. This made him seem like a rose garden. The chain stopped my fall and I was lowered the last few feet to the floor of the room. Muck or something else oozed up around my bubble. It stopped a couple of feet up the side of it. Gross, I thought, and then I heard a noise behind me.

I turned and was confronted with one of the scariest things I'd ever seen, well, next to Jagozk. I guess it had been a man at one time and a woman. Two heads and one body, part male and part female. Hugely muscular on one side and feminine on the other. That was bad enough, but the skin was the same as the Crech, and the thing had a tongue like them, very reptilian. Eyes were a bright yellow, and the pupils were vertical, just like a snake. It spit at me, and the spit bubbled where it hit the net. Acid? Who knows, and I wasn't looking to find out. I heard some more noise and saw other creatures move toward me—many deformities. Failed experiments, as Jagozk had said.

"Horrors," said Ariel. "The Crech did terrible things to my people, but nothing like this. They've reached new levels of depravity. Michael, Loren, Nazym, and I've been talking, and when you're ready to destroy your enclosure, they will be as well."

"I'm ready," I said. There was a brief pause, and then Ariel told us to go. I ballooned the bubble, and the net shattered. I extended my wings and rose back to the football field. When

I got there, I released the chain that had lowered me into the pit and turned to face Jagozk. He ordered his soldiers to shoot. They did, and well, Splut! I heard much more gunfire off toward the Smoothie King Dome.

Jagozk stood up on wobbly, spindly legs. He didn't move around much or very quickly, I guess. I heard the clink of the chain, looked over my shoulder, and saw several of the failed experiments reaching the surface. Jagozk did as well and screamed like he did before and tried to run. He fell, and the creatures from the pit swarmed him. I sailed away to the tunnel connecting the Domes and waited there for Michael.

When the creatures had finished with Jagozk, the one I'd seen first shambled over to where I stood, blocking the tunnel entrance. I reached out to the beast and found a mad jumble of thoughts, some human and some Crech. But mad. The creature reached out to touch the surface of my bubble, pushed on it, turned, and walked away, disappearing out a field door on the opposite side of the stadium. I felt sorry for it and its sisters and brothers and reached out to Ariel to see if we could do anything for them.

Except for the mother ship, we had disabled all but one of the remaining Crech ships. That ship could not outrun the star power of the Earth ships and was stopped somewhere beyond Pluto. They made a stand there but eventually surrendered and were returned to the rest of their kind on Mars, where we figured to imprison them. We moved surviving crew from the other ships to the mother ship, and then we nudged each of the smaller vessels on a collision path with the Sun.

Figurehead

The Hawking towed the Crech mother ship to Mars and beached the craft there. We permitted humans who wanted to return to Earth to do so. A very few who had made connections to the Crech crew stayed there. The rest of the mop-up went reasonably quickly. There were concentrations of Crech in several locations around the world. It took an appearance by me, one of the Hawking's sister ships, and a few shots at their gun batteries, and they surrendered. Survivors, there were taken to Mars as well. We told them that any attempt to escape the planet would mean *all* their deaths. We set a string of satellites up in orbit around the Red Planet to keep them under observation. There they sit even today.

I drifted away from the Superdome, following the spoor of the creatures that I'd freed. I found them clustered around the remains of a sewer treatment plant on the outskirts of New Orleans. As I watched, one by one, they dropped into the muck and disappeared. The last one to go was the creature I'd seen first. Again, I reached out to it. This time sadness coming from the beast in waves nearly overcame me. It and its comrades were free, but it knew they would never be happy, and the filth to which they returned now was the best that they could hope for. At least they were free. Ariel told me that there was nothing we could do to reverse what had been done to them, but she said we could at least keep watch over them and ensure that they lived out whatever remained of their lives in peace.

I settled down next to the creature and closed my bubble. I reached out with my hand to touch the beast, and it recoiled from me. I continued, and eventually, it ducked one of its heads and allowed me to stroke its greasy hair. Truth be told, it was gross, but I shielded those thoughts from the creature. We sat there for some time, and then, as the sun set, the creature touched me and slipped off into the sludge. I knew I would never see it again, and that made me sad. I wished it peace and well.

I sat there for some more time and then opened my wings and headed off to the east, to where my story began.

Michael found me there the following day as I flew around over the Gulf waves. "I brought you something," he said.

I looked up. He was carrying a surfboard.

That was the last time I was on a board.

We took the Hawking and our sister ships on to the other many worlds and attacked the Crech, defeating them in each of them. It was interesting how they organized and fell in the same way in each of these worlds. I suppose someone smarter than me will figure that out at some point, but we decided to take them on because we didn't want them to figure out how to traverse the worlds and visit us. Our Earth had fewer than 10 million people left on it when we destroyed the Crech, and we were very sure that they wouldn't survive another run-in with them, even with us protecting them.

After that, I returned to the Hawking, and Ariel and I spent a few days in her/our suite. She and her brother and sister Archangels had decided to move to a new home. They had all trained new generations of Archangels to take over for them when the Crech were gone, which they now were. When she had shaped me that time in her enclosure, I hadn't known what it would mean. Now I did, and I was of mixed feelings. The tease, I thought. She was seducing me for the job of a life-time. I guess several lifetimes.

I felt that I still had so much I wanted to do with the life I'd been given. I knew going back to my Earth wasn't in the cards, being pretty sure that a fire-engine-head red, white-skinned, and winged girl would not fit in too well in my high school. I wanted to go back to talk to my grandparents, though, but I knew my future was with my new friends traveling the stars.

The Hawking returned me to my time, and I flew from the ship to my grandparent's house under my power. We chose a time after I'd been dead for a while. I wanted to go to my grandparents to let them know I wasn't dead but not really in a position to return to them. I came with an offer from Chuck. A few days after I visited, my grandparents' friends paid a visit because they hadn't seen them at their usual haunts. The house was empty. They were not seen again.

Things turned out even better for me because Chuck took the Hawking back to a few seconds before the drunk head-oned my parents many years ago. We pulled them from the car, and now we all, mom, dad, and my grandparents, live to-gether on the Hawking in quarters that we've made to look like my grandparent's house. It took them some time, but eventually, they fit in as all the old Earth crew members did. They deserved it.

The Hawking, the biggest of the Earth ships, took some time to get to know. But once I did, I loved it. Most of the day-to-day functions of the ship run in the background. If I want to peek at them, I can, but I only need to look at them when something is going wrong with them, which rarely happens. Mostly, I just hang out. Sometimes in the tank, sometimes with my parents, and sometimes with my friends. As Ariel had promised, I also got the chance to visit other worlds. There are a lot of stories there for another time.

I am Archangel Penny and basically, I run everything.

The End

{ 4 }

The Cage

On opposite sides of the jailhouse, cell doors clanged shut. Jake Larkin, Sook Pridi, and their driver, Louis, looked at each other, and Sook asked, "What's going on? Why'd they lock us up?" Marie Larkin and Sunisa Pridi were in a cell on the other side of the jailhouse. They were also wondering the same thing.

"No idea, Mr. Pridi, no idea at all," said Louis. "We were breaking no laws, and there was no reason to pull us over."

"Well, hopefully, someone in authority will come by soon, and we can get whatever this is cleared up and us out of here. I hope Sunisa and Marie are all right," said Sook.

The beautiful day of touring the countryside had turned ugly when they were stopped at a roadblock. The wives had been separated from their husbands and taken to a cell in another part of the jail. They'd heard things about what happened to American women in these Caribbean jails, especially here in the Maldots, and they all were nervous.

With no other option open to them, though, the five sat back to wait in their different cells.

Marie and Sunisa had been friends since college. They were roommates during their undergraduate and medical school years and firm friends, practically sisters, ever since. Marie was an accomplished general surgeon, and Sunisa was an equally accomplished psychiatrist specializing in forensics. They worked together in the same large practice, sometimes closely. Marie was a large woman with an infectious smile, the steadiest of hands and sharpest of eyes. There was no better diagnostician. Sunisa was small, dark-skinned, with bright green eyes, and a very accomplished psychiatrist. She spent a lot of time in jails and was nervous about receiving jail services versus her usual role on the giving side.

She was also beautiful. She had dark, enticing eyes and very delicate features. Her hair, long and black, was usually kept braided or in a bun on her head. Police and prisoners alike with whom she worked found her thoughtful and always looking out for her clients. Her family had emigrated to the U.S. after a coup in her Southeast Asia country found them on the wrong side; they had liked it in the U.S. and so stayed, even though they could have returned home years ago.

Sunisa never had a problem finding men in college. Her exotic beauty was like an open flame to moths. Marie was envious, but both had done well. Their husbands worked together in a large bank; both were high-earner investment managers and were very well-compensated. There were no children in either of the couples, at least right then. But both had talked about it; Marie and Sunisa spent the night sitting on their bunks talking about that, among other things.

"I didn't like that Captain Grillo," said Sunisa. "He gave me the creeps, a classic antisocial personality. I didn't see an ounce of remorse about our detention, even though he about admitted that they arrested us in error. He fawned on us, especially me, but like the sexual predators I see in the jails. Telling us he didn't have the power to release us just yet is a load of B.S. He's a captain and has ample power to do that. We need to be incredibly careful, Marie."

In the middle of the night, a guard took Marie out for questioning, and when she returned, Sunisa was gone. Marie assumed that they'd taken her out for questioning as well. Her interrogator had told her they now believed they were simple tourists and would be released in the morning as soon as the dayshift came on. Given Sunisa's concerns, this didn't make Marie feel any better, and she repeatedly asked about her friend. They were trying to delay them from getting back together, she thought, why she did not know.

Another guard had taken Sunisa out of the cell, she thought to be questioned as Marie had been. Instead, she was cuffed, a cloth bag thrown over her head, and removed from the jail. The Jeep was also enclosed, and no one could see in. So, no one knew they had taken her. Her anxiety spiked, and she yelled at the driver to bring her back to the cell. He just drove on impassively.

Hours later, well after sunrise the next day, Marie, Jake, Sook and Louis met in the jail's lobby. Captain Grillo was there and re-introduced himself. "I'm Captain Grillo. My deepest apologies to you all. We'd word about four people, two men and two women, involved in drug smuggling coming down the road you were on. Unfortunately, you fit the profile for them. I'm afraid my men hadn't gotten the message that we'd captured the smugglers on the other side of the valley a few hours earlier. We know you are planning to leave this morning, so I saw Dr. Pridi in her cell while you were being questioned, Dr. Larkin, and asked her to help pack your belongings. She'll meet you at the shuttle dock or the airport. This way you won't miss your flight. I've also taken care of your stay at the hotel. You'll be met at the airport by a government representative and taken to the First-Class Lounge. It's the least we can do," he said. "Again, I am very sorry about what happened."

"Thank you, Sir," said Louis.

Marie listened, not believing a word that Grillo said.

They left the jail with Louis and headed down to the boat docks, more than a little irritated but also knowing that they shouldn't make a scene. This was a lovely country, but its leader had a reputation as an unpredictable megalomaniac who dealt swiftly and harshly with anyone who spoke out against him. Sunisa was not at the boat dock, so they passed through Customs and took the shuttle boat to the Belize airport, the next country over. When they got there, a man ushered them into the First-Class lounge as had been promised by the police officer. But still no Sunisa.

The President-for-Life of the Maldot Islands was a former non-commissioned officer. He'd led a coup a few years earlier and had won election as President-for-Life through force of will and charisma. His main campaign planks were to make the Maldots rich and free them from Western crime, mainly drugs. He was ruthless about the latter and had successfully attracted tax haven business to the islands for the former. People on the islands were frightened of the General and his secret police, but, on balance, the peace and prosperity that he'd brought to the islands made him a hero. So, they just went along with him, keeping their heads down and enjoying the fruits of his administration.

We drove for quite some time, stopping several times for the driver to talk to street people. I couldn't understand what was said, but I took the laughing and the frequent pounding on the Jeep to mean they were talking about me. We arrived at our destination, someone opened the door, and a guard whipped off the bag over my head. There were four people, all tied to poles in the jail courtyard in front of me. I didn't know who they were, not benefiting from Grillo's explanation to the others. Bullet holes pocked the wall behind them, and there were brown stains on the ground and wall. I guessed that this was blood and assumed that these people were about to be executed. I got worried about the four of us.

I'd nowhere to run, but I wouldn't let these people take me without a fight, so I head-butted the guard the first chance I got. It was a stupid move. He tackled me as I tried to run away, lifted me, and then threw me over his shoulder. He slapped me hard on my butt. "Calm down. You're just here to watch the show and to learn," he said and carried me to a cage and jammed me into it. "Want me to release the cuffs?" he asked. I shook my head yes. "Then bend over and place your hands on the roof of the cage." I did, and he released the cuffs. I rubbed my wrists.

"Is this what I think it is?" I asked.

"What do you think it is?" he replied.

"An execution." He simply shrugged. I took that as a yes.

I was now in a real cage. Different from the cell we'd been in when we were jailed. More like a pen you'd put a dog in. About four-by-four-by-four feet, so I had to stay bent over all the time or on my hands and knees. The cage had a tray underneath it that was covered with what looked like kitty litter. I knew what that was for. There was also a bowl attached to the cage wall with water in it and a slot in the door to the cage; I was sure what they would push through it. I wouldn't debase myself and use any of this. Right away, anyway. However, I also knew I needed to keep up my strength, and food and water would be necessary depending on how long I'd be here. I was sure, also, that they weren't about to tell me that.

I thought back to my study of the tactics of the murderous regime in my old country. They frequently would take prisoners and make them watch torture and murder, getting them to think they were the next subjects. The object was to make the person talk if they had anything to say without lifting a finger. Get two for the price of one: Get rid of problems and tenderize other prisoners who might have important information. That said, I didn't know what they would want out of me.

I was right about what was going to happen. A little while later, a small man dressed in an elaborate military uniform covered with ribbons and medals strutted into the courtyard with several other soldiers, all carrying guns. Several men followed them with what looked like handheld TV cameras. My God, I thought, they are going to televise the execution of these poor people.

The man walked up to one of the two women, looked over at me, smiled and waved his fingers at me, pulled out a gun, and shot the woman in the head, spraying the man next to her with brains and blood. The man started screaming. The soldier walked over to the other woman, grabbed her by the chin, and smiled. She smiled too and spat in his face. There was a brief exchange of words I couldn't hear. Then he shot her, right in the face. The firing squad killed the other two, and then they and the TV crew marched away.

The officer walked over to me and smiled. "I will leave these people out here for a while for you to study. I'll be back later for us to talk after we prepare tonight's news piece on the execution of several more drug smugglers. I may even mention we have another one in our custody." His smile turned into an evil grin like a psychotic Chesire Cat.

I was shocked at the extreme and senseless violence that I'd just witnessed. Now, I saw in real life what I'd heard about. The reports I'd read were shocking, but nothing like the real thing. I knew the Maldots were a dictatorship with a leader like Duterte in the Philippines, but I'd never thought I'd see anything like this. I became much more scared as I did what the man had asked for, thought about what I'd witnessed.

Her friends talked to the U.S. Consul to see what they could find out about Sunisa's whereabouts. The Maldot representative said he'd be available, but he could do little to help them in Belize. He'd traveled to Belize with Sunisa, he said, and then she'd gone off to change in one of those short-stay airport hotels; she disappeared after that. The airport police showed them a video of her leaving the airport on her own and heading into town. They found the cabbie who'd taken her into town, and he said he'd dropped her in the downtown market area, with a promise to pick her up in an hour, and that was the last he'd seen of her. The Maldots government man left them his card and then walked away.

The woman who'd gone to the airport was close to a body double for Sunisa. She wore some of Sunisa's clothes and ensured her face didn't show on any cameras at the airport or in Customs. When she went to the market, she met some confederates, changed out of Sunisa's clothes, and returned to the

Maldots. They had planned to have Sunisa's trail disappear at the market, which it had.

–––––––

"Jermaine Lacosta, Vice-Minister of Practice. I wonder what the hell that is?" asked Sook.

President-for-Life, General Enzo Peralta, the be-ribboned man that Sunisa had seen, had created the Ministry of Practice to help supply victims to feed his fetishes. The Ministry of Practice was a euphemistic name for something modeled after Muammar Gaddafi's Ministry of Protocol, which found girls for the Guide's harem. Peralta had those tastes but also loved to hunt and had a large, private preserve far up-country where he had many exotic animals. He hunted them and the more-than-occasional human, like in *The Most Dangerous Game*, especially enjoying those chases. The four people he had just killed were investigative journalists who'd captured him on film hunting a compatriot of theirs. Now, all of them were dead, and the President-for-Life was feeling satisfied with himself.

Peralta also loved to subjugate exotic beauties; Sunisa was undoubtedly that. Her short stature, long hair, those eyes, and curves made her an ideal candidate for the General's seraglio. He planned to break her and then wasn't sure what he'd do with her. Like he expected Sunisa to be, tarts couldn't handle the hunt after being broken, but he could sell them through auction. He still was looking for one who'd capture his heart, as black as it was. Maybe this one would be the one. He didn't care. He expected to break her, have his fun, and then figure out what to do with her over the next few weeks. If he had to discard her, so be it. The country was a wonderful place for vacationers, and there were always many beautiful young women coming to visit. Some just never left.

As promised, the man I saw kill the two women appeared at my cage sometime later.

"I hope you're enjoying your accommodations, Dr. Pridi.... I think I will call you Sunisa. That is your name, and it is so much more fetching than those Western titles of respect to which you'll find you're no longer entitled...."

"Who the hell are you?" I interrupted. "You've no right to hold me. Where are my friends and my husband?"

He smiled coldly. "You'll learn not to interrupt me." He turned and said something to two men standing behind him at attention. They jumped forward, grabbed my cage, and dragged it to a few feet in front of the bodies that still hung on their poles. Flies and other insects had accumulated on them. They ordered me to put my hands through the top of the cage, and when I refused, they left me for a few minutes and then returned with cattle prods and several buckets of something. After giving me a thorough treatment with the prods, then throwing freezing water on me, and finally dousing me with blood, they ordered me to put my hands up, and this time I did. They handcuffed me to the top of the cage and exposed me to the flies that the desiccating bodies had attracted. Great, I thought.

Figurehead

The three men walked away, talking and joking amongst themselves. I was left there until the next day. No food, no more water, communing with the bodies and flies and exposed to the tropical sun that beat down on the courtyard. It took forever for the sun to set and dark to come. Even then, the entire square was bathed in intense spotlights. There was no sleep for me. I thought I was being eaten alive. Every time I nodded off, my mouth would open, and flies would attack it. I awoke several times, choking on them.

Jake, Marie, Sook, and the Belize police were frantically looking for Sunisa. It was like she'd been sucked into a black hole after she entered the market. One or two people remembered an exotic-looking woman but couldn't tell them where she'd gone. It would take about a week before they'd give up and head home, but not before engaging a local private operative, a former American Special Forces soldier, to see if he could find her. He was confident and told them they should go home, and he would stay connected.

The man reappeared at about the same time as he left me the day before. Before he even got close, I yelled at him. My language was colorful, but he didn't look shocked. He even smiled and shook his head yes, as if I'd done what he expected of me, and it pleased him. He said something to the men behind him, and they came over to the cage. One of them uncuffed me and then opened the door, reached in, and dragged me out by my hair. I tried to fight, but the man was too strong. He pulled me a few feet and lifted me, so I was face-to-what-remained-of-her face with the second woman the man had shot. The guard pushed my face into the other woman's, and the other began wrapping rope around me so that he bound me to her, my face mashed into what remained of the poor woman's face. He then took my hands and chained them to the top of the post. They left me hanging there, now well inside the insect cloud and getting covered with fluids and the stench as the woman decomposed in the boiling sun. I squirmed around, but that released more fluids to pour over my face and down my body. I stopped moving after a time.

I tried not to think about where I was but couldn't get away from the smell, the liquids running down my face and my body, and the thought that this had once been a human being just like me. The military junta in my old country used this kind of torture to break their subjects. They'd frequently kill a member of the person's family to be tortured and tie that person to the body. I was waiting for them to hit or shock me so that I screamed and then opened my mouth. That, thankfully, didn't happen. Finally, I simply passed out, waking sometime later with a start. My mouth had opened, and... well... some of the dead woman's fluids had drained into my mouth. I vomited over and over.

Patrick O'Halloran had served in the U.S. Army across the Middle East, initially as a soldier than a contractor. As a contractor, he became, in the end, disgusted by the conduct of his bosses and the U.S. military leadership that enabled them. So, he quit publicly and told his story to several of the news services. He then disappeared and ended up in the Caribbean, to which he retired. From time to time, he took on a carefully chosen job, not for the money but to help someone in need. The story that Sook Pridi told him was the challenge he liked to undertake. Pridi had a lot of money, but O'Halloran said he'd only charge expenses if he found and returned his wife. That was the way he worked. He was paying back, was what he told Sook.

O'Halloran started where the story began in the Maldots. He interviewed Grillo, the police captain who'd talked to Sook and the Larkins. O'Halloran had an ear for the truth and felt that he was being lied to from the instant he'd asked about Sunisa Pridi He wasn't as well trained as Sunisa, but Grillo gave him the creeps as well, not that he worried about this man doing something to him. In fact, he almost wished the man would try something.

Grillo knew that this was a man to be reckoned with. He was big and carried himself like a killer. "I won't mess with this man," he thought to himself and prepared to call the President's office as soon as O'Halloran left.

O'Halloran didn't press things, though, as the Maldots had a reputation for making people who asked tough questions disappear. He played the dumb Mid-Western American grunt and left, but not before meeting with Louis, the driver, that day. "I really can't help you, Mr. O'Halloran," said an obviously nervous Louis. "I was with Mr. Jake and Mr. Sook all night, and the Doctor was gone by the time they released us the next morning."

Patrick thanked Louis and then headed back to the boat docks. He sensed he was being followed and wondered if he should let himself be taken. He decided no, at least not right away, and walked down to the docks and waited for the shuttle to the airport, staying with the crowd. When he arrived home, he made a few calls, and over the next few days, a group of people arrived there. All of them were old teammates from his time in the Middle East. He filled them in on the mission and what he'd learned and felt while in the Maldots.

Jermaine Lacosta told the General about O'Halloran's visit, and he became livid that his police hadn't taken O'Halloran. Not only was he a risk with Sunisa, but he also sounded and looked like someone the General might want to hunt on his preserve. He decided to see if he could get him to return so they could take him. He arranged with Lacosta to reach out to O'Halloran and drop a few hints so he would think Jermaine was on his side. Thus, while O'Halloran was planning to infiltrate the Maldots, they were preparing to invite him back. When he got the invitation to meet Lacosta, O'Halloran knew there was a trap in the offing and was delighted.

One of O'Halloran's closest friends was Chloë Wintergarden. Chloë was a sniper and one of the best. She never, ever missed. In the Middle East, she was up there with men like Chris Kyle—she had almost 160 kills to her record. The main difference from Kyle was that she was a ghost. Her subjects

Figurehead

never knew she was there, and she disappeared like smoke when her mission was over. No one knew who she was or what she even looked like, aside from O'Halloran. Chloë was small, maybe 5'3". She weighed around 110 pounds soaking wet, and she looked like a school kid and played on that. There were three others to O'Halloran's team: Parker Witt was like O'Halloran and a big guy. He joked that his black eyes were windows to his soul. Marc Dacks was the team logistics expert. He got them in and out of places, along with all their stuff. The last member of the team was Jered Klute. Jered was a communications and IT expert. He was their go-to guy for hacking and dropping noxious payloads into enemy systems. He was also an expert with knives and had more kills than any of them in hand-to-hand combat. They worked out a plan for Chloë and Jered to arrive as a couple for a vacation in the Maldots. Patrick would travel in separately for a meeting with Jermaine Lacosta, and Marc and Parker would come at night on a boat with all their supplies.

I had passed out because of the awful smells from the body of the woman to whom I was tied. The only positive thing was that it had rained on the second day, so a lot of smell and desiccating tissue had washed away. Still, it was awful. On the fourth or fifth day, the men returned and cut me down. I collapsed to the ground, and they dragged me away, back to my cage. They threw me in it, and pulled my hands through the bars at its top, and again chained them there. I was hosed down and washed with soapy water. Just like I was a dog.

"American whore, you will be respectful to the General when he returns shortly. He expects that. If you don't, then you could always find yourself back with the bodies. This time, the General has told me we can whip you until you bleed, and then we'll hang you back up there for a week," said a guard with a wicked smile which told me he'd love to do that.

The General came out soon after they cleaned me off. He walked around my cage and appraised me. It was clear what he was judging me for. One of the guards left and returned a few minutes later with a comfortable chair. The man arranged himself neatly in the chair, set his cuffs, and said, "I am Enzo Peralta. I rule this country and have taken a liking to you. My Vice Minister of Practice, Jermaine Lacosta, and I grew up together. He knows me well and understands my tastes. We photograph every woman who enters the country as they pass through Customs. He evaluates the pictures and passes to me the ones he thinks are women I might like. Being a beach paradise, the Maldots attract many lovely women like you. There are almost too many to pick from. Jermaine has rightly counseled me to throttle down my needs because he says that too many beautiful women like you disappearing from our country would bring the hounds of Hades down on our heads. So, I am choosy.... And, I have chosen you," he said. He smiled, and it chilled me. I also thought it sucked to be me right now. Last, I thought, a country full of psychopaths. Like attracts like, I guess. Wonderful.

Figurehead

"Chosen me for what, General?" I asked. As if I didn't know what.

"Come, come. You know very well what I've chosen you for. To be my demimondaine until I tire of you. When I do, I have many things that I can do with you. But, to give you an incentive to be the best tart you can be, nothing else that I would do to you would be as wonderful as you submitting to me as my paramour. Alternatives are many, some very unpleasant. I often sell my failed women. Who knows where you might end up? Maybe even back in your old country. Wouldn't that be precious? But the longer you keep me intrigued, the longer you put off what might be an unsavory end to you."

I thought as if what he was planning would be a savory end. His use of all those words describing a prostitute or a whore was, I guessed, his attempt to impress and demean me. I said, "I'm impressed, General, with your command of English. You seem to know a few words. Just a few. I imagine your dick is the same."

He laughed and gave me a scary smile. "I'm looking forward to breaking you, Sunisa. You will break beautifully and within the next day. As strong as you think you are, I am far more accomplished at what will happen with you. You will not resist me." He stood up and continued as he walked away, "I will see you again at my preserve. I know you will be much friendlier by then." He said something to the men, and they came over to the cage and dragged it and me across the courtyard into the back of a waiting truck. They slammed the doors shut, and, in a few minutes, it started and drove away.

Of course, it wasn't air-conditioned, and soon I was sweating buckets. I was also famished, not having eaten for several days and having vomited a lot. We drove for perhaps four or five hours. The truck finally stopped, and I heard gates opening into likely the place he called his preserve. We drove for maybe another hour and then stopped again. The cargo area doors opened, and several soldiers hauled my cage out of the truck onto a loading dock. They took me down a flight of stairs into a large area where I saw several other similar cages arranged on multi-story racks, some with people in them, all of them young women. The men lifted my cage into a slot and slid me into place. One guard released my hands, and they shoved a bowl of what looked like kibble through the slot.

"Eat. This is what's called Slave Chow. You show you can eat it; we'll take you out of the cage and give you proper food to eat," he said.

"Bite me," I said.

He smiled and walked away. He knew I'd eventually have to eat. My stomach was growling so badly.

While it looked like kibble and undoubtedly was, it smelled good, like they'd poured some gravy or something on it. I looked at it carefully and saw several what looked like pills embedded there. A guard walked by, watching me. "What's in the food?" I asked.

"Special kibble prepared for human consumption, some good gravy from our dinner tonight, birth control pills, and some drugs that will make you less resistant to what is happening to you," he said.

"Which are which?" I asked.

"You gotta take the good with the bad, so to speak," he replied. "You and the General are gonna do it tonight even if we have to tie you to the bed. Ain't no way around that. Now, the question is if you want to risk getting knocked up or not. Me, I don't care what you do. All of that's your call. By the way, if you don't eat tonight, we'll spoon-feed you while you're tied to the bed, and you won't get any birth control in what we feed you. Again, your call."

I sighed and poked my head into the dish, licked the food, and then ate it. The last thing I wanted was to have that bastard get me pregnant. I cleaned the bowl and then felt myself begin to drift off a bit. After I finished, I laid back in the cage until the guards came and ordered me out. I surprised myself and obediently crawled out of the cage and followed instructions.

They took me into a shower area and then stood around watching. Two women there disrobed and showered me, thoroughly soaping and shampooing me. One woman dried my hair, and the other kneeled and shaved my sex clean of hair. I felt some embarrassment but also no desire to fight. The one working on my hair said, "You have beautiful hair. Long and black. I'm going to weave dreadlocks into it, add some beads and then braid them together. You'll be stunning when we dress you."

As she worked, another man came into the room. That I was stark naked didn't bother me at all, or him either. These were powerful drugs. He matter-of-factly measured my neck and then left the room. In about half an hour, as the dreading continued, he returned with a metal collar, placed it around my neck, and clicked it shut. He held up a mirror to me and said as he turned it, "See no keyhole. This doesn't come off. You're now, officially the General's property, until he decides he doesn't want you anymore. My recommendation is to make yourself very tempting, so he never wants to drop you. Bein' dropped is not good," he said. That was the second or third time I'd heard something like that, and I was taking it seriously. The drugs helped with that, I guessed. I felt like I was standing outside of myself, looking in. Weird. Not good.

In another hour, they finished my hair. I'd never thought of myself with dreadlocks, but I had to say I liked what I saw in the mirror in the shower room.

"Come over here," one woman said. I rose compliantly and walked over to where she was standing next to a large chifforobe. She looked through several formal-looking white dresses, smiled, and then held one out to me. "Hands over your head." I raised my hands, and then she dropped the dress over me. It was like a serape but made from fine silk, and one tie tied loosely together, the two sections on each side of the dress. The seamstress had cut the dress deeply down to my navel. It left nothing to the imagination, and I guessed that was the point. I still felt no desire to resist or protest. I liked the feel of the fabric on my body; it tingled. I suppose that was also what they wanted.

"This will be excellent," the woman said and untied the knots, and told me to drop the dress to the floor. I shrugged it off my shoulders, and it pooled at my feet. "Go into that room and then return when they're done with you," said one of the women.

In about half an hour, I returned with my tongue, navel, and both my nipples pierced. The man in the next room had also shot a bright red tag labeled with an "S" through my right ear. I now was a fully tagged and collared slave. A part of me that was observing all of this was sickened and angered, but the part that mattered to them really didn't care. All it wanted to do was to comply and please.

"You will be one of his prettiest slaves, dear. He may even want to travel with you if you are good and lucky. That doesn't happen often. Hands up." I complied, and she re-dressed me. "You won't need any shoes tonight, my dear. Bare-foot is the way the President likes his women on their first night with him."

A formally dressed guard who I'd not noticed before came over, hooked a leash to my collar, and led me out of the dressing area, up several flights of stairs, and eventually down a long hallway to a set of double doors. Before the man knocked, he said, "I will lead you into the room. You will follow me and kneel at the feet of the President. Keep your head bowed, and do not look at him until he orders you to. Understand?"

"Yes, Sir," I said, revolting myself.

When we heard "Enter," the man opened the door and walked in. I followed like an obedient puppy and kneeled at the feet of the President, looking at the floor.

The General looked at me and smiled. They had set another place across from him, and he gestured to the man to seat me there. I did, and the man left the room.

"Sunisa, you look lovely. I am happy that you joined me for dinner." He smiled at his little joke as if I had any other option. He rang a bell, and servants came in and began serving us. The meal was delightful. Again, I wasn't sure if it was the drugs talking or something else, but every one of my senses was highly tuned. I felt *so* good. "The drugs you were given tonight have several purposes. First, there was birth control. Maybe, after we get to know each other better, I will have you carry a child for me. I will tell you that the probability of that is extremely low. You are a slave, and I do not want my seed carried by one such as you." That hurt me at one level, but I was standing outside; I just smiled and inclined my head toward him. "Second, what I call 'willingness drugs.' There are a couple of them in your porridge, but their primary purpose is to make sure we do not fight. I would rather we simply enjoyed each other. Well, I don't care if you enjoy what we do. Third, you can probably feel a need building in you. The need to have me take you. While I will, I want you to participate in this and give me heartfelt pleasure actively. Fourth, and I am sure you're feeling this, the drugs ramp up your senses. Everything you see, feel, hear, and smell is much sharper and richer. That is a gift from me to you. Finally, aside from birth control, these drugs are a first step in altering you permanently; there is more to come. I know you had envisioned a different life for yourself, but by the time I send you away, you will crave the life I have given you. You will become a complete submissive."

We finished the meal and had dessert. By the end, I was twisting around in my seat from desire for the man. I wanted him to touch me and be inside of me so much. He thought this was hilarious. He'd completely broken me and never touched me. "Come over here," he said. I practically launched myself out of my chair and hurried to stand next to him. "Kneel." I did. "Put your head in my lap." I did and breathed in his woodsy, manly scent. I couldn't wait to get more of it. He toyed with the dress's knots and then loosened them. The dress top slid down, and he bared my breasts. He played with the nipple rings, tugging hard on them a few times. I sucked in my breath when he did that.

"As I said to you earlier, Sunisa, I would break you within a day, and here you are. Completely at my beck and call. Broken."

He stood up quickly, and I dropped away from him. "Did I disappoint you, General?" I asked.

He smiled at me, held out his hand, and led me out of the room, leaving my dress behind on the floor.

O'Halloran met with Jermaine after he entered the country. "Mr. O'Halloran, I'm glad that you came on such short notice. Things are becoming very bad here. The General is becoming increasingly erratic, and there are several of us who believe that it's time that he goes."

"Really?" asked O'Halloran. "I thought you were one of his oldest and closest friends and his procurer. You were children together, right? Remind me never to trust you."

Jermaine looked surprised. He'd thought that aspect of his relationship with Peralta was a secret. He wondered about this big, supposedly dumb American. He thought about having Grillo shot at his earliest convenience.

"Anyway, regardless of your motives, I'm glad that you're on our side," said O'Halloran with a big smile. "Here, let's toast to the success of our missions."

Jermaine took the bottle of beer offered by O'Halloran, and only because O'Halloran had just opened it did he take a swallow of it. Within seconds, he knew that had been a mistake. He collapsed on the table, and when he awoke, he was somewhere else, inside of a shack. O'Halloran sat opposite him. "Good. I'm glad you're finally awake. I have a few questions for you, and you'll answer them truthfully because you won't be able to do anything else." O'Halloran questioned him in detail about the General, his strengths and weaknesses, what he did with women like Sunisa when he captured them and where they were taken and finally ended up. He was sad to hear that it might already be too late to get Sunisa out unscathed, but that crystallized things for him about what would happen next. Jermaine would not leave the shack alive, and the General would likely only live a few more days with the tables turned on him.

O'Halloran thanked Jermaine for his help. He saw the relief in him just before he lashed out with his knife and nearly decapitated him. He gathered the rest of his crew, and they headed north toward the General's preserve, leaving Lacosta, where he sat to be found or eaten by his vermin friends.

In the morning, the women who'd dressed Sunisa the night before came to take her back to her cage. This time she fought. She didn't want to leave the General's side. Peralta always loved this morning after scene. He had time to see how fully he'd broken the new slaves as they cried and begged to be allowed to stay at his side. He smiled. He loved degrading these arrogant American women and then doing it repeatedly. When that pleasure left the relationship, that would be time to sell. He'd already decided about that. Last night was a wonderful experience, and he knew he could get a lot of money for this one. He knew, too, that she was not the one to light up his darkness. She was too decent.

After Sunisa was gone, the General got up and took coffee and breakfast on his terrace, looking out over the preserve and his hunting field. He was about to head in for a shower when the captain of his guard detail came in to tell him that there was an American to see him. A man called Patrick O'Halloran. That surprised Peralta. He was the one Jermaine had said was asking questions about Sunisa and that they were trying to capture. Instead, he shows up at his doorstep. He should have been more concerned about this but was still high from his night with the woman. He told the captain to ask the man to come in and see if he wanted any breakfast. He would be right down. "Tell the dressers to dress Sunisa in something right for a few hours in the field and have her brought here."

From about a half-mile away, Chloë watched all of this through her scope. "I could have put a bullet through the scum's head, but I know Patrick wants to manage this so we can get the woman out, even if she's a basket case," she said. Jered looked up from the communications unit he'd set up and nodded.

"Well, we're the only ones that can talk now. I've hacked into the General's servers and communications systems, and they're ours. I've let Patrick know, and he said that he'd tell me when we can wreak havoc.... I'll be staying here. How about you?" Jered asked.

"I'll stay with you for the time being, but I may have to move when we start things up. Come along. I like you having my back, Jered," she said. He smiled in return.

The General showered and dressed casually for the meeting. He didn't feel that all his medals would impress this man, and he was right. They also brought in Sunisa. She was wearing a light sheer top and long pants. Not exactly clothes for a field trip, but exactly right for showing his ownership of the broken woman. The way the clothes hugged her body, it was clear that they were all she had on. He smiled and wished that they had time for another tumble but decided that could wait. He held out his arm, and she took it, lurching toward him and looking grateful for the touch.

Figurehead

"It is amazing, Sunisa, how far you have fallen in just a day," he said. Still outside of myself, I knew I should be hurt and crying, but all I felt was pleasure from his touch.

We walked downstairs. My two selves were warring with each other for dominance. On the one hand, I felt stimulation from my various piercings, interacting with the drugs I'd been given. On the other, my old self wanted to reach out and tear out the General's eyes. He smiled as if he knew exactly what I was thinking. "As I said, Sunisa, it brings me much pleasure to see how much you've fallen. I certainly am enjoying seeing you degrade yourself. Are you enjoying all of this?"

"Yes, General," I said. Shamed.

"Mr. O'Halloran," the General said when we walked out onto the terrace. "I'm glad to meet you. I am General Enzo Peralta. Jermaine has said much about you. We've also looked at your military history, and it's impressive. I am trying to find him. I'm sure that he would want to say hello."

"Thanks, General. You won't find Jermaine. He has, uh, moved on, let's say. I'm here for that woman. You release her to me, and you can live another day or two to continue your depravity," said O'Halloran, going right for the throat. The General was unaccustomed to being disrespected this way, and O'Halloran hoped that he'd do what he did. Peralta was also concerned about the implications of what O'Halloran said about Jermaine. None of what he heard made him feel good—or, more importantly, that he was in control here.

"Mr. O'Halloran," he said, producing a small revolver and pointing it at him. "I'd hoped that we could have a cordial conversation, but I see that's not possible. In any case, the endpoint of this would be the same."

"You mean a hunt?" O'Halloran asked. "I'm up for that. If I win, I get two things."

"What are those?" the General asked, again surprised.

"I get the woman, and I get to take your head as I did with that sadistic friend of yours."

The General flushed a deep red, then purple.

"Where do we start, General?"

The General gave O'Halloran a 30-minute head start into the jungle. O'Halloran could have a knife but no other weapons unless he could capture some. The General told O'Halloran that while he liked the idea of *The Most Dangerous Game*, he wasn't suicidal. He always had men with him and spread around the jungle. Little did he know that these were being dispatched one by one by O'Halloran's team.

I stood by and watched. I knew that this man was here to rescue me, but my feelings were mixed. I saw that the General saw and loved it. He wanted to see me in pain, and while I should have hated him for that, I couldn't. God, I wanted to feel him inside me repeatedly. I also wanted to kill him.

We went out into the jungle with several of his men.

"General, we seem to be having trouble with our communications systems. Our servers appear to have been hit with a ransomware attack and have shut down. I can use traditional radio to communicate with our men, but that is, as you know, slower," said the guard captain.

Figurehead

"No worry, Captain. We will quickly do this. The American is almost dead right now. I can feel it," said the General. "Tell everyone to be extra-vigilant. I don't like it that our systems go down at the same time this man shows up. There may be more people here than just O'Halloran."

I saw the captain thought it was foolish to be exposing themselves—and that we should head back to the house, but he shrugged his shoulders, and we walked on. He kept reaching out to his men, and they told him that the American was moving toward the hills about a mile ahead. He appeared to be heading toward the clear-topped one that the General occasionally used to bring in helicopters for guest hunts. This was going to be too easy, the captain thought. Once up there, the man would have some cliffs at his back and nowhere to go. If the captain had been more competent and more experienced, he would have been scared, but the General's arrogance was infectious.

We climbed up the hill to the field at the top. In the middle of it stood O'Halloran. The General's men arrayed themselves out in front of him in a semi-circle. He stood there smiling grimly.

"Mr. O'Halloran, this has been little of a hunt. You've given me no challenge," said the General.

"This was never a hunt, General. This was an assassination and a rescue," he said. At that, the guard captain fell to the ground with a bullet in his head. Quickly, the remaining five men fell as well. The General raised a weapon and pointed it at O'Halloran. There was an explosion as one of Chloë's shots hit the General's weapon and blew it out of his hand. He started to scream.

"Sunisa, I know this will be difficult, but I want you to come over to me," said O'Halloran.

I took a hesitant step toward him, but the General grabbed me and put a knife to my throat. "You shall not have her," and started to draw the blade across my throat. A few things happened: My survival instincts kicked in, and I slammed my foot down onto the General's ankle. He howled and turned away from me. O'Halloran threw his knife underhand straight into the General's throat. The shooter added a round to the General's head.

I felt sad for a moment but thought that this was for the best. He would have thrown me out eventually and to, some even worse, wolves. It still felt like a piece of my heart had been torn away, though. I cried.

We returned to the General's hacienda, released the remaining prisoners, and put the staff in the cages in the basement to await Interpol's arrival. With the death of the General, his opposition rose and took back the reins of power. It could have been a bloodbath, but the country's new leader wanted peace and prevailed on his people not to take revenge. He made the people believe the courts would do that. And they did much later. But before that, Captain Grillo had an unusual accident in his hotel in Belize as he was leaving for Europe. The strange man, for some reason, had tried to use a hair drier when he was standing in his room's full bathtub.

Figurehead

In the meantime, O'Halloran took me with the rest of his team to his base. Sook, Jake, and Marie came down to get me, but I was too badly broken and, even if they didn't see it, I did. I had been changed—and would always be—I was sure that I could never go back to my old life. I returned home with Sook and my friends, but things didn't go well for me. My appetites were now, well, abnormal. Work was impossible. I couldn't be a good doctor to my patients. I left the practice and looked around for a new job. Nothing came to mind. Slave was not a job. Sook also struggled with the changes in me and made a good try at accepting me, but, in the end, he couldn't, and I couldn't be the old Sunisa. So, one morning, he woke up, and I had gone. I hope every day that the good man is happy.

It took some time, but I worked my way down to the Caribbean and eventually to Belize and a beachside bar where I got a job as a server. I stayed there, letting myself be used until Patrick O'Halloran showed up one day. I knew he would eventually.

Shrinks would call it transference. I'm still with him. I pine away for the General, but Patrick is way more the man than he ever was. He's even offered to take me with him and his friends the next time they have a job. Maybe a way to sublimate my desires.

Action for my constantly firing senses.

The End

{ 5 }

The Lemonade Stand

I turned into my corner and almost hit the kids standing around a table, back in some bushes. They had a sign that read: "Lemonade $1" and waved as I came within a foot or two of them. I waved back, and even though it was a little dangerous, I stopped the car and leaned out the window. "Hi, kids! What're you up to?" I asked, then thought, "Duh," looking at the sign.

"Selling lemonade, Sir. A dollar a glass," said a teenaged girl, not making me feel stupid or anything. Smart kid, I thought. She has a future. I could read that.

"Give me a second," I said, "I live right there, and I'll come back after I park."

I came back out a few minutes later and bought a couple of glasses of the stuff. It tasted little like lemonade, but I gave them a five, anyway. "Why don't you guys move your stand across the street into my yard? You'll see more cars there; maybe won't get hit."

Figurehead

"Can we, Sir?" asked the girl. "That would be great. Our mom and dad told us not to go on anyone's property, and we figured that this was a good place." Which it wasn't for many reasons. They started packing their stuff up, putting it into an old red Radio Flyer wagon to bring it across the street onto my yard.

I told them my name and then asked theirs. "I'm Harper," said the girl, "and this is my brother Holden and cousin Hank." The H's, I thought. Families with a sense of humor, maybe.

They set up, and I went back into my house.

Later, I was working in the kitchen when I heard a knock at the door, and my dog started going berserk. The boy, Holden, and his sister were at the door. "Could Holden use your bathroom, Sir?" she asked.

"Sure," I said and invited him in.

I showed him where it was and told Harper to have a seat on the porch. She waved at her cousin at the stand and sat down on the steps. I turned one of the porch chairs so we could talk. She was sixteen years old and a tenth grader at a nearby private school. We talked about the usual things that you do with a sixteen-year-old: music, classes, boys. She impressed me—she was well-spoken and had a lot to say; I asked her what she wanted to do with her life. Unlike boys who want to be President or a firefighter or a cop or a doctor, she said, "I'm not sure. I have a lot of years before I have to think about that. I do like the woods, though."

"Good thinking," I said. "Don't paint yourself into a corner at your age." I talked to her more, and she stayed a while after her brother came out and went back to the stand. I spoke to her about my college and the forestry program there, one of the best in the world. She left eventually, and I went back into the house. A bit later, they came by and said that they were heading home. They'd sold their lemonade and made about twenty bucks, including my five, and were thrilled.

I wished them well but knew she'd be back at the end.

The lemonade stand was my idea, so I guess I deserved what happened to me. The nice man helped us out by letting us use his property for the stand—that helped us sell out quickly. My mom and dad wouldn't let us sell on Main Street 'cause it was pretty busy. They were the ones who suggested that we go up to one of the larger side streets and set up there, but to be careful that we stayed off people's property.

We'd done a stand like this toward the end of every one of our school years. We used the few dollars we'd make to bike down to the custard stand down the road to buy these special custards that they made. It had always been a great way to start the summer. After our success at the stand, I thought this was starting to be one of the best summers ever. I was going to find out that I was right and wrong about that.

Our property backed up on a section of woods, and we'd walked a path through it since we were little to play with friends that lived up there in the houses in the woods. The trail dead-ended on Hickory Street, a tiny one-lane road that went up toward Second Street. We didn't know that the land between our yard and the end of Hickory Street was private property but were going to find that out soon enough, though.

We'd used my old Radio Flyer all-terrain wagon, the one with the big wheels, to move our lemonade, ice chest, cups, table, and the signs we'd made up to the Y-shaped island and put ourselves near some bushes in the middle of it. We'd been there about an hour and sold only one glass of lemonade. It was hot, and we were getting a little frustrated with the poor business. Cars would come around the corner and, if they saw us at all, it was in their rear-view mirrors. Most of the cars going the other way seemed to go down the other side of the "Y" away from us. Then came the nice man, and he suggested we move to his yard across the street. Sales jumped after that, and we ran through our lemonade in a little bit less than an hour.

When Holden had to go to the bathroom, I walked him up to the house and asked the man if he could use it. He said sure, and he and I sat and talked while Holden was in the house. He was a nice guy. We talked about the usual stuff kids and adults talked about, school, boys, and my plans for the summer and after that. I told him I'd no idea what I wanted to do, though I loved the woods. He said good, not to decide too early, and mentioned that he'd gone to a college with an excellent forestry school. He had a great dog that was very friendly and looked at me intelligently, with these big almond-colored eyes. It was like he could read my mind or something. Crazy-scary, but not bad-scary.

Later, we walked back over to the man's house, said good-bye. He wished us well and said he'd see us around. I didn't re-alize until much, much later he was talking to me. We packed our stuff onto the wagon and headed back home, thinking about the custard floats we were about to get. A little ways into the woods, we talked to each other about what drinks we were going to get when a giant of a man stepped out of the woods in front of us. He was clothed all in green, had a badge, and was wearing a backpack. You could easily miss him, ex-cept for his size. He was enormous and looked unhappy.

I practically ran into him; I was so focused on the trail and the talk. I thought I heard his voice in my head rather than my ears, but how could that be? That was weird. "You know you kids are trespassing, right?" he said. "I could arrest you right here, and you'd be in deep trouble."

Holden and Hank were quicker and were further away from the man than me, so they just bolted, leaving me stand-ing there holding onto the handle of the wagon. I turned to run away as well but then heard that voice in my head again. This time, he used my name. "Harper. Stop right there. I want to talk to you."

I ran, though, leaving my wagon behind. I heard the man moving behind me. "Stop, please, stop," he yelled. "Look where you're running. You're killing them."

I stopped. When I looked around, I saw that I was in the middle of what looked like a garden, but with plants I'd never seen before. I could see that I'd stepped on a bunch of them, crushing them under my feet. Turning around slowly, I looked at the man. He looked like he was crying.

"Look at what you've done," he sobbed. "You destroyed my friends. All that work, those lives, lost."

I got the work bit, but lives, friends? "We meant nothing, Mister. We cross this way all the time. Have done it for years," I said.

"You're telling me you never saw these signs before?" and he gestured to a sign on the side of a tree. In big, red letters, it said, "NO TRESPASSING" and "Trespassers will be Prosecuted" right below it. I shrugged as we'd seen the signs but didn't think there was ever anyone around here. I knew it didn't make what we did right, but the alternative was a long walk to get to our friends. I guess I was about to find out how bad we'd been.

"Grab your wagon and follow me," he said and headed off deeper into the woods.

"Uh, Sir," I said, "My home is that way." I pointed off in the opposite direction.

"We're going to my cabin to contact the authorities so they can decide what to do about you," he said.

This was getting worse and worse all the time. Authorities? I looked down the trail and then at the man. He'd stopped walking away, and I heard the voice in my head again, "I wouldn't try to run, Harper. I know you don't want to go off with a strange man. That's smart, but you need to come with me. I will not hurt you."

GEORGE CONKLIN

Just what someone who was planning to hurt me would say, I thought. I ran but only got a few feet before the voice in my head yelled, "Stop!" very loudly. My legs stopped even though I wanted to keep running. The man walked over, grabbed me by the nape of my neck, and picked me up like I weighed nothing. He threw me over his shoulder. The voice in my head said, "Rest there," and I did, falling immediately into something like sleep. He bent down to pick up the wagon handle, and he carried me off into the woods. This all was strange, but I wasn't scared anymore. Later, I found out was that he had impelled me, and he could make someone, anyone, me do anything by talking to them in their heads.

The man carried me until we were well off the trail. He told me to wake up. I thought we ought to be getting back close to Main Street, maybe near the Corbett's house, but we just kept on walking, never coming out of the woods that we should have been out of a long time ago. Weird. Finally, we stopped next to a giant oak tree that I'd never noticed before, even though I'd been all over the woods. I looked around and didn't know where we were. It was like we were somewhere else, far away.

"Can you see the door in front of you?" he asked as he put me down.

I looked where he was pointing and saw what looked like a door only a few feet in front of the oak. I walked around it. That's exactly what it was. A door. Just standing there all by itself. "Uh, yeah. I see it. What is it?" I asked. "Looks like a door, but out here in the middle of nowhere?"

"It *is* a door, silly girl. Open it," the man said.

I turned the knob and opened the door. There was a room in front of me, with a fire in a fireplace, several oversized, comfortable-looking chairs, and a table piled with books. The smell of a wood fire came out of the room. I walked around the door again and only saw its backside in front of the oak. "What is this?" I asked again.

"Like I said, it's a door, and that's my house. Come on in." He pulled my wagon into the room and turned to me. "Do I need to use my voice on you again?"

I shook my head no and stepped into the room. When I did, the door shut. I turned around and saw only a wall behind me. "Wow!" I thought.

"Come and sit down," the man said. "We need to talk. Are you thirsty?"

"Yes, Sir, and scared."

He left me standing in the middle of the room like the fool I was. What had just happened? Was I that stupid to just go off with a guy I didn't know? Now, I was in his house, and the door we'd walked through seemed to have disappeared. Where the heck was I? I was terrified.

I looked out the cabin window for another way to escape if I needed to and saw that I had definitely stepped into something. It looked like there was a blizzard going on outside. I heard a noise behind me and then the voice in my head, this time simply sighing. I looked up at the man, smiled a little, and then sat down on one of the chairs by the fire. He handed me an orange-colored drink, and I took a tentative sip. He

GEORGE CONKLIN

then gave me a dish with an odd-looking thing that looked like an old, dry banana.

The drink was delicious. "Thank you, Sir." I thought that I might have made another mistake taking the drink. Mom and dad had drilled into both of us not to accept any food from strangers.

He smiled at me and said, "Stop this, Sir stuff. I'm Ranger. It's my name and title. I supervise work done on several sites in different places and watch out for our experiments and the animals and plants in these places. What do you think of the Spring Tangerine juice?"

"Spring Tangerine? What's that? I like it, by the way," I said.

"It's from one of my sites. I think it's better than the ones you get on your planet. Try the Pacay. That one comes from your planet. I know you wanted to get some custard, and I don't think you'll be getting any today or any time soon." He handed me a spoon, and I dug in. It tasted like vanilla ice cream.

While I was eating, he continued, "Your parents taught you right, Harper. You shouldn't accept gifts from strangers. In my case, I feel it will be a little different, but they were right about that—in general. I can only say this, but you will have to come to believe it. I mean you no harm, and you can trust I will not hurt you."

"Can I ask some questions, Ranger?"

"Sure. I bet you have a lot."

Figurehead

"You keep talking about planets. I thought we were some-place else on Earth. Where are we?"

"As I said, we're in my home. On the planet Estea. It's a beautiful place, normally, but we hit it at a bad time with the blizzard." He walked over to the table that was covered with books and brought back something that looked like a tablet. "Your planet is there, and we're here. About 1,115 of what you call light-years apart. Do you know what a light-year is?"

"I've heard of it, but not really."

"Well, it's the distance light travels in a year—about six trillion miles. That means we are about seven quadrillion miles from your Earth."

I sat back, shocked. "Huh?" I asked quite intelligently.

"I know this is hard to absorb. How did we get here, so far away from your home? We can move instantly between places, because of the technology we've developed. Your people would consider it to be magic at this point, but we are teaching you. Some of you anyway," he said.

"I have research sites on your Earth, here on Estea, and in five other locations around the galaxy. I travel to each of these and spend time there to make sure that things are going well. I was looking in on my garden on Earth when you ran through it. Do you know what those things were? That was five years of work, and I'm not sure if I can save it."

"No, Sir. Just pretty plants. Different kinds, I think," I said.

"Yes, and no. On some planets we travel to, the plants are what we call sentient. Do you know what that means?"

I shook my head no but thought I was about to learn how deep in trouble I was.

"You and I are sentient beings, though I'm not sure about you," he said with a tight but kind smile. "It means that we can perceive and feel things. Like pain. Those plants screamed when you crushed them. Maybe I should say, murdered them. They were dying on their planet, and we wanted to see if we could find them a suitable home on your Earth. You sort of ended that, at least for some of them."

He'd just called me a murderer. Oh boy, was I in a boat-load of trouble?

"I'm sorry, Sir. I didn't mean to hurt anyone... or anything."

He looked at me carefully, and I felt him in my head, rum-maging around, looking for God knows what. Eventually, he sighed. "I can tell that, Harper. But I just can't let you skate on this. We need to talk to someone else."

"Sir, you just said that I won't be getting any custard to-day or anytime soon. Does that mean I go home tomorrow?"

"I can't tell you when you'll be going home, to stay any-way. I will tell you that before anything happens to you here, you'll have to go home and explain to your mom and dad what you did and why we might take you from them for a while."

"Huh? I need to get back, Ranger. Please, please take me back." I stood up and moved back to the wall where the door had been and felt around. There was nothing there. "Please, Ranger, please." I started crying.

Figurehead

"Sorry, Harper. You and your friends are trespassers. I caught you, and you're going to be prosecuted as a trespasser and a vandal for murdering those beings and disrupting our experiment. You're actually pretty lucky. It could be a lot worse. I called it murder after all." Ranger stood up and moved across the room to a wall. He sketched a box and opened another door. "Come with me," he said, not unkindly. "Everything will be fine. Just be honest and listen to me when I talk to you there." He pointed to my head. "Also, I promise that when you learn to do this..." and he gestured to the door, "I'll allow you to go home—if you still want to by that point. Come."

He picked up his backpack, and seeing no other way out, I got up, and we stepped through the door into what seemed to be a courtroom, like nothing I'd seen on T.V., though. There was a tall woman, I guess that's what she was, sitting behind what you'd call a bench in any other courtroom. She wore a dark robe that shimmered and changed colors as I looked at it, and she had the bluest skin I'd ever seen. "Ranger, it's good to see you," she said. "What have we here?"

"A trespasser and vandal, Your Honor, on our site in Alabama on Earth. I caught her, but two other what they call boys ran off. She's young, sixteen of their years, but acknowledges that she had read our signs. She's not stupid but destroyed several of the Yiarrots and Kiflowers. I can still hear them screaming as they died under her feet."

"I am so sorry, Ranger. I know how much those entities mean to you. Let's talk to her, and then we can decide what to do," she said.

"Thank you, Your Honor, but I will have a request for you to consider before sentencing," he said.

Sentencing?

"That's fine. Please sit and young lady, come over here." The Judge stood up, well floated up as she didn't have legs. Only beautiful wings, almost like a dragonfly. "Yes, my dear, we are like your dragonflies, but, uh, smarter. Now, I speak to you directly mind-to-mind, so you don't have to speak unless that's more comfortable for you."

"Thank you, Your Honor," I said in my head, and I looked at Ranger, who smiled at me.

"I will ask you a series of questions, and you will answer them. All of what we say here will be recorded. If I read any attempt to lie, I will be very annoyed, and...."

"You don't want to annoy the Judge, Harper," said Ranger.

She smiled at him and continued, "For the court, will you state your full name and address?"

"Harper Jane Cobb, Your Honor. I, uh, live on Main Street in Daphne, Alabama... on Earth, I guess."

She smiled. "Thank you. May I call you Harper?"

I nodded, and she smiled again. I figured I needed to be as sweet as I could be. After all, I was trillions and trillions of miles from home and on trial. I was still trying to process that.

{ 142 }

Figurehead

"You just need to be honest, Harper. I don't care about you being as sweet as you can be. Honesty is what matters here for your future." I kept forgetting this was going on in my head, and she knew everything I was thinking. I was also wondering how much she knew. If she knew everything, why would we be going through this? "Let me explain. There is your forebrain and backbrain, Harper. Your forebrain is where all your thinking goes on. That is what I can see. Your backbrain is where, let's say, your soul lives. I can't see that directly, but I can get a picture of it from our conversation and behavior. If I interpret blackness in your soul, you will be incarcerated and put to work. If not, then many other possibilities open up for your service."

"Service, Your Honor?" I asked.

"I'm asking the questions, Harper. Next question: How old are you? I want you to confirm that for the record. We have different ways that we treat people of different ages."

"I'm sixteen years old, Your Honor."

"Did you see the 'No Trespassing' signs when you were walking through the forest preserve?" she asked.

"Yes, Your Honor. We'd been walking through there since I was a kid, and...." There was a snort from behind me, and I turned to see Ranger trying to stifle a laugh.

The Judge glared at him. "I'm sorry, Your Honor. I was just laughing..." he started, looking very embarrassed.

"I know what you were laughing at, Ranger. I thought it was funny too, but you don't see me making the young lady uncomfortable, do you?" she said sternly.

"No, Your Honor. I'll watch my mouth. I apologize to both of you."

"Go ahead, Harper. I apologize for the Ranger. He spends too much time away from people and has forgotten his manners," the Judge said.

I looked at Ranger, not understanding any of this. "Anyway, we'd been walking that way since I was a kid..." and I turned and looked deliberately at Ranger, who smiled at me, "and it's only been in the last year or so that you, I guess, put these signs up. Since we'd always been walking through the area and we did nothing there, except pass through, I thought nothing of it. Until now. I know we were wrong, and I apologize."

"Apology accepted, but that doesn't mean that you get off without a service sentence of some sort. How many times did you walk through the forest do you think, and how many of you walked through the area do you think?" she asked.

I felt a gentle prod in my head, I thought, from Ranger. "Be careful how you answer this question, Harper," he said.

I didn't know what he meant but was as honest as I could be. "Maybe once every week and at least me and my brother. Sometimes other people, but mostly just us," I said. I thought I heard a sigh in my head.

The Judge frowned and asked, changing course, "What do you want to do with your life, Harper?"

"It's funny that you ask that question, Your Honor. A man that let us use his yard to set up our lemonade stand asked me just the same question." She smiled at that, and I wondered why. "I told him I didn't have any actual idea now. My brother, who's a year older than me, wants to be a cop... I mean a police officer. I'm not sure about myself. All I can say is that I enjoy being in a forest."

She looked directly at Ranger, smiled, and nodded. "What about being in the forest do you like, Harper?"

"The quiet, the smells, the way the light moves through the trees. In our area of the country, our soils are deep and moist; they spring under your feet when you're walking, especially when you're barefoot," I said. "I love that feeling and everything else about it when I am alone out there."

"Are you willing to take responsibility for breaking the law, Harper?" she asked, abruptly changing course again.

"Yes, Ma'am." that question made my gut turn a little. I knew we were getting close to whatever the Judge meant by a service sentence.

"All right, then. I have two options open in front of me. One is to sentence you under the laws of Alabama, and the other is to sentence you under the laws of the Confederation that we are all part of. Your case is kind of tricky, too, as, at 16, I could sentence you as an adult and should, given the severity of this incident. Harper, please leave Ranger and me to talk for a moment. He'll be right out. I'll consider your sentence when he leaves me."

Things sounded worse and worse by the minute. I was scared out of my pants.

Ranger came out of the court a few minutes later and sat next to me. "I asked for her to judge you under our law," he said, "I was trying to get you to be a little less precise about the many times you crossed the property. I appreciate your honesty, and I know the Judge does too, but you could be eligible for as much as eight and a half years in jail under Alabama law. Maybe not because you're so young, but you would be looking at almost three years in a juvenile facility. It might not sound better, but your jails are not good places."

"Understand," he said, "we are on your planet with the full agreement of your government. They know who we are and the importance of our work for your planet's survival."

"Earth's survival?"

"Yes. You've probably heard of global climate change...." he said.

"Right. We read about it in science class. Some people don't believe it exists," I said.

"They're idiots. All you have to do is look at the year-on-year data to see that something is happening to your Earth and that it's not good. Your own United Nations released a report just a little while ago. It says that it will take centuries, if not thousands of years, to undo the problems that you have caused on your planet. In the meantime, your planet is going to be a mess. That assumes that someone has the guts to start to fix the problems. Most of the people who are loudest about this have reasons, mainly greed, to argue about the cause of it. We're pretty sure what the cause is, but don't get into that argument because it's so political and distracts from the problem, the reality of what is occurring to you. As far as

I'm concerned, the damage is already done, and now we need to mitigate it. Do you know what mitigate means?"

I shook my head no.

He said, "It means to make something less severe. The effects of climate change are going to be unbelievably bad. We've seen it on some planets where worlds that seas had covered are now deserts. I have an experiment going on on one of them. Anyway, all we look at is the data, and that is extremely clear. Weather is changing. In a few years, the storms that you've been seeing are going to get much, much worse. Wetlands will get wetter, and drylands will get drier. The fires you see out West are going to get worse and worse, and they will not be able to grow foods anymore."

"These floods and droughts are already forcing massive migrations of people from some lands to safer, healthier places, which puts stress on food supplies; you will see famines and many, many people dying. You'll also see increased terrorism of many kinds and wars over the best farming and grazing lands. Sadly, most of this can and likely will happen in your lifetime, Harper. I'm there on Earth and working elsewhere to see if we can soften the impact of it. There's no way we can stop it. We can lessen it. Many people will still die. Needlessly is my political statement. Your area may well be underwater before you're even thirty years old. That's how bad things are."

"There are," he continued, "several of us on your world. Like you know, I'm Ranger. There are also ones of us called Guardians. They watch over things and keep us informed about the environment. There are other creatures there, usually with the Guardians, called Protectors. Most of the time, they look like something benign, maybe even friendly, like a big goofy dog. But you wouldn't want to get crossways with them. They watch over the Guardians and help them accomplish their missions."

I sat there, stunned, at the death sentence Ranger just gave my planet, family, and friends. He saw and reached out with his mind to soothe me. "We're doing our best to make the impact of these changes as little as possible. Maybe you can help."

Ranger looked up and then stood, "The Judge's asking us to come back into the court. I'm there for you and will stick by you, Harper, regardless. I like you." He said that as we walked into the courtroom.

The Judge looked up as we walked in, and she said, "I like you too, Harper, and have decided not to refer you back to the Alabama penal system. Instead, I will sentence you under our law to a term of service to be no less than eight and a half of your years...."

"Excuse me, Judge," I said, moaning, "Eight and a half years? How is that better than maybe three years in a juvenile facility where my parents and family can visit me?"

"Let me finish. I know this is disturbing, but our view of crime and punishment, unlike yours, which is all about breaking the mind and body of the jailed, is to provide guidance and training to be a productive member of our society. So, look at this like a tough college years before when you are supposed to go to one. Tougher than that in all ways, but school, not jail. You will continue to be schooled in the basics like what you are doing in high school and then in your area of specialization over the next eight and a half years. There will be a lot of learning packed into a short period for you. You have maybe two more years of high school, as you call it, back on Earth. We will pack that learning into the next six months. We will focus the rest of the sentence on what we call an Assistantship." She paused as she saw I was having difficulty grasping all of this.

She resumed when she saw me settle down a bit. "You said you like the woods, so we'll give you that and more experience. Once that's completed, you'll qualify as a Ranger Assistant, basically have a bachelor's degree in forestry, and you can voluntarily seek additional training to be able to, eventually, take on a job as a licensed Ranger Mentor, like Ranger here, yourself. That would usually be another three years and would look like what you on Earth call a master's degree. Otherwise, you can go home and pick up with college there. They fully accepted our degrees at most any Earth university."

"Now," she said, "as to visits with your family, there's no reason that you can't see them. Maybe not as often as you think you want right now, but you'll be able to see them as much as your mentor allows."

"Mentor?"

"Every person convicted of a crime under our law is placed into a one-to-one training program and assigned someone who, for the term of that sentence, will ensure that you are safe, disciplined—in all senses of that word—and receive the training necessary for you to take on the responsibilities for which you're being trained. That person is what we call a mentor. They have, in your case, because you are still a minor on any planet in the universe we know of, parental responsibilities. I will require you to obey that person like they are your parent. When you're with your parents, I'm afraid it'll be a little complex, but we'll give them the training to understand their roles relative to your mentor's. The mentor's word is final in all cases."

"In your case," I could tell she was finishing now, "your mentor will be...."

"The Ranger, I hope," I said, again not able to keep my mouth shut.

She smiled down at me, "Yes, the Ranger. He will take you to be processed in a few minutes. You might find aspects of processing demeaning, but you need to remember that we have convicted you of a crime, and, in exchange for the education and experience we will provide you, you'll lose a little of yourself, your dignity, for a few years. As you grow and show that you're capable, you will be rewarded, and we will restore your independence to you."

"Last thing, Harper, I've greatly enjoyed meeting you. We will see each other many times over the eight and a half years. As your Judge, you will see me every few months so we can all talk about your progress and any needs that you might have. I know that this isn't easy, and there will be things over the next eight and a half years that will be distasteful to you, but

Figurehead

I know you'll get through it and become as qualified a Ranger as your mentor. Ranger is one of our very best. I look forward to the opportunities we will have to get to know each other better."

She was correct; processing wasn't fun. Ranger couldn't stay with me for it based on their rules. They brought me into a room, took many pictures, and I gave them all kinds of fluids. A medic gave many almost painless shots and what I think were vaccinations. The processor also shot me with a little gun that embedded a chip in my shoulder; now, I felt like my dog. He was a nice enough man; I think it was a man, but he had a job to do that involved what Ranger told me was devaluing me. I felt like a piece of furniture by the time he finished. They gave me a tattooed barcode on the inside of my lip and butt, and an ornate drawing that looked a little like a sun surrounded by stars tattooed just above it. The man told me that meant felon in one of the Confederation languages. Last, I was given a metal collar that supposedly could be used to track me literally anywhere I went. There I was: Sixteen and a felon, collared, tattooed, so for life, I guess.

When they were done with me, Ranger picked me up in the exit lobby. It was still snowing. "Care to take a walk in the snow, Harper?"

"I'm not really dressed for it," I said. I was still wearing my tee-shirt and shorts from Alabama.

He opened the pack he took when we left his house and brought out a pair of hiking boots, a pair of pants, and a heavily lined cape. The shoes were a little large, but he also gave me some heavy socks and the pants, thankfully, had a web belt I could pull tight around my skinny waist. The cape was something special. They lined it in some kind of material that Ranger said would heat or cool me depending on the weather; had all sorts of pockets, some of which had stuff in them already that Ranger said was the survival kit; and shrank to fit me all on its own. It had been the property, he told me, of someone a little taller than me.

We walked for some time in silence, and then he turned into what looked like a restaurant like we had back at home. Ranger was well known there, and we got a table right away, far back in a corner. Dinner was pretty good though I had no idea what I was eating. I couldn't read their script, and so Ranger said that he'd order it for me. He also said that I'd start language training tomorrow as there were ten of them I'd have to be reasonably good at quickly.

"Oh, and there is no summer vacation here. You work all the time. When you're not studying or traveling with me, we both will work around the house. I'll be working right along with you, Harper. You're not a slave in this relationship. You're my student, and you'll be learning a lot. This next eight and a half years will not be easy on you, but I hope you see everything that happens as valuable and treat it as the learning experience it's supposed to be." Little did either of us know what was to happen to us and the significance of the learning experience to occur.

Figurehead

After dinner, we walked back through the blizzard toward Ranger's home. He was fiddling with his communicator thing that looked a lot like my old, now useless phone, but better. He dropped a little behind me.

"Harper?" I turned, and he hit me square in the face with a snowball.

"So that's the way things are going to be," I thought. We had a snowball fight and arrived home thoroughly exhausted and cold. But I felt a lot better. I was feeling better and better about Ranger and all of this.

"Ranger, can I ask you a question?"

"Sure, ask anything you want. You don't have to bother to ask me that every time you have a question, by the way."

"How old are you, and where's your wife? I thought I saw pictures of her here in your house. She's beautiful. Is she away somewhere?"

He paused for a moment and looked sad. I thought I might have stepped in it again. He sighed and said, "I'm 26, so about ten years older than you. I *was* married, as you saw from the pictures in my house. My wife was a warden and worked on another set of planets. She died."

"I'm so sorry, Ranger. I shouldn't have asked. I apologize. I just thought she's so beautiful."

"Yes, she was…. You need to know this. Being a Ranger, even on your Earth, is not a safe job. We have a problem on almost every one of our planets with what you call poachers. These people capture or kill exotic animals for sport, skins, meat, and other organs, sometimes just for that and sometimes for supposed magical properties. There's a big market on your Earth for rhinoceros' horns, for instance. Supposed to increase sex drive or something stupid like that. Your poachers have driven the rhinoceros almost to extinction. Anyway, Anya, my wife, worked in an anti-poaching squad on one of our planets, and her squad was ambushed. She was captured alive but died later in the most horrible of ways. It is better for poachers on most planets to kill the wardens and rangers than to let them live. So, they do."

"I am so, so sorry, Ranger. What happened to the poachers?"

"They got away—for a while—they aren't alive anymore. I hunted every one of them down." The look on his face told me that this was one man it was best to have as a friend.

We walked into the house. "Anyway, you have a long day tomorrow. We'll be up early, and I'll take you to where I work out to keep up my manly physique and where you'll build up yours."

"I'm a girl, Ranger. Not a man," I said before I could stop myself.

He glared at me, and I thought it not wise to mess with your jailer, "Then, like I said, your basics and then language training. It's not as hard as you may think. We're, as I think you've guessed, a super-advanced group of races. We'll then take a short trip to Alabama to talk to your parents, so they know that you're all right. Your room is here."

He opened a door, and I walked into a large room with a bed, desk, a computer like I'd never seen, and a chair setting around a fireplace that had a small fire in it to keep the room warm. "Over there is a bathroom, and there are clothes in that closet and in that chest. They were Anya's but should fit you okay until we can get something for you, maybe tomorrow or the next day, or when you stop being a smart-ass." He glared at me for a second, then smiled and started to laugh. "Don't ever stop being yourself, Harper. I love your mouth and your smart-assedness."

I looked around in the closet and chest and found what looked like a flannel nightgown. I was a little chilled from the snowball fight, so I went into the bathroom, filled the tub with toasty water, and soaked in it until I was warm. I dried myself off, put on the nightgown, and climbed under the heavy covers. I was asleep in seconds. My last thought was about how far I'd gone, aside from the 1,115 light-years. A nice little girl in a decent school with a good life ahead of her to a branded felon. With that said, I slipped off to sleep feeling happy and optimistic about everything.

I woke up suddenly to hear pots and pans crashing. I shot out of bed and ran into the kitchen. Ranger was standing at the sink, running his hand under cold water. "What happened?" I asked.

"I was going to make us a nice breakfast, and I burnt myself pretty bad," he said. "I don't normally cook when I'm home. That restaurant we ate at last night makes some great breakfasts. It looks like we'll be back there tomorrow."

"Let me look at your hand," I said and reached out. His hand was bright red from where grease splattered on it. I didn't see that it was that bad and thought, "Wuss."

"Why don't you sit down and soak the hand in some cold water. I'll make us breakfast."

"What's a 'Wuss?' Something not nice, I assume," he asked.

Well, I thought, started the day off smart-mouthing the jailer again.

He smiled at me and said, "One of these days I'll teach you how to keep things private in your head. Not for a while, though. I love reading your thoughts."

Breakfast was something I was good at. Actually, I was a pretty decent cook overall. I liked the order of kitchens and recipes. So, I excelled. I had a lot of questions about what the different things were in the refrigerator, which looked like something out of a sci-fi movie, but I made us a pretty good rendition of bacon and eggs.

"Look, I need to contribute here as much as I can. Why don't I do the meals and take care of the house? You can pitch in, but let's say those are my jobs." I fingered my collar as I said that.

"You're not a slave, Harper. Do these things because you like to do them," he said. "The collar is to make sure you stay safe."

"Okay, but I look at it kind of like survival. If you cook every meal as this one started, then we'll both starve," I said with a smile.

He smiled back.

Figurehead

"Get used to my smart mouth," I said.

With that, he launched himself from his chair, grabbed me, and threw me out the back door into a snowdrift. He slammed the door in my face. "The front door is unlocked," he said through the closed door. I guess he wanted me to start the day off cold. My smart mouth gets me in trouble again. I shrugged, walked around toward the front of the house, got to the side gate, and found it locked. I had to climb over, and by the time I got to the front door, I was soaked, chilled to the bone, and spoiling for a fight. I knocked on the door, even though it was unlocked, and then stepped away. Ranger stepped out on the porch and made a big deal of looking around for whoever knocked on the door.

"Hello? Someone here?" I heard him ask as I slipped in behind him and closed and locked the front door. "Very funny," I heard from behind me, and then a pair of hands grabbed me. I'd forgotten about his ability to make doors. He hauled me into the living room and onto his lap. He pulled up the nightgown and down my underpants, and then proceeded to give me a thorough butt whacking.

I stood up afterward and said, "I'm not sure that I deserved that."

"Maybe not, but I bet you'll think things through better next time, right?"

"I suppose so." I walked off to my bedroom, took another hot bath, and hung my wet clothes to dry in front of the fire. When I got back to the bedroom, there was a pair of athletic

{ 157 }

shorts, what looked like a jogging bra and underpants, a tank top, sneakers, and socks on the bed.

"We're a little late, so we have to get moving," he said as he walked into the room without knocking. There I was stark naked. He turned around and walked out. "Sorry," he said.

"Ranger, come back in here."

"You dressed?" he asked.

"No, but you need to get over seeing me naked. I won't parade around in my birthday suit, but you certainly will see me undressed from time to time. Like I'll see you. Like I saw this morning. Your robe didn't cover up much. You sleep in the buff all the time?"

As I made this little speech, I was dressing. "Okay. Ready to go," I said.

He drew a door, and we stepped into the middle of a large exercise facility. The ceiling of it was open to the stars. I was gaga. There were many different types of creatures there. "Where are we?" I asked.

"This is an exercise facility called Galactic Fitness on a space station near my old home planet. Like it? There's a bunch of them around the galaxy, and we have a membership in all of them."

"It's incredible," I said.

"Here's your ID badge. Go over to that terminal and scan your card and your lip barcode. It'll spit out your exercise regimen. Every time you move to a new machine, just remember to scan your lip barcode. That will make sure you get credit for the work you do. It'll also show the others here who and what you are."

"Credit? Scan my lip? Are you trying to embarrass me?" I asked.

"Yup. You have specific goals that I set for you so we can work together in the field. I don't want to have to carry you around. You need to understand that you are a student in a mentorship program and have only limited rights at this point. You shouldn't be embarrassed. It's a fact of life you have to live with."

I did what he said and found that my first exercise was a two-mile run on a treadmill. I hadn't ever run two miles, and here he expected me to do it on Day 1. There was a list of about twenty other machines he expected me to hit today as well. I wanted to talk to him about his expectations, but he'd already disappeared.

I felt a breath of air pass my head and looked up to see the Judge floating next to me. "Hello, Harper. How has your first day gone?"

We talked as I ran on the treadmill, and she drifted next to me. I was through all my machines before I realized the Judge had helped to distract me. "That wasn't so hard now, was it?" she asked.

"No, Judge."

"You should be proud of yourself. I am. I understand that you and the Ranger are going to talk to your parents today. That'll be difficult, but all will work out. By the way, unless you are standing in front of me, and the Lords help you if you do, my name is Opal."

"Thanks, Opal. Are you here often?"

"Every day before court. Come and let's play again soon." She flew off. I didn't know what to think about all of this, but I didn't think I'd be feeling this way in juvenile detention in Alabama. It was going to be hard to explain to my parents, for sure. I needed to compose my thoughts before we got there.

We returned home, and I took yet another fabulous bath, put on some other clothes, and straightened up the house. I didn't want to touch any of Ranger's books or personal stuff, but I picked up dishes and dusted around everything.

"What are you doing?" he asked.

"Some of my jobs, Ranger," I said.

"Let's figure out all of that later. Right now, we need to get you fitted for a translator, and you need to get back to your basics." He walked over to me with a box, pressed a button on the side of it. He ran a light that came out of it over my ears, and a few seconds later, what looked like a hearing aid like my uncle Eddie wore popped out. "Try it out. It might pinch a little, but let it marry into your ear. You should never have to take it out."

I put it in my ear and felt a slight pinch as it fit itself to me. Ranger walked over to the computer, played with it for a minute, then said, "Come over here. This is one of my colleagues on one of our planets. Listen to his report and tell me what you hear." I could see a creature, wearing a uniform just like Ranger's, who looked like a large, blue lizard with six eyes. He was talking, but the language I heard was English. It was like one of those dubbed movies. The English was a portion of a second behind the creature's speech.

"I can hear him in English. This is amazing," I said.

"Good. That's part one. Now, part two." He pressed a few keys on the keyboard, and a window opened to the same creature looking at us.

"Ranger, it's good to see you. I just sent you a report. Did you get it?" he asked. "Who's that with you?"

"Yes, Srim, but I haven't listened to it yet. I need your help with my friend here, though."

In English, I could hear both the creature and Ranger talking and the creature's speech, which sounded like a bunch of hisses and clacking sounds. Boy, I wish I had this for French class, I thought. Ranger looked at me and smiled. I kept forgetting that he could hear my thoughts.

"Srim, this is Harper. She's my mentee and is training to be a ranger, maybe to take our jobs someday." They both laughed at that. "I need to get her some experience using the translator to listen and speak. Could you help?"

"Definitely. Harper, very nice to meet you. What are you? Not quite what Ranger is, but very close."

"I'm a human, Srim."

"Ah, from Earth. What brings you to work with us?"

Before I could answer, Ranger interrupted, "Now, Harper, these do more than just translate. They also understand everyday language and context and translate your language as you speak or listen based on that. So, you'll always sound like a native speaker and listener. Just relax and have a conversation with Srim. Answer his question and then ask him to tell you about his work."

I did and, over the next hour or so, learned how the translator worked. It was too cool. While Ranger had ten languages I needed to know, I now knew how to speak hundreds of languages; now, I would just need to learn how to read and write the ten he wanted me to understand. I thanked Srim for his help and he said that he was looking forward to meeting me face to face sometime soon. He also invited me to call back when I wanted to have a meaningful conversation with someone who knew what he was doing. The dig wasn't lost on me, though, I didn't believe him. He seemed as fond of Ranger as everyone else was.

"He's a funny man," said Ranger. "I have a surprise for you." He walked away a few feet and opened a door. Sitting there was a box. He picked it up and brought it in. All my textbooks and the contents of my desk at school were there.

"How'd you get those?" I asked.

"Easy. Remember that I said that your government and ours had signed various treaties. Each of us has several contacts with our respective governments. One of mine went to your school this morning and picked up your stuff and your books for next year. Go into your room and study for a while. Your teachers will send homework and tests, and I'll be checking them over. You better do well, or we could have a do-over on what happened this morning." My butt still hurt a bit. I went into my room, looked at my homework, and did it in a few minutes. Like Ranger had said, I wasn't dumb, and all this stuff was easy for me.

I told him I'd finished it. He looked it over and made a few suggestions on one of my geometry proofs and English composition. He is a bright guy, I thought. I could have done a lot worse.

"Ranger, a question. What will my friends and people at school be told about me not being there? Remember, that I have to live with these people again sometime," I said.

"They're going to be told that you were offered a scholarship to study abroad, which I guess is sort of true," he answered.

"Sort of. Thanks."

With my homework done, it was time to bring the lemonade stand home. I wasn't looking forward to this trip.

Ranger opened a door to our back porch, and I pulled the wagon through after me. We'd agreed that I'd go into the house first and start the conversation with my parents. He said he'd listen and come in when I asked him to or if he felt that there was a problem he could help fix. I opened and stepped through the back door into the kitchen.

"Hi," I said, not able to think of anything more profound. My parents, brother, and another man were sitting around the table, eating, and talking. They stopped and looked at me like I was a ghost.

My father jumped up from the table and ran over to me, closely followed by mom and Holden. It was so good to be with them, even if it would be for a short time. After a few minutes of them loving on me, I asked the other man, "Who're you?"

Ranger answered, "Don't be abrupt with the poor guy. He's a federal agent, my contact here, and a friend. I think anyway."

"Sorry, Ranger," I just blurted that out. Everyone looked at me and then around to see who I was talking to.

"Paul Hicks, Miss. I'm glad to see you back here," he said. "I guess you're not alone?"

"No. Uhm."

"Is he outside?" Hicks asked.

"Yes."

And Hicks left through the back door. In a few seconds, we heard voices—friendly voices from what I could feel from Ranger.

"Who's with you?" my mother asked.

"A friend," I said. "The man who I need to talk to you about."

My mother and father looked at each other. I could read in their faces and minds—I was growing a minor talent at this—what they were thinking. "Ick, no. That's not what I meant. Can we all sit down?"

Holden asked, "Want something to eat or drink, Sis?"

"Sure, Holden. Lemonade would be good. Funny. That's what got me into trouble," I said.

"What sort of trouble, Harper? Whatever it is, we can get through it," my dad said. There were many reasons I loved these people, and this was one of them. Always there for all of us.

"Thanks, dad, but this is something that I need to get through on my own. Let me explain," I said.

I did, and everyone's jaws dropped at the story about Ranger, Estea, the charges against me, the trial, and my sentence. There was silence when I finished. My father was the first to speak. "You're a child. They can't do that to you. Eight and a half years? We have to fight this."

"It's what I want to do, dad. I broke, as it turns out, interstellar laws and murdered sentient beings; they don't recognize age as a mitigating factor." I smiled to myself at my use of the new words that Ranger had taught me. I sensed him smiling as well. "I should have read and obeyed the signs and had to admit to the very nice Judge that.... I'm responsible." I paused and took a breath. "You need to meet my mentor, Ranger. That's his name and title. He's a good guy."

The two men came in. Hicks was a big man, but Ranger towered over him. He looked at my parents and brother, whose eyes were popping out of his head. Ranger smiled at him and said, "I'm not here for you, Holden. Not now, anyway. Just read and obey the signs next time." Holden shook his head yes.

Ranger got Twenty Questions in a big way. Hicks inserted himself in here and there. He explained he worked for a special branch of the National Park Service. Not a cop, but a cop, and was a liaison to the Confederation. He'd come here as soon as he'd heard about my "kidnapping," sure about what had happened. He told my parents that the treaties between the Confederation and us were explicit about violations of law. If Ranger or another Confederation member violated a law here, they were as much subject to our laws as I was to theirs. Here, as Opal had said, there was the double whammy of me violating Alabama law *and* Confederation law. He agreed I got the better deal, given how I'd experience my sentence and where I would end up after all this was over, eight and a half or so years from now.

My parents sat there with open mouths mostly because they wouldn't see me every day, partly because I/we had broken the law, and partly because I was handling this so well. I was excited about this opportunity and could make them understand that. I didn't tell them about my chip or tattoos, thinking as I'd heard my dad say once, that might be TMI. They saw my collar, though, and asked about that.

"It's for a few reasons, mom and dad. It identifies me as a mentee wherever I go in the Confederation, so they can help me if need be; it also has a locator in it for me when I am in the wilds; and I think it's a pretty cool piece of jewelry, not that that's why they gave it to me. You gotta remember that this isn't camp. I got arrested and prosecuted. At least, I'm not in a jail upstate somewhere and am going to get some incredible experience with Ranger here," I said.

"Good girl," said Ranger in my head. "Almost completely true." I sensed a smile there.

"What about her education, Ranger? You said that you were her mentor. Are you going to see that she continues with her education?" my dad asked.

"Yes, Sir. In fact, it'll be a lot tougher than what she's been doing and probably a lot more compressed. We will do the rest of her high school in the next six months. No time off at all for the next eight and a half years. That means we'll be packing almost two years of learning into every year that she's with me. She'll be taking college courses by the end of next year. She will have her apprenticeship certificate within two years. I hope we can her fully licensed as a Ranger within six years. Maybe before the end of her sentence. You should be proud of her; she's very bright and learns quickly."

In my head, I heard him say, "Don't let that go to your head, mentee."

"We'll be living together in my home on Estea," he said, "when we're not traveling to one of our research sites, and she'll have chores there as well as doing remote and on-site learning, which I understand from Harper, she's got plenty of experience with. Before the end of her term, she'll be qualified, I hope, to work independently as a Ranger like me. You're welcome to visit at any time. Just give us a little warning, and we'll be back home for you."

"Ranger and I go back many years, Mr. and Mrs. Cobb. I knew his wife very well." I could see that my parents were a little uncomfortable with the business of me living with Ranger, and I let him feel that. Hicks saw that as well. "You can trust that Ranger will treat your daughter with respect if she behaves and then like you if she misbehaves. I'll be engaged and keep you informed on her progress. I think you ought to visit Ranger at his home. It's lovely, and Estea is a planet a lot like Earth, but it's not."

I didn't like this behave-misbehaving stuff, but I figured that went along with the territory. I was Ranger's at this point and would have to do what he told me to do. I suggested we visit, and Ranger agreed. "I'm setting myself up for a lot of work," I told him. "When my mother sees your house, she's going to tell you to put me to work on housecleaning."

He smiled at me, "I'll tell her it's all stuff you volunteered to do anyway and that we'll do it together." He turned to Hicks and my family. "How'd you like to see where your daughter will live? There's not much to see outdoors right now; we just had a blizzard."

They said yes, and he explained how we traveled, that Estea was well over six quadrillion miles from Earth, and they would simply step through a door to get there. Ranger drew the door, opened it, and we stepped through into our living room as he and I had done only a day or so ago. My parents looked around and were impressed and shocked. Holden ran up to the window and saw the snow. "Cool," he said, "Can I go out?"

Ranger said, "Sure. There're coats and boots by the door. They'll be a little big on you, but you're not hiking. Maybe Harper will go out with you."

Figurehead

I retrieved my cape from where I'd left it to dry in my room, and I walked out onto the porch with Holden. "So, Sis, I'm sorry about this. Eight and a half years. I can't believe it."

"I'm still getting my brain around it, too. Ranger is tough on me but a good guy. He's making me work out every day. I've got a good friend, I think. Her name's Opal, and she was the Judge at my trial. So, I guess a friend unless I mess up."

"He is tough. Ranger told me...," said Holden, "...I won't recognize you when I see you next time. He wants to bulk you out so you can carry the load of the work you'll be doing."

"I'm not sure about that workout stuff, but I guess I'm kind of excited. I'll never be as big as him, but from what I saw of his wife, I'll end up being a lot like her. He's a good man. And he's challenging. He loves the outdoors and lives to be out in them at one of his, I guess our, sites now. He lives for the freedom he has as a Ranger."

"I should turn myself in, so you don't have to do this alone, Harper," Holden said.

"Don't be stupid. Then mom and dad would be without two kids for the next eight and a half years. You be with them, and I'll take care of this. I'm not alone. You'll be able to visit, and I'll be back now and then to work with Ranger in the woods. Just keep yourself out of trouble."

"What's he doing out there? It just looks like some woods and plants to me," Holden said.

"Experiments," I told him about the climate change work we were doing in several locations around Earth and other planets. "Sooner than later, Ranger tells me, the work we're doing will become essential."

We found the adults sitting around the living room in front of the fire when we returned. They all had steamy drinks in mugs. The smell from them was something spicy. Like nothing, I'd smelled before. "There's a pot on the stove with some more kerek in it," said Ranger. "Try it. Kerek is a spice grown on one of my planets. A little like your nutmeg and chocolate all in one."

We poured some drinks and came back into the living room. "Come sit next to me on the floor," said Ranger in my head. I walked over and sat down with the drink, and took a sip. "Wonderful," I said.

Holden had waited for me to take a sip and then did the same. "Love it," he said. "Thanks."

We talked for another hour or so, and I saw that my family was sad about losing me but had become comfortable with Ranger. Ranger gave them a device that he told them would allow them to communicate with us. Like a phone: the "1" button was me, for a communicator he said I'd get tomorrow, and the "2" button was him.

After they left, Ranger said, "Well, I think that went pretty well. Your mother says that she expects you to work hard to clean this place up. I told her that was a job we were both going to take on, and she said that you deserved that one all on your own. So...."

"Yes, Sir." I picked up the mugs and started to clean up the living room.

Figurehead

"So... Harper. She's not *my* mom. We'll do this together, like I said before. That'll be our little secret. You just tell her I'm a hard taskmaster," he smiled and picked up some more of the litter. We worked side-by-side for several hours, and then he said, "Time for bed, I think. We're back to exercise tomorrow, and I want to get you outfitted with your travel kit."

"Ranger, did you tell Holden that you were going to make me look different by the next time he sees us? That true?" I asked.

"Yup. Between the exercises and some additives in your foods, you're going to bulk out a bit. Right now, I think you're too scrawny," he said.

I'm sure that my face told him I wasn't happy with this.

"Us Earth girls like being thin. Don't make me a monster, please, Ranger," I pleaded.

"Look, Harper, over here." He pointed to a picture of his wife. "You see what Anya looked like? I will not make you her, cannot, but that is the kind of bulking I'm talking about. You need to be strong to survive in the worlds we're going to, and I will make sure you are. This is for your own good."

"Yes, Sir." I smiled. "I told Holden basically the same thing."

"I believe that you only say 'Yes, Sir' when you don't like what I just said. That right?"

"Yes, Sir."

"Good to know, but that changes nothing. I just hope you come to like how you feel about yourself and look," he said.

The following day, we got up early. I made breakfast, and there was a lot less drama than there had been the day before. We worked out and then went to a large building like a warehouse but where the Rangers got their outfits. Ranger's uniform was green, and mine was brown, showing that I was a mentee. I got a badge, too. It said "Ranger Mentee" on it under a starfield like on Ranger's badge. I thought, "Cool." I also got a pack like Ranger's, a range of great camping equipment, some high-tech communications and mapping stuff, a knife and sheath, and a gun that Ranger told me was like a Taser on my world. He said it would knock someone or something senseless, at least long enough to get away.

He showed me how it worked on me. Funny man.

Life with Ranger was hard, but, by and large, I loved it. He was deeply respectful and, in his way, affectionate. Months, then years flew by. I got my High School diploma from Mr. Hicks about a year and a half early. I graduated second in my class but obviously could not be able to be the salutatorian. My family frequently visited at first, but then it became difficult to coordinate schedules given the travel that Ranger and I were doing. Times between visits got longer and longer. Not that they cared less about me, but that they knew I was safe and were relieved. I was too.

Ranger taught me how to "slice" was what he called it. Using what he taught me, I could have private thoughts that were truly private, even when my mind was otherwise open. He also taught me to selectively release thoughts from that personal slice so we could both see them and then put them back. It was wonderful to be able to do that, especially when I met with Opal as the Judge. She and I met outside of Galactic Fitness once every six months to follow my progress. Ranger frequently attended those sessions. Those were exciting. She was proud of what I was doing and pushed me to do better and better. I felt good about my progress as well.

Ranger was right about my physical development. I got stronger and bulkier but in all the right places. He showed me some pictures they took when I was processed and compared them to ones he took a few years later, and I could barely recognize myself. And what I saw, I liked. So, a win-win.

Early in my time with Ranger, he took me back to Earth and the garden where I murdered the Yiarrots and Kiflowers. He gave me personal charge of their survival and to learn how to communicate with them. It turns out learning to tune into a foreign, sentient being was going to be very important to me in the future, but I didn't know that then. Anyway, he had me get down and dirty with the plants, sometimes spending days on my hands and knees tending to them. At first, all I sensed from them was fear of me, and it was a potent set of feelings—almost overwhelming. Once or twice Ranger found me fast asleep next to the plants. He told me that was a defense mechanism when they felt threatened. After a while, though, they became a lot less scared, and eventually, they forgave me for murdering their brothers and sisters. That was an important day for me, and both Opal and Ranger congratulated me for showing the Yiarrots and Kiflowers love, even in the face of their fear and resistance.

"Perseverance in the face of hardship matters, my dear. You've done well," said Opal. "The Yiarrots and Kiflowers are mighty creatures. They can make the strongest beings fearful. You overcame that to show them you were repentant. Good girl."

I found the other worlds we worked on amazing and sometimes scary. One of them, the one that we were on right now, was a desert world that was always extremely hot, the one Ranger had told me about that had once been very lush and wet. The animals there today had adapted to the conditions and could go weeks without water, pulling the little moisture they needed directly out of the air. There was a giant, cat-like creature there, a terrifying predator. Ranger called it a Giant Scimitar Cat, and they could weigh in at over 400 pounds. It was like the old saber-toothed cat, the Smilodon, from our Pleistocene era. Just bigger and fiercer.

We lived in a tent in that world, Besepra, which was over 300 parsecs from Estea and 600 from Earth. Ranger had taught me to use parsecs versus light years as they made the numbers a lot smaller. Anyway, one of my many jobs remained breakfast every morning. So, one morning, I got up, put on my clothes, and stepped out of the tent. I heard several pots clang against each other and looked up to see this thing that looked like a saber-toothed tiger on steroids standing a few feet from me, the Giant Scimitar Cat. I froze; it froze. I reached out to Ranger, who was instantly awake. "Don't move," he said. "It'll be on you in a second if you do. Stand your ground but look down and to the side. I'm going out through the rear door of the tent and will slip around behind it. Don't panic. You'll be fine."

I was looking forward to turning twenty next month, but I thought I might not make it right then. The cat stepped toward me and growled deep in its chest. It kept advancing, and I looked down and away. I put my hand on my knife in the sheath on my hip, realizing it was like a toothpick compared to the teeth of this beast. It stopped about three feet from me and then extended its neck forward, so its head was inches away. It huffed once, covering me with its saliva. "Gross," I thought. "I'm being basted before being torn apart. Great."

It huffed again and then laid down in front of me, observing me. Slowly, I squatted down, so I was looking into its eyes. It looked back, and then I felt a nudge. It was trying to communicate with me. I felt no aggression from it and so sat down next to it. I tentatively reached out and scratched behind its ear. It rewarded me with a purr rather than a bite. I opened my mind as I had done with the Yiarrots and Kiflowers and saw the world from the cat's perspective. It wasn't an intelligent being like Ranger and maybe me, though one would question that about me given why I found myself here, but it had powers like what Ranger had and what he'd taught me. Sentient, I knew. And it appeared to like me.

It was a primitive being. History was only meaningful to it, as that was how it learned. It did not know a future. I saw Ranger come up behind us and told him I was all right and that he might want to come around at us from the front.

He did, and the cat stood back up again, growling deeply. I reached out, caressed it, and let her see Ranger was no threat. Like she had litter mates and a mate, I let her see that Ranger was a friend. It was then that I first felt I wanted more than just to be friends with him.

He kneeled, and the cat laid back down again. We spent a few more minutes with it, and then it got up and walked away. It stopped once as it walked away, looked over its shoulder, and then was gone. We saw her a few more times in the next few days. We never saw each other again after that.

"That was amazing, Harper. And dangerous. How did you know she wouldn't attack you?" he asked.

"I didn't, but when she was a few feet away from me, I didn't think I had anything to lose. I felt a nudge, and I knew she was trying to communicate with me. So, I reached back and got a brainful of images. Obviously, she's not like us, and her gift's not like ours. More primal, I guess. But still very rich."

We planned to spend the rest of our time on Besepra, looking at the various experiments scientists and naturalists were conducting. Besepra had no intelligent life forms on it, unlike our other planets—though perhaps the cat was not wholly un-intelligent. Scientists had found evidence of ancient, advanced life on Bespera back when the planet was more fertile than it now was, with several gigantic oceans. The scientists searched for why the planet had become a desert and any further evidence of the life forms. Ranger's and my role here was purely support, gofers for the scientists. They would send us lists of things they needed, and then we'd bring them with us when we came through.

The research so far had turned up little. A party of scientists was working in some very rugged hills about two hundred miles away, 1.04×10^{-11} parsecs, I jokingly told Ranger just before he pushed me down a dune. When I came back up to the top of the dune, Ranger was finishing a conversation with the main expedition leader. He pushed me down the dune a second time and then yelled, "Would you stop fooling around? We need to go check out the other scientists."

Now, with sand pouring out of every pore of my body and deep into my now very long, light brown hair, I came back up the slope toward him. "I'm sorry to have upset you, Master. Do you want to punish me one more time before we go?" He looked at me for a second, and I followed that with, "I just want you to try it." He drew a door, and we stepped through. We came out at the mouth of a large cave on a hillside. The cave mouth was strangely, perfectly round, like a piece of mining equipment carved it. The cave itself was dark, of course, and nicely cool inside. "Oh, this feels so good, Ranger. It's good to be out of the oven."

"Hopefully not into the fire," he said. "Look, over there."

I looked to where he was pointing, and I saw the group of scientists standing in a circle, all facing each other. They didn't move even when we called to them, and as we got closer, we saw their glassy eyes. "I wonder what happened here," said Ranger as he pulled out his communicator. "No signal. I need to go outside and call back to the camp. Wait here and touch nothing or any of them." He stepped outside, and I saw him make a call.

I felt a hand on my shoulder and turned to see a very tall, skinny, silver-skinned man, I guessed, with large bug eyes. He had three fingers on his hand. I also saw the cave's mouth slowly start to close like the sphincter-mouth of the Giant Ginger Suckerfish we watched on one of our expeditions on Estea. I called out to Ranger, and he turned, took a few steps toward me, but then I lost sight of him as the sphincter snapped closed.

More tall creatures appeared and picked up the scientists and carried them out of the room and down a passage that had opened. It looked curiously like an esophagus, I thought, just as the thing that had closed its hand on my shoulder pulled me along. The tunnel or whatever it was down which we walked looked more like the gullet of a creature that Ranger had me dissect in one of my classes. I reached my hand out, touched the wall, and came away slimy; it reacted to my touch by closing behind us and pushing us ahead of it, closing as we moved, just like peristalsis. I hoped these creatures wouldn't dump all of us into an enormous stomach up ahead of us somewhere. Finally, we stepped out into another room, or what I thought might be a room.

The scientists were all placed in a circle on the other side of the room from me. The creature stopped where we were and then pulled me out of the room, down another of those esophagus-like passages. We finally stopped next to a sac in the tissue's wall, and it pushed me in. I tried to fight it, but it was far stronger than me, and it grabbed me by the throat, lifted me in the air.

It regarded me with its enormous eyes for a second or two, then I saw these hairs coming up out of its skin and felt dozens of pinpricks on my neck where it held me. I felt white-hot pain, but before I could scream or fight, I passed out.

When I awoke after God knows how long, tissue surrounded me. In the sac, I guessed. Wonderful. I pushed and kicked. It was like they trapped me in a great big leather bag. It wasn't going to open for me. I laid there a bit, and then I noticed tiny bubbles of liquid forming on the inside of the sac. These rolled down its side and pooled at the bottom. Soon, my pants were soaked with a liquid that smelled very sweet. I got woozy. When the liquid reached the middle of my chest, and it completely soaked me, I passed out. My last thought was, "I hope that this isn't digestive fluid."

I was still in the sac when I awoke. It felt like I was outside of my body, looking in, though I knew I was still there. I didn't feel scared at all. I could feel that the liquid was in my lungs, yet I hadn't drowned and still felt like I was breathing. Then I felt the nudge in my brain. "You are awake. Can you hear us?"

"Yes. Where am I?"

"In a preservation pod where we will keep you for the time being."

"What about the others?"

"We sent them back in a trade."

"A trade?"

"Yes. A trade. The one you called Ranger broke into our body and threatened to do damage if we didn't release the scientists and you. We told him we could release them, but not you without damaging you."

"Huh? Damaging me?"

"You ask a lot of questions."

"Yes. I'm young, and about all I have are questions."

I thought I heard a sigh. "You are inside our body, in one of what I told you is a preservation pod. The pods protect you while we are in motion like we are. We will be in motion for quite some time, so I am going to put you back to sleep."

"No, wait, what about Ran...." And I drifted off.

I came to spewing my guts out on the floor of the passageway. Across from me was Ranger. He looked worse for the wear, as I'm sure I did.

"You okay, kid?" he asked.

"Yes, I think so. Where do you think we are?"

"I don't know, and that's a problem."

"Why?" I asked.

"Without knowing where we are, I can't tell how we get to where we want to be. I need to know both ends of the line to open a door for us. The best I can do now is to open a door to the big room we came into. That gets us nowhere. So, I think we sit tight for now."

"Good that you are not foolish," said another voice. "We are called the Sykywr. You are inside one of our living constructions."

"What are you?" Ranger asked.

Figurehead

"You would probably call us fish. On the girl's planet, yes, that is what we are, but on the world, you just left, the one you call Bespera, we were the Alphas before the seas dried up. A few of us remained in the caves you found to await other Alphas and take you to our new homeworld. I'm the last of us. With my departure, we are completely gone."

"What about us?" I asked.

"I'm sure you know what a zoo is," the voice said. "We wanted to find breeding pairs of Alphas and have brought many back here for our study and entertainment. The affection between you is more than clear. So, the two of you will be our latest and last breeding pair for the time being. Our minions will come for you shortly. They will see that you are fed and can get into something else more suitable for the zoo and your roles."

Ranger and I looked at each other. Not that I hadn't had those kinds of thoughts in the last year or so, but I wasn't exactly looking at things from the perspective of us being a breeding pair like sloths or hippos or something like that. I reached out to him, but then I felt something happen, almost like a shutter had closed, and his mind was no longer there. Now, that was truly scary.

Two of the silver creatures, the voice had called minions, showed up a little later and forced us down the passageway to another larger enclosure. This one had what looked like a bed in it. We walked in, and a transparent panel came out of the wall, closing us in. "We're in a cage in the zoo," said Ranger and looked at me despondently. "I'm so sorry, Harper. I want you to know that regardless of what happens, this is not what I wanted for you."

"Same here, Ranger, at least not in this way," I said. He looked at me, surprised.

"The clear window in front of you," said the voice, "prevents you from leaving your cage, but you can receive and remove inanimate objects through it. Take off your clothes and push them through the window."

"No way," I said. "You can't make us do this."

"Yes, we can. If you do not immediately follow our instructions, we will punish the other one of you." Ranger collapsed and thrashed in pain. "The pain he is experiencing will stop when you disrobe."

"Don't Harper. Please don't," gasped Ranger.

"I can't, Ranger.... I can't let you suffer," I said and took my clothes off. All I now wore was my collar, and, well, they didn't design it to cover anything.

When I was standing naked, the voice said, "Male, now you disrobe."

I was hit by what felt like a massive electric shock and collapsed to the ground, howling.

"I'll do it. Stop hurting her," said Ranger and got undressed. He bent down, picked me up, and laid me on the bed. I had to admit, from my position on the ground, I still liked what I saw. Those muscles... that chest.... I needed to stop thinking this way.

The voice said, "Do what comes naturally to you." The wall opposite our cell went transparent, and outside we could see water and dozens of what looked like gigantic, whale-sized creatures, with monstrous black goggle eyes, staring at us. I cried, and Ranger brought me into his chest and held me tightly. We were both hit with shocks, and the voice repeated, "Do what comes naturally to you."

Later, after we did what came naturally to us, the window opposite our cell returned to its former opaque skin. Food was brought to us in trays by the minions, and they took our clothes away. After dinner, the voice returned. "Leave your bed. We need to clean the blood off the bed and shower you." Warm mist-like rain fell in the room, cleaning the bed and us. I didn't know what I was supposed to feel like, but the maid-enhood I'd protected was now gone. As much as I was glad that Ranger had taken it, I felt dirty and cried myself to sleep.

A bell rang, waking both of us. "You will perform at least three times each day until the female is pregnant. We will test you, female, daily until we detect you are pregnant. In the cell's corner, you'll see that pillar with the screen on the top of it." A light illuminated the pillar. "You will go over there and give us what you call a urine sample. If you resist, your male will be punished. The viewing window will be open when you give the sample. Male, you stay on the bed. If you move off it to obstruct our view of her, you will both be punished. You will perform directly after she passes urine, and then you will relieve yourself, male, and we will give you food."

I reluctantly went over to the pillar as it called it, sat on it, and peed. It surprised me that a small jet of water and then a warm blast of air cleaned me after I was done. That didn't feel so bad, except for the dozens of creatures that were gawk-ing at me. I returned to bed, and Ranger made warm and slow love to me. At the end of it, he said, "If we have to do this, we might as well get as much enjoyment as we can out of it." I smiled and snuggled into him. The wall went opaque, and Ranger got up and walked over to the pillar, peed, and returned to bed. Two minions delivered our breakfast, which was more of the same that we had at dinner the day before, and they stood and waited until we finished. The minions re-moved the trays, and they left us alone for a few hours until our next performance.

I counted. We performed thirty-six times before my urine declared me pregnant. I was brought to the front of the cage, and the minions took various measurements and posted them on a panel next to us. I remembered when the hippo at a zoo in Dallas was pregnant. The Zoo published regular re-ports on its website on the progress of the pregnancy, includ-ing videos and interviews with the vets and animal handlers. The same sort of thing was going on here, I guessed. A video showing everything from when they placed us into the cage and shocked us until we disrobed and then shocked until we made love played on a loop, day and night. They didn't show all 36 episodes, but enough for their brethren to get the pic-ture. I suppose they did this to keep us in line, partly. Maybe it was a fundraiser. Who knew?

The routine was the same day in and day out. I now knew what animals in cages must have felt or people in jail. Being locked up was awful for me but took a much more severe toll on Ranger. He became withdrawn and eventually just took to standing in the corner, facing away from me and from the creatures that came to observe us. Painful shocks didn't have an impact. He'd get shocked and then simply get up and stand in the corner again. He also wouldn't eat as much as I tried to get him to do that.

The voice spoke to me, "What is wrong with your mate, female? We monitor all his signs, and they do not look good. He is unhealthy."

"What else would you think, you useless piece of chum? You capture us, lock us up here in this cage, and turn us into performing animals. That's not what we are. Our kind dies in prisons like this. If you kill him, then I promise you—I hope you understand that word—I will kill myself and my baby, and all of this will be for nothing," I said.

There was silence for a long time, and then the voice came back, "Would returning you to the surface to live help him?"

"Yes, it would help both of us."

"There is a single island on this planet. We could place you there, under guard and under our protection, to live if you think that would help. But you would have to come back for the birth of your child, and both return to create another. Then you could return to the surface again."

"So, an incentive to stay barefoot and pregnant?" I asked.

"I don't know what that means, but the more children you make, the more time you spend on the surface, yes."

Minions came a little later that day and brought us clothing and took us to the surface. They constructed a camp with us, and the Sykywrs saw we had plenty of food beyond what we caught for ourselves. They were reluctant to give us weapons at first, but after I got pregnant with our third child, I think they thought that we'd fallen in line. They gave us weapons to use when we went hunting.

Ranger's color and strength returned, as did mine. We had no mirrors aside from each other's eyes, and so we looked like we'd been shipwrecked. Ranger's hair got awfully long, and I braided it and worked to dislodge lice and other things that nested in it. He did the same for me, though my hair was over three feet long at this point and so harder to clean and groom. He was all thumbs on braiding my hair. One day, one minion came over, shoved him out of the way, and gently braided my hair itself. That behavior shocked me as I thought these creatures were robot jailers. I had to rethink my conclusions about them. They seemed to have some capability for independent thought and kindness we hadn't realized.

We knew we were constantly watched on the island by the Sykywrs. We saw cameras in the trees, drones in the air, and we were very sure that whatever the minions saw was transmitted somewhere to be spliced into movies for the watchers. "They must love this. We're like monkeys in the zoo grooming each other," said Ranger glumly.

"Shh. You said this to me years ago. Everything will work out. Be patient. In the meantime, we have each other," I said, hugging him tightly.

One morning we awoke to a loud alarm blaring in the forest. I was about seven months pregnant with child three at that point, so I couldn't move fast. My minion, the one who did my hair, opened the tent door and gestured to us to come out quickly. When we did, I looked up and saw a large silver ship hovering above us. Several bright lights projected from its bottom, and armed men appeared where they hit the ground. Except for my minion, the other minions were cut down; it had shown me kindness, so I felt I also needed to protect it.

"Srim, what took you so long?" Ranger asked.

"We can always leave if you're not going to be grateful," he said and clapped Ranger on the back. "It took us a while to find you, but then we picked up the signal from Harper's collar. We sent a team through to do a survey here and then figured out how to get our ship through a door. All that took time to happen. I see you've been continuing your biology classes while you've been here," he said with what I took to be a smirk.

"We have three children, Srim, counting this one. Two of them are with the Sykywrs," said Ranger.

"We know. We've been negotiating with them. They're open to releasing the children back to you if we promise not to boil their oceans away," he said with what I thought might be a smile. "They'll be here shortly."

The minions, who'd been the kids' nannies, came up to the surface with the kids in two Sykywrs bubble vehicles. The voice said that we could take them with us if we wanted them and that they had returned all our faculties to us. It sounded very apologetic, if not downright scared. "I'd like to take the three minions with us if you think that would be safe, Ranger," I said.

"It will be safe. We love our lives here and will be good citizens," said the voice. "You know where we are, and we want to keep our oceans where they are."

So, our new family returned to Estea and our now too small house there. We all set to building an addition. Opal, my family, and Hicks came and helped. My parents said nothing, but I could see that they were awkward with what had happened to me. I don't think that they'd ever thought that they'd be the parents of a zoo star and grandparents of zoo animals. I knew they'd get over it, though.

Ranger and I re-started up our daily exercise regimen, I went back to school, and we went back to our experiments. One day, when I was working out, I felt the flutter of wings behind me and turned to find Opal there with another creature like her. "Harper, you've never met my mate, Sapphire. I wanted to introduce you."

Sapphire bowed to me and said, "I've heard a lot about you, Harper, especially what you've been through. It made me very sad."

"Thanks, Sapphire, but I have three beautiful children with the man of my dreams—literally. I'm happy. I've also made some decisions about what I want to do after my sentence is over. Obviously, I'll stay here with Ranger...."

"That's what I want to talk to you about, Harper. Can you come to my court later today?"

Figurehead

"Huh? That sounds scary, Opal, or do I need to call you Judge, now?" I asked.

"Just be in my court at two this afternoon." She turned, and they flitted away.

That ruined the rest of the workout for me. I found Ranger and told him what had happened, and he looked surprised and a little concerned. "I'll be with you, Harper. I'll always be with you," he said.

We went home, and I tore through my closet in our bedroom, eventually settling on a very understated dress that had been Anya's. "Excellent choice," said Ranger, "Anya called that her lucky dress. She was wearing it the night that I asked her to marry me."

"Should I put it back?" I asked, concerned about the memories it triggered for him.

"Nope. I hope we don't need it, but it was my first love's lucky dress, like I said. It's right that this love wears it."

Since we'd been home and since I was pregnant for a couple of months of that, Ranger had spent a lot of time teaching me to make doors. With his bosses' permission, he got me the devices to make the doors and then taught me its science. All it was, was fixing in your mind a picture of where you wanted to be and then drawing the door with the device. Easy-peasy, I thought. I traveled home quite a few times, as he had promised I could long ago. But, as he also said back then, I had also stayed with him and continued my work and education. I even have been back to the Sykywr planet to show off the third child. We'd now added little Harriet to our little H family of Hill, Hallie, Harper, and Ranger. Well, almost all H's. The Sykywrs were enthusiastic and held a reception in our honor. We go back a lot to visit them.

I opened the door to the court. Unfortunately, I plopped us right into the middle of a meeting the Judge was having with two men, one in a Ranger's uniform. "Sorry, Your Honor. I'm still kind of new at making portals. I meant to land in the hallway."

"It'll get better, Harper. You're here now, and you both may as well come forward," said the Judge with a small smile.

Ranger and I walked to the front of the room and stood below the bench with the two men. "Ranger, I assume that you at least know of the Ranger General."

"Yes, Ma'am. We've spoken several times."

"Very good to see you face-to-face, Ranger," said the Ranger General.

"And this," she said, gesturing to the other man, "Is our secretary of state, Algo Miggle."

I shook hands with both and then turned back to the Judge. "You know, Felon, that I sentenced you to eight and a half years under the mentorship of Ranger when you were last in this court. That sentence would have ended when you were almost 25 years old, and at that time, you could have returned to your home or stayed here for advanced degrees and licensure as a Ranger. Well, circumstances have changed. Your performance in the first years of your sentence gave us all great hope you would be a success."

Figurehead

I wasn't sure where this was leading, but I thought I heard an ax about to fall.

"Well, that's not where we find ourselves today. The thirty-month vacation you took with the Sykywrs was...."

"Please, Judge... none of that was my fault... please let me try again." I felt a nudge from Ranger.

"Just shut up, Harper," he said.

"Thank you, Ranger. Shut up, Harper. Do you think we would be so cold as not to recognize the skilled work you've done and what you've undergone while prisoners of the Sykywrs? I think you've been called this before, 'silly girl.' You are treasured by us, well, me in particular, and all of us. When things were at their worst in that cell, you stood up for your partner and made things as right as you could with what you had at hand. Truly creative, and we all believe well-deserved of recognition." She nodded to the secretary of state.

"Harper, I'm here today because our Confederation President couldn't be here. He asked me to stand in for him but wants to meet you as soon as you can figure out how to open the door to his office." I heard a snort behind me.

"Do I have to admonish you, yet again, Ranger, to not make the girl uncomfortable?" said Opal.

"No, you don't, Your Honor," he said, "but I'm sure that I'll be made more uncomfortable tonight when we're home."

"His behavior would justify that, Harper," she said, looking at me with a smile.

"In any case," Miggle said, "The Judge has requested that the last two-and-a-half years of your sentence be commuted.

We agree with that, and as of right now, you're free. The President also wants to recognize the great sacrifice that you made during your time in the zoo, and we want to grant you and your children full citizenship in the Confederation." He handed me a few pieces of paper and shook my hand.

"Now, Harper. At the end of your sentence, you were to be offered a Ranger Assistant license and the opportunity to train and be licensed as a Ranger Mentor, like Ranger here. The Ranger General wants to talk to you about that as well," said the Judge.

The General turned to me and smiled. "I've watched your work as you've studied and worked with Ranger. He's one of our toughest mentors, and you've performed as well, if not better than any of our current classes of mentees. That and you suffered through imprisonment and, what I view to be torture, while there." He held his hand up. "I know what you're going to say, and the children are a wonderful outcome, but the fact is that they forced them on the two of you. I also know because Ranger and I had talked about it that he wanted to take your relationship to, uh, the next level, so to speak, before you were kidnapped and that you had significant feelings for each other."

I blushed.

"You need to gain proficiency in shielding your thoughts and feelings, Harper. It'll take some time, but it will come," he said with a smile. "Ranger and I had talked about this as well: We felt that you'd learned all necessary to be an Assistant and so were going to petition the court to issue that license and then put you into the advanced program for your Mentorship license. At your rate of progress, we feel that you'd finish that in short order." He smiled, "I expect to see you graduate from the Ranger Mentor program in a year, maybe less. You could have been our first Ranger Mentor who was in the mentorship program. But we don't need to worry about that now with your sentence commuted."

He handed me two pieces of paper. The first was my Ranger Assistant license, and the second was a scholarship to the Ranger Mentorship license program. "Fully paid by the Confederation. I hope you accept it."

"What else could I do?" I asked, overwhelmed by what they were giving me.

I stepped onto our porch back in Alabama. I carried Hallie and Harriet, and Ranger brought Hill.

"You got us here in one piece, Ranger Assistant. I'm impressed."

"Watch it, big boy."

The next morning Holden, Hank, and I brought things full circle: We resurrected my old Radio Flyer wagon and carried the lemonade stand to the same corner where we met the nice man. He was sitting on his porch, looking no older than when we first met him, six-plus years previous, and he had the same big, white dog. Now that was impossible.

I walked over and started to speak.

"Shh," he said and then spoke in my mind. "I knew you'd be back. It looks like you found your path. I am happy for you," said our Guardian.

The End

{ 6 }

Reminders

I'd shot an unarmed man dead.

A few minutes before I pulled the trigger, I'd stepped into what I thought was my apartment after a tiring workday, a double shift. I'd flicked on the light switch as I stepped into the living room, and nothing happened. Because the T.V. was on, I stopped in the vestibule. "Is someone here?" I asked.

A voice answered, "Who're you?" and a large man stood up from the couch and turned toward me. The streetlights back-lighted him, and I couldn't see any details except to know that he wasn't someone I knew. He had some things in his hands. I took a defensive posture as I'd been instructed, thinking the man might have a weapon.

"I'm a police officer. Put your hands in the air and stay right where you are," I ordered as I reached for my service piece and removed it from its holster. With the gun pointed at the floor and my finger off the trigger, I said, "I have my weapon out. Put... your... hands... up." The man still didn't raise his hands, but he took a step toward me. "Please stop. I don't want to shoot, but I will," I said, not too believably, I thought afterward.

"I don't know who you are, but you're in my home. If you don't get out right now, *I'll* call the police," he said. He took another step toward me. I saw a spark of light from something in his hands and raised my weapon, centering it on his chest.

"I'm aiming my gun at your chest. Take another step, and I'll shoot," I said.

He did, and I did, twice. Solid hits, center mass. The man collapsed to the floor, and I moved toward him, tripping on a piece of rug that shouldn't have been there. What I thought had been a weapon turned out to be a large spoon, and the thing I saw him carrying turned out to be a bowl of soup that was now spreading out on the floor, mixing with his blood. I bent down next to him, checked for a pulse, found a weak one, began CPR, and called 911 on my phone. It was only then I realized I wasn't in my apartment and that I'd just shot an innocent man watching T.V., having a bowl of soup in his apartment, relaxing. Oh God, I thought.

It took less than five minutes for other officers to show up and another five for the EMTs. The man was pronounced dead on the way to the hospital. They took me to a car, and the officers took my weapon, bagged it and my hands, and prepared to take me to the central station where I'd been just an hour earlier as a cop. This time in custody, though not in cuffs—yet. They treated me well but processed me for gunshot residue and then put me in an interview room.

I was a basket case. I'd only used my weapon once before with a drug dealer, but there was a lot of gunplay that night with many people involved, cops and criminals. This was something different. I'd made a colossal mistake—several of them. I was so tired after 16 hours on duty I walked like a zombie past my floor and went to the one above my apartment. The apartment I'd entered wasn't mine. And I'd shot and killed an innocent man simply watching T.V. in his home.

All I could think of was what I'd done to him and his family. It was quite a bit later, that I thought about myself.

In the past few years, there had been a growing focus on "IncarceAmerica," as many activists called it: That America was the world leader in incarcerations, at 25% of all incarcerated in the world, should have been an embarrassment to our country, but it wasn't. More than that, a large number of incarcerated were people of color or the poor; that, too, should have been an embarrassment, but it again wasn't. Many pointed to it as a sign that "those" people were incapable of civilized life and needed to be managed. The fact that more than half of the prison population were white didn't mean anything to these people who cherry-picked the statistics to justify their racist beliefs.

A new government, led by a progressive President and supported by a Congress from the same party and with the same beliefs, had developed, passed, and begun implementing an "abolitionist" agenda. This agenda charted a multi-year plan to close almost all prisons and change how criminals were treated. Not rehabilitation, though some of that, but focusing on keeping criminals in their locales where they would provide restitution to the community at large for their crimes and ultimately reintegrate positively. Okay, rehabilitation, but something different from what people thought of when you said that word in the near past. To learn to be different.

To become a more permanent feature of our society, Congress passed a Constitutional amendment, number 31, that described the new criminal justice system and where the authorities for its administration were based. The states ratified it after a very long and heated debate. Overall, the program's administration was under the U.S. Department of Justice, but the states each had responsibility for the delivery of the program aligned with the intentions of Congress. One Amendment provision around which there was a lot of debate was that around what was called "Reminders." Reminders were to be administered to convicts locally and could range from periodic public shaming of the convicted to corporal punishment or some combination of those things. At no time, though, were the convicted to be subjected to corporal punishment that permanently damaged them. As many saw it, Congress permitted reminders to sate the bloodlust of crime victims and their families and gain their support for the amendment.

Of course, not all the then-incarcerated could just be freed for community service. Some people had been so thoroughly institutionalized that they couldn't simply return anywhere to work. Others were just plain evil and would need to be supervised carefully. Over time, we might reintegrate these people as they showed behaviors that proved they could return to community service. Jails and prisons would still be required for people who committed genuinely heinous crimes and could never be released. But these were the tiny minority of the currently incarcerated.

"Release" was also a relative term. Those people not going to prison still had sentences, now called Corrections, to serve as set out at the end of their trials. They would live out their Corrections in communities where they would have work assigned to them during sentencing; live in segregated housing, halfway houses; wear uniforms that would single themselves out as convicts in Correction; and be subjected to periodic public Reminders that they were serving a sentence for the crime identified on their uniform. At the end of their terms, the prisoners would return to society into jobs for which they had been trained during their Correction. While society still had some maturing to do, the former prisoners were told that, unless they repeated, all would be forgotten. The permanent brand of being an ex-con would no longer be there. It would be a great idea if society could forgive and forget and if the former prisoner kept up on their end of the bargain.

Three drivers for the new program were reducing the number of people in prisons, addressing the abysmal conditions in these prisons that only seemed to breed more criminality, and preparing to send back the incarcerated to the community when they had fulfilled their Corrections. They hoped that the right balance of punishment and forgiveness would reduce the amount of violence in society. The proposals were met with equal amounts of support and horror and near rebellion. Family groups, municipalities, churches, and states were torn between accepting the proposal as a significant step forward and fear-mongering about releasing bad people into the community to do whatever the opponents to the legislation could fantasize to women and children. The fact of the matter was that research had repeatedly shown that the released incarcerated were far less likely to commit crimes than what were called "normal" people in society if you took out the sociopaths, career criminals, and others like them. But, just like the mentally ill, people wanted to believe that ex-cons could never redeem themselves. Hence, how they ended up in a revolving door.

So, the proponents of the legislation left some prisons open as a deterrent to those undergoing Correction so they wouldn't act out in communities. The remaining prisons would be little better than the infamous Black Hole of Calcutta. Next, they would require all convicts to wear monitoring devices while serving their Correction. They made three types available: a wrist cuff, an ankle bracelet, and a collar. They assigned devices based on the kind of community service to which the convict was posted. Finally, convict's uniforms would show the crime of the person. Like Nathaniel Hawthorne's *The Scarlet Letter*, there'd be a large, garishly colored letter affixed to each uniform ("S" for any sex crimes, "T" for theft, "A" for assault, "M" for murder, "E" for terrorism or any form of extremism, "N.V." for non-violent crimes like embezzling, computer crime and things of that ilk, "R" for a misdemeanor, and "O" for other).

I was one of the first to process through this new program. I got an "M" on my uniform as they sent me to my community service for a fifteen-year Correction. Because I'd been a law officer and my case got an enormous amount of press, they sent me to another city for my servitude; no one there was supposed to know that I'd been a cop. While this took trust on my part, it was better than being in a prison where I could've found myself with a shiv in my back, even in a protected area. Better, too, was that I was outside all day on my job versus the enclosed conditions in prison. I'll get to my job soon.

My trial came at the end of a summer of many discontents. The man I'd shot was a young Indian, a bright and up-and-coming accountant at a large consulting company. His shooting came when there'd been a spate of shootings of people of color. Thus, it made the newspapers in a big way. Demonstrations and riots were going on countrywide against cops who'd committed these crimes. My picture was all over the T.V., Internet, and print services—worldwide. They grouped me in with a bunch of corrupt cops who'd gone way beyond the pale in carrying out their jobs. This was no complaint about what happened to me, just observing the conditions at play when they tried me.

I was relieved to be in jail at first, and when bail was set, I decided not to pay it. I was kept sequestered in the jail and so not in the general population. It was tedious being in solitary, but I looked at the alternatives, and none were particularly good. The second or third night I was in jail, my apartment was broken into and trashed by a group of demonstrators. My stuff was taken out of the apartment and burned on the lawn in front of the building. If I'd been home, things might have gone bad for me and maybe some people who broke in.

My attorneys, who were supplied by the police union, tried to get me to fight. I refused. I'd done evil, and I expected to be punished for it. I was ready to take whatever sentence the courts dispensed. The prosecutors were seeking a minimum sentence of one year for every year of the life of the man, Sumit Kamath, who I'd killed. That would have been 30 years. Not the way I'd expected my life to go—I'd expected a husband and a family and maybe becoming a detective someday—but I felt it only appropriate that I reaped what I had sown.

Sumit's family did not like all the attention people gave their son's and brother's murder. They wanted nothing to do with the demonstrations and notoriety. They'd made it clear on a couple of news shows that they saw what had happened as a horrific accident and wanted to forgive. However, the municipal and State governments were concerned about the backlash of doing what Sumit's family wanted to do and pushed for the maximum sentence, which would have been 99 years. Parole could occur after 45 years on a 99-year sentence so that I would be 73 years old, and after 15 years on the 30-year sentence the prosecutors wanted, I'd be 43. The guts of my life carved away by my immoral action. I believed I deserved it, even though it made me very sad to think about being locked up and away from things and people I loved for such a long time.

I readily admitted in court that I'd made a mistake and killed Sumit. My attorneys tried to make a case that this was not entirely my fault to soften what I'd done. They described an array of contributing circumstances like the design of the apartment complex, my exhaustion after the double I'd worked, and that Sumit had left his door unlocked. I told them I wanted to take the stand, and against their wishes, took full accountability. They convicted me after the Jury deliberated less than 12 hours over two days. During the sentencing portion of the trial, Sumit's family said they wanted me to do no time. They said that they'd felt that I'd suffered enough and would for the rest of my life—they were undoubtedly correct. My father spoke on my behalf, and the court called me to apologize publicly for what I'd done. I didn't stop crying during this phase of the trial. All the confidence and strength I'd developed over the years evaporated the moment that I pulled the trigger in Sumit's apartment. I almost looked forward to getting on with the punishment I faced, whatever it was to be.

The Judge came back and surprised everyone. He sentenced me to 15 years, the minimum, for a murder conviction and parole after seven and a half years. I could still have some kind of life ahead of me. The Judge thanked and released the Jury. He then cleared the courtroom except for the attorneys and me. He lectured the prosecution about falling for the public's bloodlust and assigned me to the new Alternatives to Prison Program, or APP, in another city across the State where I could be treated anonymously. I wondered, given all the publicity and the fact that my face had been everywhere, if that were indeed possible, but assignment to the APP was worlds better than being in prison, at least I thought initially.

They hustled me out of the court to be processed into the APP. The intake unit created my APP ID, assigned me to a job working in Parks and Recreation in my new hometown, and gave me my new uniform, with a large, dayglow "M" on it. My stigma, my brand. Because I would work outside, moving around a lot, and using my hands, they gave me a metal collar versus a wrist or ankle bracelet. The collar was not just that; like the electronic ankle or wrist bracelet, it would show my location all the time for the next fifteen years. I'd still have to wear it even when paroled, they told me.

My days settled down to the same routine. Our halfway house was in an old high school. The 40 of us, men and women, slept on three-high bunk beds in the old gym they'd made into a dorm. Bathrooms and showers were down hallways on either side of the gym, labeled "Boys" and "Girls." Staff supervised the dormitory at night, so there was no hanky-panky or something worse. We were up at 5 AM every morning for a group session where we talked about our crimes and our thoughts as we went through our sentences. I admitted to the group early on that I'd been a cop to get that behind me. I found these sessions, initially, painful and like a pity party. But, after a while, I came to cherish these early morning opportunities to relate to people in the same boat as me. I picked up some reading on such groups and found that the stages I went through were the expected ones, like with the five stages of grief popularized by a famous psychiatrist. They turned out to be very helpful to almost all of us.

After group, we'd have breakfast; the prisoners alternated responsibility for cooking and clean-up and everything required for the house's upkeep (laundry, cleaning, and so forth). By 8 AM, we'd be out for our assigned work crews. Again, for me, it was Parks and Recreation Department. Sometimes I'd be raking, weeding, cleaning, sometimes planting or trimming, sometimes garbage removal, and sometimes all the jobs on the same day, day in and day out, seven days a week, summer or winter, rain or shine. They provided lunch from a truck from the halfway house, and dinner was like breakfast, at about 8 PM. Between 8 and 10 PM every night, we had free time. The school's library was open to us, as was a second gym next to where we bunked. There were even a few P.C.s connected to the Internet. They heavily monitored those and reviewed any emails we wrote before they sent them. My parents were not Internet-savvy and so I didn't have a lot of people that I corresponded with and these few folks, after a time, stopped responding to my emails. I was a little sad about losing those connections but also figured their lives were moving on and I was now part of the past for them. More importantly, I used the Internet and the library to research my job and learn about plants and ground management. Bedtime was no later than 10 PM. The work was exhausting but good. You saw something accomplished. Had pride in finished products that others gained value and maybe wonder from.

Periodically, we were subjected to the "Reminders." These were for both us and the local citizenry. It was a continuation of our public shame and was also supposed to deter anyone contemplating a crime. In the center of the city park was a large stage and on this stage were several pillories. They pilloried convicts due for a Reminder based on a formula that set out the frequency and length of time in restraint. They recorded all of this in the convict's punishment book kept in each municipality. Also, the formula dictated what other forms of abuse were possible during a pillorying. Murderers were top or, depending on your point of view, at the bottom, of the list. We were pilloried for an entire day, once every two months for our whole sentence, and the public could heap whatever abuse they wanted to on us, short of anything that would kill or severely injure us so that we couldn't work. So, no sticks and stone. But lots of name-calling, a good paddling, and rotten fruits and vegetables were thrown at us, usually all three. In fact, an entrepreneur sold rotten fruits and vegetables from his farm to be thrown at us—good old American ingenuity.

Figurehead

Six times a year, they would subject me to this until I was paroled. Forty-five times if I was lucky enough to be paroled in seven and a half years, up to ninety if I wasn't. I was resigned to the sore bum I'd be having for days after my Reminders. The good news was that there were several limitations on paddling. A specific paddle on the stage was to be used; the number of whacks was five per person; the swing a person could use with the paddle limited the strength of the whacks. The worst part was the whacks, of course, not just pain but the humiliation of being spanked in front of hundreds of people, as it turned out. The first time I was out there, forty people whacked me. The guard on the stage managed it as well as one could expect. It still hurt like hell. There were still twenty people, maybe, lined up when he stopped the paddling because he saw it was getting near to damaging me. I thanked him.

"Toughen yourself up, convict. I may not be here the next time, and I can't tell all these people to go home every time. My kindness is because this is your first time, and it's our first time dealing with a murderer like you," he said.

"By the way," he said in a sympathetic voice, "I don't think they should have convicted you of murder. You got guts, that's for sure. I'm sorry that you have to go through this."

"Thanks, Officer," I said, "I don't like it either, but I killed a man and feel like I deserve this."

He shook his head, and I might have seen a tear.

Reminders occurred rain or shine, hot or cold, all seasons of the year. Maybe they would have delayed one if there'd been a tornado or an earthquake or something, but I almost doubted that. Given that I worked seven days a week, the Reminders were almost and perversely a welcome break in the routine. It was hard to walk around for a few days after each one, though. You'd have also thought that foul weather would have cut down on the whacks. Not the case. I still got 200 or so at every Reminder. The worst Reminders were when it was sweltering and humid, which it got in our area of the country reliably, sometimes for months on end. You got pilloried and beat, then baked in the sun.

I was one of two murderers in our Unit, as it was called. The other, a man, was assigned to work in the computer services department of the municipal government because he'd those skills. His name was Ted, and we became friends; he was serving a twenty-year sentence. He came after me to the Unit, so his Reminder dates differed from mine. We could commiserate with each other after we suffered through them.

Ted had been an I.T. executive with a large company. He and several of his coworkers were out one night, and one of them started a fight with some people in the bar that they'd been at. When Ted stepped in to calm things down, a man took a swing at him, and Ted pushed him away. The guy fell and hit his head on the edge of the bar; he died. Two of the man's buddies said that Ted had used a bottle on him though there was no evidence of that, and so he was arrested and tried for murder. As with me, he could have been sentenced to up to 99 years but was sentenced to 20. He got to spend his days in an air-conditioned room. Me... well. I had a great tan. He was a little sallow. I frankly wasn't sure who had the best gig. Most days, I thought I had.

"Lexie, you sure got the raw end of your deal. I read about your case and feel you should never have been tried, let alone jailed. It was a terrible accident," he said.

"Thanks, Ted. I was a trained police officer. I should have known better. I should have seen the instant I walked into the apartment that it wasn't mine. The overhead light not coming on should have been my first clue. Furniture in the apartment the next. This was entirely my fault, and I live with the consequences. I think about Sumit's family almost every day and the pain that I've caused them. The worst part of this is the pillory and the spanking. I could do without those, though," I said. "You don't deserve what you got, either. Your coworkers are jerks."

At the end of my first year, I figured I'd been spanked a little over 1,200 times. Looking out to the full seven and a half years, that would mean they would spank me over 9,000 times. "Ouch!" was all I could think. But as that first guard had said, my behind was getting tougher, and it didn't hurt as much as it had initially. The humiliation, though, was something else. I recognized a few of the same people coming to almost every Reminder and videoing me being spanked. They seemed to get some jollies out of that and my tears. The same ones would throw rotten vegetables at me and yell and curse at me, calling me, "Murderer!" or "Slut!" or "Killer cop!" or something like that. I'm glad my parents didn't have to see this. I found out later that they posted these sessions on the Department of Corrections Internet site, again as a deterrent. I never knew if my parents saw any of them. I found out later that one or two of the people videoing my Reminders were uploading them for sale on one of the light porn sites. One guy had created "The Lexie Reminder Series" and sold a subscription so followers would automatically get my Reminder when the jerk uploaded it. Again, American ingenuity, I guess.

On my parents: At my request, my aging parents never made the trip to visit me. Any travel would have been difficult for them. The Department of Corrections had set up a video-conferencing link for remote visits, especially for me, because I was almost 1,000 miles away from them. I appreciated that consideration. It was good to see them, but hard not to touch them as I saw others doing with their visitors to the Unit.

"Hi, mom and dad. It's great to see the both of you," I said over the link from the office in the halfway house. They asked how things were going, and I told them as well as expected, and they said that I looked fantastic. Had excellent color and looked like I'd been working out. I explained the job and that it was almost all hard, physical labor, so I didn't need to work out. They laughed, and we always parted with us crying. I got to see them about once a month this way on the link.

Every month, convicts got a day off to tend to personal business. I had none, so I hung out at the gym. One of those times, a Unit Supervisor—a guard—asked me to spot him as he worked out. I was strong and nearly as buff as this guy was. He told me he'd been a professional fighter until he got hit in the eye and lost sight in it. He threw in the towel at that point and took one of the newly advertised Supervisor jobs. He was a nice enough guy, but I had to be careful not to appear that I was getting close to one of the staff. I thought my fellow convicts might look at me poorly for that.

I was holding the heavy bag for him one time when he did a triple punch and kick combination that I wasn't prepared for. It knocked me on my tail and the wind out of me. "Whoof!" He came running over to me, worried. "Jeez, Lexie. Are you okay? I didn't mean to knock you down. That was one of my favorite combination punches and kicks when I was fighting. Hard to defend against," he said as he helped me up.

"Damn right, that would be hard to defend against, Officer. I saw stars for a second or two," I said because I had when I hit the ground. I was rubbing my butt when I said that and thought it might have hurt a lot more if not for the Reminders. Good with the bad, I mused.

"I'm so, so sorry. I'll give you a warning if I'm going to do something like that again if there is an again," he said self-consciously.

"Don't worry. There'll be an again, Officer," I said. "I enjoy the exercise."

"Well, you're not getting much exercise spotting and holding the bag. Want to work out with me?" he asked.

"I'm not sure that's a good idea. The other convicts may not like it."

"Gotcha. Well, let's ask and see who else might join in. Also, when we are 1:1 like this, the name is Jaime."

"I'm *definitely* uncomfortable with that, Sir."

"You may have murdered someone, Lexie, and I'm frankly not sure of that, but you're still a human being. The entire purpose of this new justice system is to take the impersonality out of it. Call me Jaime."

"Okay... Jaime," I said, smiling a little nervously.

Later that day, after all the convicts were back in the halfway house, Jaime called us all together. "You all work a wide variety of jobs. Some of you get a fair amount of physical exercise in your work, some of you not so much. I talked to the other Supervisors, and we all agreed that we would start a voluntary group exercise program. All us Supervisors will exercise along with you as equals. We spot for each other and get some tension of the day out. We'll exercise at night after dinner and before lights out. Anyone wants to take a shower after, we invite you to have at it. Anyone interested?"

I waited until a few hands went up, and then I stuck my hand up. Ted did after me.

"Good, about ten of us. This'll be fun. We all know each other and what you did to get here, but no uniforms to level the playing field. I'm going to pass around a piece of paper. Put your name and sizes on it, and I'll get some gym clothes. We'll start tomorrow night."

Figurehead

The exercise turned out to be fun. Even though we all knew what the others had done, not having that big "M" out front during the training made me feel more comfortable. I think everyone else did, too. There was a lot of joking around, and we burned off a lot of steam and calories. Relationships developed that looked like friendships. I didn't need this exercise but did it for the comradeship and to work parts of my body that I didn't have time to work on my job. I worked out a lot on the various punching bags we had, frequently with Jaime spotting for me and me for him.

A few months after our opening, authorities began adding new prisoners to the Unit. Some of these were new to the system, but increasingly, people were coming in from the big prisons that were being shuttered. These latter people had a lot of issues and could disrupt the day-to-day activities on the Unit. Some of them wouldn't share the work; others tried to influence and bring jail gang culture into us. The Supervisors watched these new inmates to make sure that they didn't wreak too much havoc. Even with that, they missed a lot.

Maria Theresa Lopez was a large, muscle-bound Hispanic woman who I thought was one of those. She'd been in jail several times before. This time, she was doing eight years for a drug offense, with two years of that already behind her in a conventional prison upstate. She led a small group of other Hispanics who were kind of scary. I kept my distance from them mostly, though one or two of them were on my rotation in food service. One day, when I was heading to the shower, she came walking over to me with two of her enforcer-types. "Hey, Gringa, I want to talk to you." I kept walking. "Stop walking away, or you get your butt kicked," she said.

Knowing I had few options, I stopped and turned around. "What's up, Maria Theresa? I was just heading for the shower. Can this wait?"

"Only if you want me to spread word that we have a cop here," she said with a nasty, gotcha smile on her face.

"You won't get a big rise out of that revelation, Maria Theresa," I said. "I let everyone know I'd been a cop in one of our first group sessions. I figured I'd better do it before someone else spread the word. My case was pretty public. I didn't have any choice."

She shrugged and walked over to me, stopping well within what I would have called my personal space. She was so close that I had to look up to talk to her eye to eye, and I was tall. I supposed that was her intent. She sniffed a few times and then said, "You smell like sweat. I like it, but you need a shower. We'll talk later."

"Looking forward to it," I said, though I wasn't.

When I finished my shower, Maria Theresa was sitting in our common area, alone. Her enforcers were both nowhere to be seen. Continuing to dry my hair with my towel, I walked over to her and sat opposite her. She looked me up and down. Amazingly, I didn't feel threatened. She was appraising me for sure, but I didn't think for anything bad.

Figurehead

"I read all about your case when I was upstate, Gringa. Lexie, right?" I shook my head yes. "I thought you got a raw deal. But I gotta give you credit for taking it the way you did. Most people would have blamed anyone but themselves. You got my respect. Let me know if you need anything."

She stood up. I reached out and put my hand on her arm and said, "Sit for a second, please." She did. "You're not what I expected, Maria Theresa. I thought we might have a problem, and I'm glad that we don't. You'll find that we all need friends."

"Especially after our Reminder, I know," she said. "I'm not looking forward to that. Been a long time since I had my butt spanked."

"You don't get used to it," I said, "but a friendly guard told me after my first one, it toughens up. Mine has. It still hurts, but not as much. For me, it's the pillory that's the worst part."

"Yeah, I can see that too. Along with these letters," and she gestured to the "D" on her uniform shirt.

"Well, try wearing an 'M' and see what's that like. Not to minimize the shame any of us faces, but us murderers get it worse of all. Mothers see me working in the park, and they grab their kids and run away with them. Like I'm carrying the Plague or something," I said.

I was there for Maria Theresa after her first paddling. She didn't take it well, even though it was far fewer than I got, and she was up there for a shorter period. She was a proud woman, and the humiliation of being paddled and then left there for more abuse hurt her. While I knew it was something she'd get used to, it stung me to see her brought so low. She buddied with me after my Reminders. It was good to have a shoulder to cry on after a Reminder.

Integration of the existing prison populations, as I said before, into these new settings people knew was always going to be tough. It was complicated with the brutal gangs like MS13 and the various white supremacist groups. The opportunity to break these gangs up when the convicts were distributed out to the community units was something the states and the federal government looked forward to. The problem was that there were only a few APP settings, and there didn't seem to be any end to the numbers of these gangs and people in them. That meant that you sometimes had a few of these guys from one or another of these gangs in the same Unit. The powers that be were stupid about it, as they usually are about these kinds of things. Always acting according to their prejudices. They thought that the gangs, especially the nationalists, were all separate, so one or two guys from different groups in the same Unit wouldn't be a problem. The trouble with that was that they were adapting, getting together, and collaborating everywhere—strength in numbers, I guess. Or maybe they thought they would deal with their differences after reaching their objectives; that was more likely. The January 6th insurrection that I watched was an example of how they had collaborated, even though the professionals said there was no evidence of that. A load of crap, I thought. All these guys showed up with bear spray, poles, weapons of other types, and radios that just so happened to be tuned to the same frequency so they could talk. Again, crap. They hurt too many people that day because of the incompetence of government, senior law enforcement, and intelligence leaders who, as always, decided not to take responsibility. Or shoveled it at someone else.

We had guys from the Aryan Brotherhood and the Oath-keepers, and a woman from the 3%'ers join our unit. They all got along great with each other and made it clear that some of us were not welcome in the place we called our home. There were a few fights and a couple of hospitalizations before the Supervisors intervened and separated the groups. The nationalists were moved to a disused wing of the building and placed on their own work detail, a road gang. When one of them tried to make a break for it and was brought back, it became a chain gang. That ratcheted up tensions in town and made the rest of our lives a little trickier.

Unlucky me, I was scheduled for a Reminder right after the escape attempt and creation of the chain gang; lousy timing to be the first Reminder after that and a murderer. They defined Reminders in the federal legislation, but state and local law dictated what made up a Reminder. With the appearance of these new, more brutal criminals, the townspeople were rightly scared, and the new Reminder rules echoed that. They changed from a paddle to a leather switch or a strap, like they used to use in Texas prisons. Also, the pillory was replaced with an instrument called a cangue. The cangue was primarily used in Southeast Asia; one of the townspeople had read about it and adapted it for use here. They put me in this cage and put my head and hands through holes in its top while standing on wooden blocks. Once in there, the guard removed the blocks, so I had to stand on tiptoe to stand at all. My scrub pants and underpants were rolled down to my knees, so I was exposed, and then my tank top was rolled and pinned up, exposing my back and butt. They then used a strap on me for 50 lashes on my butt and back. I suppose that was better than a few hundred with the paddle, but I still have trouble believing that. After the lashing, they made me stand in the cangue for the entire day.

People couldn't whip me, but they could touch me, so I got a lot of slaps on my butt and back. Thankfully, the guard stopped anything more intimate since I was so exposed. About two in the afternoon, based on the clock across the plaza from me, about 8 hours after the Reminder started and maybe halfway through it, it rained. That drove the crowds away, and so I just stood there and got wet. The only good thing about that beyond the crowd dispersing was I could drink my fill of the rain.

The Supervisors protested to the local government the savagery of the punishment. They were told the Reminders were the states and town's business, not theirs, and if they kept making noise, they'd increase the number of days in the Reminder punishment. Jaime apologized to me, and I told him I appreciated their try, but I could endure the punishment. He let me know that the town considered increasing the number of days in the Reminder so they'd be watching the other convicts to make sure that they didn't provoke the town to make more changes.

Our medic, not a doctor but an EMT, put me on bed rest for a couple of days after the Reminder and made that a regular thing for the other convicts. He applied a cream to my back and butt, and it cooled and helped heal the welts and wounds, a couple of which had bled during the strapping. I was okay after about two days and went back to work, a little stiff but glad to be out of the dorm. And I was not looking forward to my next Reminder.

Maria Theresa didn't take my whipping very well, both for herself and me. She was upset and crying and was clearly scared about her time on stage in a few weeks. Lucky for her, our Supervisors registered a complaint to the State about the whipping I took, and they put a hold on these new ones until the Department of Corrections could conduct an investigation. So, Maria Theresa got the paddling. Still upsetting to her, but not like a whipping would've been. As my luck would have it, though, the State had looked at the whipping rules and reinstated them when my turn came again, except for the cangue, which they said *was* barbaric. The town took it out on us by adding a day to all subsequent punishments. So, I got 100 "strokes," as they politely called it over the two days, and got to spend overnight in the pillory, unguarded but not alone. That was the worst part.

Ted fared worse than me. He didn't take any of the beatings well, having been a professional his whole life. As with the rest of us, the disgrace of standing in front of the crowd was overwhelming. His wife divorced him, and then people he knew started getting copies of his videos from his Reminder sessions. While he never expected to see these people again, all of it was too much. A Supervisor found him hanging in the showers one morning. I mourned the man. He'd been a good friend.

I'd been a prisoner for five years when the State changed the rules for Reminders, moving them to every quarter versus bi-monthly. That was fine by the other convicts and me. The State also set out a list of permissible punishment devices based upon surveys of those used at other Units. That was not good news because the town experimented. You never knew what you were going to—literally—get hit with. More straps, a Texas Prison Bat, cat-o'-nine-tails, the bullwhip, floggers, paddles, single tail whips with and without weights, and a collection of brushes used bristle side in or out. I got to experience a couple every Reminder-session. The single tail whips with weights were probably the worst. The guards who administered the Reminders didn't like them either, but the town, to whom they reported, wouldn't listen to them. Their response was to barely strike us with those whips, for the most part anyway.

Figurehead

I liked the work outside more and more, though. The Park manager put me in the greenhouses after he found I had a green thumb. I liked the life in the greenhouse. There were many days where I was alone there, and aside from the quotas and tasks that he assigned, I could do anything I wanted.

I used our Internet connection to research different gardening projects and proposed some of those to the Parks and Recreation manager. He thought playing with grafting and my idea to try out bonsai were great ideas. I experimented a lot with grafting and with bonsai. That took very steady hands. I could see myself doing this permanently when I got out. Later, I came up with an idea to sculpt some of our bushes and trees. That got the notice of the town, and even some kids came to help me out. Eventually, one of the kid's parents came to me and my boss and told us I was not the evil butcher that they'd heard that I was. A positive thing this ended up being, I guess.

The manager asked if I'd consider staying after they paroled me, and I said that I would, though I was frankly concerned about trying to live in the town after they'd seen so much of me. I wasn't sure that I'd be accepted or at least treated with any measure of respect. Then again, the experience with that parent told me that anything was possible.

Year six came and went. By my calculation, I'd gotten 1,500 butt whacks and over 2,000 whip strokes. My back and butt were a mass of scars from the whippings, mainly. Other than that, I felt I looked good. Hefting 50-pound bags of dirt all day and doing all the digging and planting I did outdoors left me in good physical shape as well, with fantastic color, just like my parents had said years ago. I also kept up with nightly exercises at the unit and, until Jaime retired, he and I would spar on my days off. I thought that all-in-all, this had been a good thing for me. I wished, though, that it was this good for other reasons.

My calls with my parents continued. Unfortunately, bad things were going on with them. My father admitted that my mother was suffering from dementia during one call when she wasn't there. He also said that he'd been hospitalized and had surgery for a tumor on his liver. The surgery was a success, and he was under treatment but looked washed out. Later in my sixth year, my father told me they'd institutionalized mom and that his cancer had reappeared. I tried to get a compassionate release to visit with them, but my father had died by the time it was granted. The staff at the Alzheimer's center where my mom was said that I shouldn't visit as that would likely impact her treatment, such as I imagined it was. All of this was too much for me—another consequence of my actions that night over six years ago. The only one to blame was me. Maria Theresa rallied to me to help me through this. I loved her even more for how she stuck with me.

At the beginning of my seventh year, I got a request from Sumit's brother, Vineet, to meet with him and his family. I hesitated and told him I was reluctant to meet them. He said not to worry, that the family wanted to see how I was doing as they were formally supporting parole for me. I was apprehensive, but I met with them at the local courthouse several times over a few days. They were very friendly to me, much more than I would have been had one of them killed someone I loved. Vineet went with me to the park and saw where I was working. He even bought one of my bonsai plants. I wanted to give it to him, but he Googled bonsai plants and compared what he saw to those and then paid me the highest price. That touched me and gave me a little spare cash.

It was soon after that they called me to meet with the Parole Board. I was the first murderer sentenced under the new laws, and they wanted to spend time with me. They did, grilling me for three days. It wasn't easy. They asked many tough and emotional questions, some of which stressed me as they wanted to see how I'd respond. In the end, they told me that the earliest they could release me was in about six months, and they would let me know well before then. In fact, they let me know the following week that, given the support of Sumit Kamath's family, they were going to parole me when I reached seven and a half years. I was, as you can imagine, thrilled and sailed through the next six months. I even walked up to the stage for my last Reminder, smiling. The guard there knew why and said that he was going to miss me. I wasn't sure how to take that.

I took the park manager up on his offer and stayed in town. It wasn't easy. While I didn't have to wear the uniform with the big "M" on it any longer, I was still collared and would be for the rest of my sentence. I'd become attached to the collar and wouldn't have turned it in if I could have. It labeled me again my deserved stigma. I was okay with that. Maria Theresa told me I was a "masoquista." I guess maybe I was a little.

The manager helped me find a one-bedroom apartment near the park, in a modest area and well within my budget. I could even afford some new clothes. People were friendly or unfriendly, much like when I'd been a cop, I thought. I still had women taking their kids across the street when they saw me, maybe, but I thought that was going to be my lot in life if I stayed here or until the people who knew what I'd been left town. Freedom, though a relative term, in my case, was an exciting experience. Before going to jail, I'd never really understood what it meant. My boss at the park and I talked a lot about what it was like being free after being one of the first people in the APP. I told him about my feelings about freedom and that you never really miss it until it's gone. He agreed and gave me a copy of a book by Robert Heinlein called *Stranger in a Strange Land*. He told me to think about the word "Grok" that Heinlein had coined there. Now, when I talk about anything that I feel, I say that I "Grok it," feel it in my soul.

My workday started at 6 AM when I walked from my apartment to the park. I had my own keys to the greenhouse and would work there on my projects until the workday started at 8. I oversaw the convict contingent at the park and doled out and supervised the work they did. I loved the job so much that I jumped in on it with my old brothers and sisters. With a push from the Parks and Recreation manager, we also started a tree and bush sculpting class. It surprised people to see an ex-con running the class, but they got past any concerns quickly when they got to know me. My worries and shyness about being out in society also faded away as I was accepted.

Maria Theresa was there, and she liked the park work as well. She was due out in another year, and I talked the manager into offering her a job too. When she was released, she gratefully lost her collar; she hadn't become attached to hers like I had to mine. I got her an apartment in the same building as me, and she and I would walk to work in the mornings. We ate most meals together and would hang out in each other's apartments. We pooled our money and bought a T.V. and a laptop computer so we could entertain ourselves. I wrote this story on it.

Little did I know what direction my life was about to take.

One night, after dinner and a few movies with Maria Theresa, I headed up to my apartment, exhausted from the long day. It surprised me to find my door unlocked, but this was the country, and I frequently left it unlocked when I was in the building. I opened the door, and standing there was Vineet. He had his hands in the air.

"No need to shoot, Lexie," he said.

"Not funny, Vineet," I said. He smiled and walked over to me.

"Sorry. I wanted to see you outside, and here you are," he said. "May we talk?"

"Of course. Want something to drink?" I asked.

"I brought us some tea. We grow this on our farm in India."

He brewed the tea, and we sat back to drink and talk. I lost track of time, and when I looked at the clock, it was well past 2 AM. "Vineet, I need to go to work in a few hours. How long will you be here?" I asked.

"I've nothing pressing me to be anywhere. I'm staying at the hotel downtown. I fell in love with it when we came to meet you, and I bought it today," he said.

"Huh? Just like that? You bought it?" I was shocked.

"Yes. My family is what you call rich," he said with a bit of smile, "astronomically rich. So, I will stay here for a while. I hope we can see each other again." He stood up to leave and headed over to the door. But before he exited, he stopped. "Can we meet tomorrow after your work? At the hotel. I have a proposal that I'd like to make to you." He walked out the door before I could answer either way. It seemed more an order than a request, anyway.

The next day, I met him at his hotel as he'd requested, still dressed in my Parks and Recreation uniform. I walked up to the front desk and asked for him. The woman there must have recognized me because she hesitated before picking up the phone and said, "There's someone here who says that she has an appointment with you. Do you want me to send her away?" I could hear her whispering to Vineet, "She's one of those convicts. A murderer!"

She blushed over something he said and stated, "Mr. Kamath said that he'd be right out and that you were not to move." I bet she added on that last part to save some face.

Vineet came out of the back and gave me a hug and a kiss. As we walked away, he said, "Sorry. I hope that affection didn't offend you, but that woman was not being pleasant."

"That's fine, Vineet. You took me a little by surprise, but I saw her face, and it was worth it. There are many people like her here. It's changing, but I'm used to the looks and people talking behind my back."

"Too bad that you have to live through that. Now, come with me."

We walked back through a warren of offices to a large corner suite overlooking my park and greenhouse. The bonsai he had bought from me had a prominent place on his desk; that touched me. "So, what do you think? I get to watch you every day, as it turns out. I'm a very early riser and have seen you coming in just after I get here. I'm not stalking you or anything like that, but I do believe in fate. My people would call it Karma."

"Truthfully, Vineet, it is a little creepy. What's this about?" I asked. I'd always been direct, but being in prison only sharpened that, I guess. I mentally thwacked myself on the back of my head for being so disrespectful to such a nice man.

I started to apologize for my rudeness, but he spoke. "Nothing or everything," he said. "I have some paperwork I want to share with you, and then we can never see each other again if that's what you want. Be clear. It's not what I want. Please, sit and read through these." He pushed a couple of pieces of paper across the desk toward me. I took them and sat down to look at them. I had to look twice. The first one was the deed to this property. The owners of the property were Vineet Kamath and me, Lexie McGrath. The second was a contract to work for the Kamath family as the owner-manager of this hotel at a salary that made me, well, I guess, obscenely wealthy by my standards.

"Vineet, why?" I said, tearing up.

"Remember when we first met in the courts how my family and I said we didn't want you to do jail time and that this was all a horrible accident? Well, we feel we failed you by not persuading the court that they should not sentence you as you were. This is a paltry attempt to pay you back for that loss and what you still have in front of you," he said.

"Vineet, the fact is that I killed your brother. That I was wrong. And I needed to pay for it. I..."

"Stop. Your definition of paying for it and ours is quite different. Our parents and I feel that your honest, heartfelt acceptance of responsibility for Sumit's death was all we needed. You were, unfortunately, sucked into the maelstrom of social unrest occurring here at that time, and what they did to you was wrong. That is, in our opinion, and given that my brother was killed, we were all that should have mattered. But we did not, like you did not. What you have suffered—and I truly know that you have, I've seen videos of your Reminders—was very wrong and went far beyond compensation for Sumit's death. We *want* to give you this," he said. He gestured at the papers.

I was speechless. I stood up and walked out. As I stepped through the door, I turned to him and said, "I need to take a walk. I'll be back soon." He nodded, and I walked out and down the street to the park. I stepped into the grounds that I'd fallen in love with and looked back up at the office. Vineet stood there and was watching me intently. I walked a little more and then came back to where I'd seen him. He was still standing there, and I waved at him to come down.

"Vineet," I said when he sat down next to me, "I'm grateful for what you've done, but this is where I want to be. I could never run a hotel, especially one as nice as that one. I'd do everything wrong, and I don't want to hurt you and your family again."

"Lexie, I meant what I said when I said that we were wealthy. The cost of this hotel is what you would call chump change to us. It's not the money that's important here, but you, as far as we're concerned. The hotel could fail tomorrow, and it would benefit us from a tax perspective. You shouldn't worry about that. You've lost a quarter of your life, not working and living on the outside. You've had much taken away but have come through the experience, I think, a better version of your old self."

"You're not ready to run a hotel like this," he resumed. "I know that, and I would never place you in that position. Plus, I know you love this park. I could see that in your work in the greenhouse and out here. I wouldn't want you to stop that work. You create beautiful things, like this place," and he gestured around us, "your grafts and sculptures, and those beautiful bonsai. No, the ownership and manager status is for three purposes. One we've already talked about, another is to give you a backstop should anything go wrong in your life, and last to give you money for you to fashion a life for yourself here or wherever you want to be," he said. "Actually, maybe a fourth reason, I want to see the faces of the hotel staff, in particular that woman, when I introduce you as my co-owner."

He took a breath and then continued, "I'll be staying to run the hotel. I hope you would see fit to let me see you and maybe, eventually, for that to develop into something else. We have got a lot of affection for you, and my mom and dad have said that you would make a wonderful daughter. I won't rush that. You've been out of circulation for quite a while. You make whatever decision you want to make when the time is right, and I will be there to support you whatever it is."

I hadn't yet put behind me the need to settle up for Sumit's murder, but this put me on an entirely new track. Somewhere I would never have expected, even a few months back.

I had never expected the Kamath's forgiveness, and now I had that in the most solid of forms. Maybe eventually, I'll do the same for myself.

The End

{ 7 }

Retriever

The bicycle I was riding would've crashed if it wasn't for the farmer guy I ran into. I apologized to him as we both scraped ourselves off the ground. Still and all, he looked none the worse for the wear and said, "Not to worry, young man. I'm glad you didn't run into that wall. That might've killed you."

"Sorry again, sir. The brakes on this thing have been warning me that they were going to give out for the last twenty miles. I'm in a rush. Gotta get to my sister. Thanks for understanding," I said as I jumped back onto the bike and raced away.

"Get that thing fixed as soon as you can, boy! The next person you hit might not be as understanding," he said as he waved goodbye, smiling and dusting himself off.

I hit the city streets and turned toward the slave markets showing on the map on my implant. I'm a Retriever, First Class. My name's Cass. You might ask, "Cass what?" and I'd have to say, "Cass." That's all I've ever known. My trainers told me that meant I was clever, which I am. I'm also genetically and physically modified so that I can change my appearance at will. Right now, I look like a skinny fifteen-year-old boy, not my standard thirty-something-looking giant enhanced with a variety of augments. Those are all buried inside me right now. I can call them up when or if I need them. Otherwise, aside from the bike wreck, I'm forgettable—intentionally. In fact, I bet the guy I hit couldn't remember if I were tall or short brown or blonde-haired right now—a feature of my augments.

I hit the city's main streets and began working my way toward the markets. They were scheduled to open in about two hours. I planned to get there, rescue Sheela and get out of there to rendezvous with the Amalgam Spaceship Venable. Every time I think of the names of our spaceships, I have to laugh—the A.S.S. Venable, at least it wasn't named for that Norwegian physicist Njål Hole or that Norwegian detective, Harry Hole.

Anyway, Princess Sheela Jessen was out with friends when slavers took her. Her friends got away, but Sheela was too slow, maybe too drunk based on what I'd heard about the poor little rich girl, and she got caught. We were in port and were tasked with tracking her down and bringing her home. The slavers cut a wide swath, making it easy to track them to here, the planet Doter. Doter is the only planet in this section of the Amalgam that has commercial and public slave markets. All worlds allowed slavery, to one extent or another, but Doter was the only one where the markets were all above ground and public. That was the good news. If they had taken Jessen to one of the other planets, we might never have been able to track her down once they landed her there. She would have been gone for good.

So, why take her here? Easy answer. These public markets, because they were that, attracted big credit buyers interested in legitimate purchases. She could command a higher price here than in the underground markets that had a lot of overhead.

The bad news was that once a deal was closed on an "asset," as they called the people they sold, it was almost impossible to get it undone in a legal market. There were few avenues to reverse a legitimate sale, and it could take years to move through the Doter courts. And, meanwhile, well, a slave's a slave. So, me and a retrieval. I had license to do what was necessary, even if it broke local law to steal her back.

Slaves to be sold on any day were listed in an online catalog with provenance and many pictures. The catalog listed the starting bid price and a rune, in the Princess's case, showing that this was a reserve auction. That meant the seller, the slavers, knew who they had and would withdraw her from the block if they weren't getting the money they wanted for her. Another bit of bad news because they would likely expect a rescue attempt. Oh well, I thought, that's why I get the big bucks.

GEORGE CONKLIN

I don't get big bucks for anything I do. I'm a sailor. I get my pay; that's all, well maybe something else. I do this because I love adventure. I came from a planet called Aeliv, close to beyond the borders of the known galaxy. Aeliv is a minor planet, a little smaller than Mars in the Sol system—that's what we use for all our comparisons and measurements, planets in the old Sol system. The big difference from Mars was that Aeliv is lush. They officially classed it as a bread-basket planet, so most of us that lived there were farmers like the guy I hit with the bike. My parents didn't need another son—or a daughter for that matter—and so they had me enlist in the space Navy as a child. I was selected for the Retriever program after I turned 11. Our job is, as the title implies, to retrieve lost things—and people. There is at least one Retriever on each cruiser. In the Venable's case, there are two of us. This is an active part of the galaxy, what with many populated planets and energetic slaving rampant, and the Venable is an enormous ship, one of the largest in the fleet.

I've been a Retriever now for over sixty years. I know I said that I am thirty-something, but I said "looking" in there. We are so expensive that they also figured out how to slow our aging to get as much out of us as they can. By the time I retire, I'll be well over 200 years old, with another 200 years or more left in me. I personally think that's kind of cool and a decent trade-off for the things done to my body and the pain I undergo every time I change to one of my appearances.

Figurehead

I arrived at the auction yards and parked my bike. Well, I ditched it because I didn't think I'd be using it again. It had served me well for over a hundred miles from the Venable drop-site. No way I could ride it with the Princess. We'd need to find some other transport when I rescue her, or worse case, with an entitled and likely whiny royal, walk. Maybe one of the slaver's vehicles. I like that. Balanced. Maybe with the slaver's head on a pike instead of a hood ornament.

I'd brought a few other sets of clothes in my pack—some for me as disguises and some for the Princess. I took a nice pair of pants and a tunic out for myself. I put a few weapons—guns, knives, Billy clubs—and grenades on a belt underneath the tunic. Be prepared, as I always said. And I carried the rest of my stuff in the pack I hefted over my shoulder.

The catalog gave the Princess's lot number and approximate time for her auction, so I headed into the market to inspect the merchandise, so to speak. They had chained her to a pole with her hands over her head. She looked drugged. I tried to reach out to her through her implants, but all I got was a hum. They'd probably found them and disabled or removed them.

She was fourth in line to be taken to the block. I thought about buying her, just for the heck of it; her father was paying for all of this. My actual plan was to wait until they released her cuffs and leg irons to take her to the auction block and then to intervene. Over the next twenty minutes, I appeared to meander around the yard and stashed a series of smoke and incendiary explosives, all set to go off on a signal from me. I figured that would cause a riot and allow me to change one more time and rescue her.

The Princess's time on catalog came up. "We have a special prize today. A real princess," exclaimed the auctioneer. "Princess Sheela Jessen from Enia. You may know or have heard of her father, the king of Enia, Lackmore. I'm surprised that he doesn't have representatives here tasked with buying her."

"As you can see from the catalog, her starting bid price is set extremely high, one billion credits, and that this is a reserve auction. If the seller," and he gestured to a man standing off to the side of the auction area—my hood ornament I guessed, "is dissatisfied with the price we're getting, he can withdraw her, right up to the instant I strike the gavel. Are we all ready? This one would make a wonderful addition to any harem."

As he spoke, I signaled the explosives, and they ignited around the plaza. People screamed and ran for the exits. I saw the slaver run toward the block, drawing a gun. I transformed into my base shape, intimidating on a good day, and launched myself toward the block as well. Sheela was looking around, bewildered by the chaos, maybe coming out of the drugs. As the slaver reached her, she lashed out with her foot and connected with his chin, sending him sprawling back, and he lost his gun in the crowd. I reached her, and she turned on me. I caught her foot, twisted it, and she sailed off the block into my arms.

Figurehead

"I'm retrieval Princess. Don't fight me, or I'll have to put you to sleep for a while," I said to her. We headed toward the exit.

We were about out the door when someone grabbed me from behind and twisted me around. The slaver, backed by two other men. "She's mine," said the man, and he advanced toward me. My augments gave me many advantages. Bullet-proof wasn't one of them, though. I had a Kevlar chest plate under my skin that would stop most ordnance. All three of the men carried pistols that might carry armor-piercing ammo, though. I wasn't about to let them get a shot at me to find out. One of my other augments gave me speed and agility that I was sure that these men couldn't match. I was right, too. One of them got a shot off my eyes could see as it left the barrel of the gun. I moved around it, disarmed the man with a chop to his throat, and then took out the second man as well the same way. The slaver said, "Damn. A Retriever." And I knocked him out.

"Can you walk, Princess?" I asked.

"I can run too. Can you, carrying him?" she asked.

"I wasn't planning on carrying him. If he comes, he comes on his own two feet. Otherwise, I kill him here," I said.

"Well, I want his balls first," she said. I could learn to like this girl.

"Now, I need to get you out of those clothes and that collar. You stick out like a sore thumb, undressed like that," I said. We moved out of the auction house and to the alley where I'd left the bicycle. It was still there. I was impressed with the honesty of the Doterians. I opened my pack and handed her the clothes I'd brought for her. They toned down her good looks and made her look a lot younger than she was. Meanwhile, I transformed myself and put my other young-kid clothes back on. "Come here, Princess. I want to get that collar off you."

She came over, and I pushed out my steel teeth augments and brought my face down to her neck. She cringed away. "Just stay right there, Princess. I don't want to cut you," and I bit through the collar. She stepped back, shocked. I smiled at her as my augments retracted. "You never know when you might need to eat your way out of something."

We heard a moan. The slaver was waking up. "Good. You're awake," I said. "I wanted you to see me when I cut your head off."

His eyes flew open, and he backed away from me. The Princess stepped behind him and kicked him in the head again, but not hard enough to knock him out. "You bastard," she said. "You were going to sell me? I ought to let him cut your head off, but I want to castrate you first."

She had spunk and a sailor's mouth to go along with it. I told her that, and she smiled. "I keep telling my daddy that I need to go into the military. He just won't agree."

I turned back to the slaver. "Your name?"

"Nicolas Finnsson," he said.

"Well, Nicolas. Do you know what I am?" He shook his head yes. "They have given me a broad license in this rescue, so your life's hanging on a thread. I had visions of stealing your vehicle and using your head as a hood ornament, but I'm not sure that's a good idea. So, I'll just settle for the transport. Once we're out of the city, I'll release you. Nothing fancy meant there. I'll let you go free, but if we ever see you near Enia, the Princess, or me, that'll be it for you. Understand?"

Again, he shook his head yes and said he'd take us to his car and out of town to wherever we wanted to go. Men guarded the car, and he asked that I not kill them as they were his kin. I said I'd try not to, but that depended on them and him. We reached the car, and the three of us walked up to it.

"Nic," said a good-looking young man who eyed us suspiciously, "we thought that something had happened to you. Where'd you go?"

"I'm fine, Theo. I ran after the big guy who stole the Princess. He turned on the guards and me and took out the two of them. This boy and his sister were walking by and yelled, so the guy ran off with the princess," said Nicolas.

"Really? This girl looks a lot like her," said the man he called Theo. "Anyway, we need to get out of here. Too bad about losing her. She was going to be a big payday for us."

"I know. We'll find someone like her and get that payday. I promised these two we'd give them a ride out of the city for their help. They live... where was it, Adam?" asked Nicolas.

"Pier City, Nic," I said, looking at the map on my eye screen. "Eve and I live outside of the city, but if you can get us there, we can get home on our own. Can I throw my bike in your trunk?"

Nic's transport was a large vehicle. It looked armed and bulletproof. And it was utterly silent inside. I kept my killing steel in my sleeve and waited for them to pull something, but it turned out that Nic was a man of honor, pirate that he was. They left us on the west side of Pier City. We said our good-byes, and he thanked us again for helping him out. We walked off toward the south. Only for about two miles, and then we turned west again.

"My ship will rendezvous with us about thirty miles from here. So, maybe two days away on foot, if we don't run into any trouble. Are you okay with that, Princess?" I asked.

"Sure. Can we stop that, by the way?" she replied.

"Huh?"

"This Princess B.S. Never Princess. I rather like Eve, so let's stick with her. When we're home, I expect that you'll call me Sheela. What's your real name?"

"Cass."

"Cass what?" she asked.

I laughed. "Just Cass. I was raised from a youngster to be a Retriever. My mother and father enlisted me in the space Navy when I was a kid, so no last name. Just Cass. It means clever."

"That you are," and she put her arm around my shoulders as we headed off into the sunset. I was a little shocked at this kid's behavior, but I was warming to her as well. She had spunk and was pretty regular. Gorgeous too.

We stopped a few hours later in a small thicket by a stream and in front of an immense pile of boulders. We backed up against them, and I took a couple of ration bars from my pack. We each took one and munched quietly. I also started a small fire with one of the fire packs I carried. We warmed ourselves by it and chatted pleasantly. Sheela, I mean Eve, was not the spoiled, whiny rich kid that I'd imagined. She was practical, not into the charade of royalty, and said that she loved this escape. That's what had got her into trouble. She had ditched her security detail so she could spend time together with her friends the day Nic had shanghaied her. As I had guessed, she had been drunk, so when the slavers hit, she was too disoriented to get away. In fact, she said, she ran right to them.

"Maybe getting caught was subconsciously intended," she said. "It's a little wicked, I guess, but I was also looking forward to being sold. I figured that would be about as low as I could go and was excited by it. I'm not too fond of the royal court and all the protocol stuff there. I'm like sixth in line for the throne and so will never be on it. You can see how unimportant I am by the fact my father sent no one to bid on me."

"Well," I said, "He sent me, and I've never lost a retrieval."

"Maybe," she said, "but he should at least have made a show of having someone there for me."

I stared at her.

"Don't look at me like I'm crazy. My life as a Princess is just about like being a slave. I have to follow all these rules, and I'm expected to toe a very narrow line, so I don't embarrass my parents and the monarchy. I'm also expected to marry to increase our family's holdings and power and have children who'll be unable to ascend to be king at any point unless everyone in front of me and all their families are at the same party that gets blown up. I've got to smile and make nice and make babies. It makes me want to puke when I think of what's ahead of me," she said.

I didn't know what to say. I'd thought life of privilege was a good thing, but I guess, like, with all of us, there were problems there, too.

"I'm sorry, Eve. I thought you had a good life. But I see now.... So, I guess I'm taking you back to something not so nice," I said.

"Not to worry, Cass. I'll survive. They brought me up to understand that I would not be happy. I've resigned myself to that. Maybe why I've been such a whiner to everyone around me. Time for me to grow up," she said.

I looked over at her and saw tears in her eyes. She turned away from me and looked like she was going to sleep. I got up and walked away from the fire, and took a position to see anyone who might try to approach us. I called up my infrared augments and looked out at the countryside. Sometime later, I heard steps coming up behind me, and she plopped down next to me. "Sorry that I'm such a downer, Cass. I do appreciate your coming to retrieve me and also for this adventure."

"I'd not thought about it before, Eve, but what I'm learning is that what I see you're going through, I'd give my life to have those problems. That's not the point, though, is it? It's what you live and experience that's important. So, what I might want to have as a problem doesn't matter. It's what you're experiencing that is."

She looked at me a little curiously. "I could fall in love with you, Cass," she said. "Never thought that I'd say that—sober anyway—to anyone."

She fell asleep next to me as I kept watch, her head in my lap.

When the sun rose, we ate another ration bar and then headed out. My implant maps charted a path to the meeting with the A.S.S. Venable that was more or less direct. We still had a little over 25 miles to go, not having made much distance toward the location the day before. The weather reports from the implants said that today was going to be a swelterer. By mid-morning, we were both soaked. I'd stripped down to my tee shirt and gave Eve one of mine to wear as well. I admired her body and how the clothes clung to her now-sweaty body.

"Stop staring, Retriever," she said, looking over her shoulder with a smile. She wiggled her hips and butt and then laughed.

I looked away, flushing red.

She turned around, saw that I was embarrassed, stopped, and fell in next to me. She put her arm around me and hugged herself to me. "Stop just staring and just looking, Retriever, was what I meant," she said and pulled me into a small stand of bushes off the side of the game trail we were following.

I'm not a virgin—and neither was she—but I'd never made love to someone who was an animal like that. She was ravenous, and we spent several hours in the brush. The sun was well past noon when we finally started walking again. "We keep that up, and we may never meet the Venable," I said.

"Every cloud has a silver lining, Sailor," she said. "That was the most fun that I've had, well, ever. Thanks, Cass."

"No thanks necessary. I had the best time, too," I said.

We walked along in silence for a while. "This makes me not want to return, Sailor. What can we do?" she asked. "I don't mean I want just to disappear, and you go back to your ship, but I want to be there with you. Any way we can do that?"

"Not that I can think of," I said. "Besides, what the shrinks tell us Retrievers is to watch out for just what's happening with you. They had some complicated terms for it, but it all comes down to you falling for me because I rescued you. That's all you're experiencing. Let's just have fun and not talk about this being anything like permanent."

"Boy, do I wish I could change myself like you," she said. "I'd make myself into something else and enlist."

That gave me some pause. "This isn't a simple thing, Eve. Changing is very painful. I'll live a very long time, but it is at the cost of lots of pain whenever I change," I said.

"How-so?" she asked.

"You saw me as my, what I call my base self, or near to it at the auction. I'm now in a much more acceptable, human form. My base form, as you saw, is a giant. Enormous size. This body is a lot smaller. Every time I add or subtract size, it forces me to change my muscle and bone structure. It hurts to do that. They bred me for this, and I live with the knowledge and the pains. That's the downside. The upside was that the augmentation process added centuries to my life. It was, they told me, a cost-benefit thing. I was extremely expensive to build. So, to make sure they get their money's worth, they slowed my aging. I'll be hundreds of years old when I begin to die, and that could take a century or two as well," I said.

She looked back and teared up again. "I'm so sorry for you, Cass."

I smiled at her, and we continued our walk. "Don't be. While I didn't have much say in what they did to me, I like this job and changing myself to help people like you. Maybe that was psyched into me, I don't know, but I'm happy with this life."

We continued to walk. At sunset, we barely had made fifteen miles. I sent out a message through my implants that we were making slower time than I'd projected, and we wouldn't be at the meeting place for maybe three more days. I also said that I needed to see the ship's genengineer when we got back. I told them that a couple of my changes had not gone smoothly and wanted a check-up. That wasn't really why I wanted to talk to him, but it would do to get some time alone.

We passed a small town as the day was ending, and I told Eve to hide out in a broken-down barn that we'd found and went into town to look for something to eat other than my dwindling supply of ration bars. I bought some bread, cheese and sausage, and a bottle of wine and headed back out of town. I wanted to walk a few more miles before stopping for the night just to get away from any prying eyes from the town. Eve was sitting in a corner of the barn, looking out over the old fields. "Wouldn't it be nice to have a place like this? Just the two of us?" she asked.

I smiled and said, "We shouldn't be doing this. You know that. When we get back to the ship, you'll have to go back home. We shouldn't make that harder than it needs to be."

She smiled to herself and then nodded.

"Let's move on a few miles. We've still some good light before we need to bed down," I said.

We walked a few more miles and then found a clearing next to a stream. Just upstream, we also found a small waterfall. I stripped off my clothes and jumped in. She was a few seconds behind me. We swam around for a few minutes and then climbed out of the water and dressed. "That was great," she said.

"Yes, it was. What I like is the way your clothes hang on you when you're soaked like that," I said. That was a signal for another tumble... and then a nice dinner by the waterfall. I kept watch again. She asked if she could spell me, and I told her that I didn't need to sleep like ordinary people did when I was in the field like this. My body was constantly awake. I'd crash when I got back to the ship and went into a hibernation chamber.

"What's that?" she asked.

"The hibernation chamber?" She nodded. "It's a special bed on the ship for us modifieds where we're immersed in fluids, and our modifications are tuned. Looks like a big fish tank.

Figurehead

I'm awake the whole time, breathing through a hose and a mouthpiece. They customize each bath for the modified based on an assessment that's done in the lab. I like it because it's very relaxing. I hear this time they have some updates on my augments that they want to apply. Those make me faster, stronger, and all-around better."

"Interesting. Could I try it?" she asked.

"Sure. Non-modifieds don't get the entire set of benefits that us modifieds do, obviously, but it's a good way of relaxing and rebuilding when we've been running around like this," I said.

She slept with her head on my lap as she had the previous night. We left early the following day and walked all day with only a couple of stops to rest and have some water. Eve was quiet, and I suspected she was thinking about what was in store for her when she arrived home in a week or so. That night, she made intense love to me, and when we were done, she cried and wouldn't talk to me about what was making her so sad. Though I pretty much knew what was happening. I started to curse myself for getting attached to her. She didn't come out to where I was sitting, unlike the previous nights.

The following day, she was even sadder. I had to force her to eat something, and as we walked, she seemed lost in herself. I tried to get her to talk to me, but she wouldn't. When we were about five miles from the rendezvous, I stopped us. "Eve, talk to me. I don't want us to part like this."

"One last time, Cass?" she burst out crying and folded herself into me. And we settled down in some bushes and made love again and again. When I woke up, she was gone.

There was a brief note. I said, "I just can't go back, Cass. You've made me feel what it's like to be in love, and I want to see if I can rediscover that. Love, Your Eve."

"Damn," I said. I sent out a message and told the ship what had happened, that I'd lost the Princess. The response was terse, "Retrieve her, Retriever. No warm-up until you do."

I headed out after her.

Finding her wasn't difficult. I spied her walking ahead of me toward a town a few miles away and stayed back as she entered it. She went toward the town square, where there seemed to be a festival of some sort going on. There were many people, stalls selling various things, and a large stage where a band was playing. I transformed back into my fifteen-year-old body, changed into the clothes I'd worn earlier, and walked into town. I wandered around looking like I belonged there and bought a piece of fruit at one stall. I munched it as I walked around a few rows from where Eve was also wandering, looking at the food. Of course, she didn't have any money so that she couldn't buy anything.... But that didn't prevent her from trying to steal something. She got nabbed almost immediately and taken away, fighting two big burly men. I kept up as they dragged her to a group of men standing next to the stage.

One man turned and talked to the two men. He then turned to Eve, put her hand under her chin, and lifted her

Figurehead

face. He spoke to her for a few minutes, and she started yelling again, this time in apparent panic. The burly men took her behind the stage to what looked like a holding cell with several other people in it and threw her in. They walked away.

I strolled up to the people standing over there and asked what was going on in my best fifteen-year-old country bumpkin voice. A spectator told me that this was the annual Festival of the Planting, one of their biggest celebrations each year. The other being the Feast of the Harvest. So, I asked what was with the people behind the stage. They said to watch and enjoy the spectacle. "It's where we offer the gods our homage, and they will hopefully smile on us and deliver a good crop this summer."

While they were talking, several men had worked on the stage, assembling what looked like large crosses without a top on them. On the crossbar for each were a pair of cuffs and another pair of cuffs at the base. I had a feeling that I was going to witness a pagan display of some kind. I looked in my backpack and saw I still had three grenades, my guns, and knives. I hoped that would be enough to break Eve out again. I wandered away from the friendly people and found a dark place to transform again, back to my base self and size. I knew I'd need to be intimidating.

Unlike the slave auction, this was going to be more challenging. I only had offensive fragmentation grenades left, so I'd need to be careful about where I put them. Starting a riot here would mean that a lot of innocents might get hurt or killed. I looked around for options.

A man walked up to the stage and began speaking, "Welcome all to our annual Festival of the Planting! Tomorrow we begin the annual work of sowing our fields, expecting a wonderful harvest in a few months."

As the man prattled on, I saw the workers move large steel pans under each cross. It became clear what they were going to do. The poor people in the cage, Eve included, were going to be whipped on the crosses until they bled, and their blood was going to feed the town's harvest. Once the men finished assembling the crosses, they went to tables at the end of the stage and came back, each of them carrying a long, curved, wicked-looking knife. I'd heard about this kind of thing but never thought I'd see something like it. This would not be a flaying with a whip but a peeling of skin from those poor people. No harvest was worth this horrendous violation of other humans as far as I was concerned, and I now had another reason to interrupt this ceremony.

Okay, we were all given non-intervention orders, but that said, Amalgam planets lived under a constitution that reflected what we called progressive values. And that did not include what these folks were doing. Savagery like this had been outlawed in the Amalgam centuries ago.

I flashed a message to the Venable. They had returned to orbit and said it would take them about half an hour to get to my location. I knew I had way less time than that. I told them to come in and dispatch some marines as soon as they

Figurehead

got here. I worked my way up behind the stage as they led the people out of the cage. They all fought until they hit the bottom step of the stairs to the platform when all resistance seemed to deflate. Except for Eve, she fought right to the top. Good girl, I said to myself. She was so distracting that I got me under the stage near the place where I saw and heard that they were tying her. She was raised to the cross, and they cut her clothes away.

"People, now the moment we've all been waiting for: The shedding of the growing blood. Thank these people who give their blood so we can all flourish," said the man. The crowd applauded and hooted at the poor sacrifices tied above me.

I threw my first grenade toward where I estimated the master of ceremonies was standing and waited five seconds before throwing one of my last two in the same area. In the meantime, I heard screams coming from the people tied to the crosses over my head. The first grenade exploded, taking down the front of the stage, nearly on my head. The man who was speaking fell near my feet. He was a bloody wreck and quite dead. The second grenade exploded taking down even more of the stage and giving me the distraction I needed. I heard screams from the crowd and the beginnings of panic. I backed away from the stage, went around to the stairs, and made my way to the top. The men had continued to cut at the prisoners. Eve's back was a bloody mess. Pieces of flayed skin hung from her; blood pooled in the pan below her.

I shot the man flaying her through the head and did the same with the others. I cut Eve down and put her over my shoulder. She was nearly unconscious but smiled when she saw me. "Behind you, Cass," she said in warning.

I turned, and the two burly men who had taken her were coming toward me, both brandishing knives. I smiled and raised my weapon. They dropped their knives and ran away. I walked down the platform, cutting the ropes holding the other sacrifices. People ran up onto the stage and took them away, presumably family members or friends. I walked away, disgusted. No one tried to stop me—smart of them.

Eve continued to bleed as we walked out of town. There was so much damage; there was little I could do to stem the bleeding. She was wounded everywhere. As I left town, a Venable shuttle materialized in front of me, and a squad of heavily armed marines rushed out to help me and to take us back to the Venable. When we got there, we took Eve to the sick bay, and a doctor took one look at her and put her in a hibernation tank. I walked off to talk to the captain and the genengineer.

He came down to the sick bay later. "You're sure you want to do this?" he asked. "You're the best tracker and Retriever we've ever had in the service. But I'll go along with this for you."

We walked in to talk to the doctors and Eve.

After a while, we returned to Enia and talked with now "Eve's" father. We'd created her an identity while she was in the tank, and her augmentations were registered to that identity. She was now a registered Retriever like me and a space

Figurehead

Navy Sailor. Her dad was unhappy but, with nudging from his wife, agreed to make a statement that his daughter had died from injuries sustained during the abduction. He was sad to see us go but happy that Eve, now, had found a way through life that mattered to her. They come to visit us when they can slip away discreetly.

Many years later, Eve and I were sitting on the porch of our home on Tolara, a small, Pluto-sized planet in the far reaches of the quadrant. We were the only family within miles, mainly because of what we raised. Carnivorous cats, bigger than Nicolas's vehicle. He said it scared him to death when he visited to drive through the plains surrounding our home. I told him not to need to pee before he got to our compound.

We still are Sailors and do retrievals when there's an especially difficult one. That was the *quid pro quo* that the captain and I had agreed to. Eve had gone into the hibernation bath, and the captain had ordered that she be modified and our bodies synchronized so we could be sure of a long and happy life together. She comes with me on every retrieval. We found our ability to transform and long-liveness was conferred on to our kids—what a surprise to us and the scientists.

Our oldest was out with the big cats right now. Nowadays, she spends most of her time out there. We had named her Elizabeth, but she decided she wanted to be called Kat for obvious reasons.

The End

{ **8** }

Probably the Safest Place to Be, It Turns Out

I was helping mom can some fruits and vegetables.

She loved working with me because I was better at it than her and quicker. I knew it; she knew it; and I loved getting my hands into the beans, cherries, tomatoes, peaches, apples, and everything else we canned. I was not nearly this good a nurse, but, heck, I'd just gotten my degree, and I'd been canning since I could stand. The canning, this time, had coated my hands with cherry juice, and I knew it would be a few days before the red color left my skin. Oh well, I thought. I had nowhere else to be.

"I'll see you guys later," my brother Jake said as he walked out the door with his bag and racquets. "A guy called about a private lesson for his kid." Jake was a champion tennis player, just graduating from high school, and was thinking of turning pro sometime soon. He was 18, four years younger than me—a good-looking guy with bright green eyes and sandy blonde hair bleached by the sun.

"Have fun," I called to him. We were always close, he and I. I was the academically gifted one, and he was the sports maniac. We didn't compete on a thing aside from who could be the better friend. I turned back to my work.

My cell phone rang about an hour later.

"Emma Hyde?" asked someone on the phone.

"Yes, this is she," I replied, wondering what this was about. I'd about had my fill of spam calls, but something told me that this wasn't one. "Can I help you?"

"We have someone here you'll want to speak to." There were several clicks on the line like the call was being transferred, and then my brother came on the phone, sounding scared.

"Emma? These guys grabbed me after my tennis lesson today and told me to tell you, you need to do what they tell you to do, or they'll hurt me. They look serious, Sis," he said, and then the call clicked off.

The first voice came back on the line, "We *will* hurt him if you don't do what you're told. Understand? Are you with anyone else?"

"Yes, my mother," I answered.

"Okay. Talk to no one. Walk away. Go somewhere outside the house. I'll call back in two minutes. No fooling around, or he gets hurt bad," the man said.

"All right. All right. I'm going outside," but the line was already dead.

What was happening, I asked myself, panicking as I left the house. The phone rang, and I answered before it completed its first ring. "I'm here. What do you want? I don't have any money. I just started a new job and don't have any money," I said.

"I know that and don't care about money. What I want you to do is to get in your car and drive up to the shopping center up near the highway. Park your car near the front of the electronics store. Leave your car keys on top of your car's rear driver side wheel after you lock it up. Then walk around the back of the stores to a rusty brown pick-up truck up. We'll move your car back to your house, maybe later if it's still there. You won't be needing it anymore, anyway," he said.

"The truck keys are on top of its right rear wheel, and there is an envelope there for you. Follow the instructions there to the letter, and after we'll release your brother. Things are going to happen to you today, and you have to go with the flow. Understand?"

"What do you mean 'things are going to happen'?" But the line had gone dead again. The guy had been clear about not talking to anyone, so I followed instructions and got into my car. The old, rusted brown pick-up was behind the big-box electronics store, and I found the keys right where he said they'd be on top of an envelope. I got into the truck and started it up. It took three or four times before the engine caught. There was no A/C, and I was soaked with sweat from the long walk from my car to get here. The engine rattled as I tried to put it into gear, and then the truck stalled. I tried again and got the vehicle to roll.

The note was brief. It said:

> *Drive back toward your home and to the shopping center next to the highway there. Pull up in front of the hardware store and go there. Pick up this list of materials and hardware. When you've got everything, leave the store, and load it into the truck. Do not bother checking out.*
>
> *Drive away.*
>
> *We expect and direct you to be arrested. When you are arrested, we expect you to fight with the police or security. Fight, curse, and be as loud as you can be. We will be watching and what happens to your brother depends on how well you act.*
>
> *Destroy this letter before you leave the store. Throw away your phone when you leave the store as well. Remember, I will be watching everything you do.*

The second page was a lengthy list of things.

What? I thought. Arrested? I'd never been in trouble my whole life. I stopped and reread the letter. The truck rattled and then stalled again. My phone rang.

"I can see that you're having trouble with what you've been tasked to do. It's simple. A smart girl like you, with a B.S.N., ought to be able to follow these instructions. Do you need an incentive? I can reconnect you to your brother, and you can hear him get punished because you can't follow instructions. Want that?"

"No. No, I don't. You want me to steal things and get arrested? Why do you want to do that to me?" I asked.

"Because it's what I do. Bet you thought you were going to have a great life. Well, I take pretty little things like you and make sure that you get broken on the wheel of life. Badly broken. By the way, the truck you're sitting in. You just stole it. That's a Class B Felony, 2-20 years when you're caught at minimum. After you're arrested for all of the other things I've got planned, I will see that you get an attorney. You're to do everything he tells you to do. Now get going, or I'm going to hurt your brother."

I was sobbing. He was right. I had big plans for my life that he was ruining, just like that. I started the truck and drove away toward the shopping center. My phone rang again. I picked it up, and he came back on the line. "See that big trash bin in front of you?" How the heck did this guy see so much, I thought. "Stop there. Open the door on the top and look for a paper bag in there. See it?"

"Yes."

"Good. Open it and follow the instructions in there."

Inside the bag were some clothes: A filthy and stained old Aerosmith cropped tank top tee and a pair of equally dirty shorts, and a greasy old ball cap with an embroidered logo on it showing two hands and the letters C.S. The instructions

Figurehead

were simple, disrobe entirely, put on the clothes, and throw out my scrubs and underwear. I did what the instructions had told me to do quickly so that any passersby wouldn't see me. After about five cranks of the old truck's engine, I got it started and headed off, feeling extremely uncomfortable and vulnerable in these filthy and revealing clothes. They looked like someone had worn them who didn't care about hygiene.

The phone rang again. "Just thought that you might want to know that the ball cap you're wearing carries the logo of an anarchist group called Common Struggle. They have a government overthrow wing; it's going to look like you just joined. When you get arrested, make sure that you let them know that you're a member of Common Struggle. Say something about your brothers and sisters, and you will bring down the government or something saucy like that. Enjoy, Emma," the man cackled as he hung up.

It took about fifteen minutes to get to the hardware store. I looked at the list. Whoever had written it, helpfully, put the lanes where it displayed the objects I was to take and their prices. All told, I was going to steal more than $5,000 worth of tools and other stuff. I'd no idea what that would mean, but I knew it would likely be terrible.

When I finished my "shopping," I headed out toward the checkouts, watching the store staff to see if I could slip out undetected. As instructed, I threw away the letter and my phone, and then, when no one was looking, I made a quick dash out the door. As soon as I passed the entry, an alarm sounded. I ran, weaving my way through the parking lot, losing, I thought, any pursuers. I arrived at the truck and quickly threw all the loot I'd taken into the truck's load bed. Of course, it wouldn't start until a police car from the substation about a hundred yards away pulled up in front of me. Another blocked me from the rear. Two officers approached the truck with guns drawn but pointing down.

"Hands up and on the steering wheel. Don't move!" said one officer. Another reached my door, pulled it open, and dragged me out of the truck. They ordered me to lie on the ground with my hands behind my head. An officer grabbed me by my wrist, twisting it behind my back. I remembered then that I was supposed to fight. So, I did, knowing that the man would be watching. I kicked the police officer standing behind me and then tried to headbutt the one in front of me. They jumped back, and I got to my feet, backing away from them.

"Now, miss. You don't want to be in any worse trouble. Just calm down," said the officer.

"Kiss my...," I said and launched myself at the officer closest to me. What I didn't see was a third officer who was furthest away had taken out her taser. In mid-flight, I got zapped and fell to the ground, writhing in pain and screaming even more obscenities at the officers. I was quickly cuffed and thrown into the back seat of a car, where I waited until the officers inventoried everything in the truck. During that search, they found a bag full of a white powder they eventually determined was cocaine, enough to charge me with the sale of a controlled substance. So, they charged me with three

Class B Felonies, making a terrorist threat and assault on a law officer. A whole lot of trouble, as I had thought I would be in.

"I'm your attorney, Ms. Hyde. My name is Dash-Ed Hopes," said a handsome and well-coiffed man. "I was asked by a mutual friend to defend you, though I'm not sure what help I'll be. You're in a load of trouble. The only thing we might try to do is to get the sentences for these offenses to be reduced through some maneuvering that I'm pretty good at," he said, sounding full of himself. "Consecutive sentences, you're looking at maybe 80 years, with a chance of parole in 45. You'll have spent almost two-thirds of your life in jail by that point." He smiled at me, leaned across the table, and whispered, "Think of my name, girlie. Dash-Ed Hopes." He giggled, and I finally realized that this was the guy I'd been talking to.

"How's my brother?" I asked.

"Doing well unless you mess up. As soon as you're sentenced, and we see what that looks like, he'll be released. If the sentence isn't good enough, I might have to hold him a little longer until you can add more years on," he said.

"Why are you doing this? What've I ever done to you?" I asked tearfully.

"Absolutely nothing. Like I said to you before. I look around, find a fine young person heading off to a good life, and then I derail them. I'm what's called a serial sadist and get pleasure out of this. I've done things like what I'm doing many times. You're not my first, and you won't be my last. I can tell you, though, that you may be my best so far. I'm going to do well for you, and I'm a damn good lawyer, but you're still going to go away for a good chunk of the rest of your life. My personal best on these sentences, probably," he said, sounding proud of himself.

Continuing, "Before you go to court and when you're there, I want you to mouth off to everyone, especially the judge. Say lots of anarchist things. Curse at them and make sure that you get at least one contempt citation. That'll add maybe a year, but you'll be required to do that before the clock can start on your other offenses. I want you also to assault at least two more people, preferably cops or guards. You're going to be an old lady when you finally get out if ever you do."

Arraignment went badly for me. At the end of the session, I had two contempt citations and two years added to my sentence. I assaulted a couple of guards in jail and got two more assault charges tacked on to all the others. A week later, Dash-Ed Hopes met with me to give me the deal that he'd worked out. I would enter a new prison program that the state was implementing for long-term first offenders like I supposedly was. I was going to be sentenced to 40 years for the criminal offenses and two years for the contempt citations with a chance for parole in year 27, or when I was 49 years old. The good news was that the new prison program would use my skills as a nurse. I was given a provisional license for my term to practice in prison under a physician who was also a long-term first offender like me. After release, that license would end, and I would have to work as something else, maybe as a nurse's aide, Hopes told me. He giggled again at that image. He ordered me to accept the offer and make another scene, and I did when we went back to court. I got two more contempt judgments and two more years added to my sentence. So, the earliest I could get out would be in 29 years, when I was 51. Well more than half my life gone.

Hopes was ecstatic, and I was suicidal.

The government had built a fifty-foot-tall circular steel wall around an area of land that was to be our home for our terms. The interior wall of the prison was completely smooth and slanted inward, so climbing out would be near impossible. Armed drones circled the prison day and night to keep us in. There was a little over three square miles of land inside the prison, including two artificial and well-stocked lakes, a forest, again well stocked with animals, farmland, and space to build our habitations and support buildings like our hospital. After we did the things we were supposed to do to build our homes, we would be entirely on our own and only successful if we learned to work together. We would need to be self-sufficient they told us. A way to teach us nasty felons what it was to be a part of society.

There were no doors through the wall. The only way in or out was by airlift, though there was a complicated system for channeling rain to run off and not simply drown our enclosure. They airlifted us sixty prisoners, forty males, and twenty females, into the prison. It was pretty clear to me what we females' extra-curricular roles were, besides our assigned jobs. They gave each of us women to two males, our "gang," they told us, and we were to take care of them and them, us. In addition, we all had jobs where we cared for everyone else in some way. Me, again, I was the prison nurse. There were other professionals in the group: One was a vet, and several were mechanics. They told us they were seeding the prison with the talent that they believed was needed for a subsistence life in the prison.

Several "guards" were dropped in along with us initially. These were people with skills who would teach us the basics for survival, how to build, how to cook, sanitation, government, and so on. They were to live with us for the first twelve months of our sentences, teach us what we needed to know to survive, and then leave us to our devices. Their support—tents, etc.—was airlifted along with them and then came load after load of lumber and other materials we would need to construct our home for the next decades.

The first task they put us to was digging the latrine. It was to be ten feet deep, eight feet wide, and twelve feet long. So, almost 1,000 cubic feet of earth to be moved. I volunteered to work on that project because I wanted to make sure that we built the thing right and it wouldn't poison us all. With ten of us working on it, the guards told us to expect the digging to take three days around the clock. At the end of that, we needed to pour a cement wall and floor inside the pit, add the lime necessary to keep us safe, install the drains for the waste, and construct the latrine building itself, a six-hole one, according to our guard-construction trainer. It took us about two weeks to build the whole thing. We had a christening ceremony, as you would guess.

While that work was going on, the others were clearing spaces for our habitations. There was to be a kitchen, rest area, and a sleeping area in each of them. We wouldn't have electricity, gas, or any of the other facilities we'd become accustomed to in the polite society that we were no longer part of. Every habitation had a coal stove to be used for heat and cooking and oil lamps. It was like we were being sent back to the 1800s for our sentences.

One thing that the Department of Corrections brought in from the outside regularly was a supply of coal for the stoves, being that coal wasn't mined anywhere near here. Otherwise, we probably would have been digging it up ourselves. The lumps they brought in were large, so we did have to break them up, though—no rest for the weary.

We built a barn and a chicken coop and fenced in some fields for horses and cattle that were moved into the prison as we were, in cages suspended below helicopters. They brought in manual farm equipment, and the guards taught us to plant and rotate crops so that we didn't overwork the earth. Turns out, one guy was a trained blacksmith. We built him a smithy, and he helped make things we needed around the prison or fix things that got broken.

The hospital and a common building where we could go for medical care, relaxation, and entertainment were next on the list after doing all this other work. All the buildings, habitations, hospital, common areas, and barns surrounded a square called "The Commons." We set the Commons up as an athletic field where we could exercise and play sports. The guards drove us to complete all this work substantially while they were there. They were hard taskmasters and great teachers. They said they wanted to see us survive and flourish so that we'd all be better citizens when they finally released us. I couldn't fathom that, given that I would be 51, at the youngest, when that happened. I was pretty sure that I would look at being outside in 29 years like someone who time-traveled from the past to whatever today looked like then.

Several of us already had other skills that we needed. Aside from my skills as a nurse, they put me to work cooking and canning foods so that some things would be available all year round. I dug a root cellar with help from a few guys from my and one of the other gangs. It helped us to keep things cool all year and was a great storage area. The guards said they were impressed and left us on our own as we did the work.

The guards told us, women, that part of our role was "stress relief" for the men, them included, while they were with us. I successfully lobbied with them to get us on a progesterone implant, so we'd have no little surprises, at least early on, and then only intentionally. The implants were good for three years, and all but two of us could take them. They gave the other two other devices to ensure they didn't get pregnant because of our "stress relief" duties.

I need to say that I was angered, initially, by this humiliation, but I enjoyed the connections that "stress relief" duty helped me and the other women establish. Reduced my stress,

Figurehead

I guess, too. I made a lot of friends, as you might imagine. I was perhaps the tallest woman there, at nearly 6-feet, and my long, curly black hair and brown eyes made me an attraction.

Our first year was a rough one. No one died, but there were a couple of close calls, and several people came down with a mysterious flu-like disease that raised fears in the doctor and me of something like COVID-19 hitting us. If it had been COVID, I'm not sure we would have survived. It was scary, but whatever it was, burned out, and no one died or had any long-term impacts. Other than that, we saw cuts and bruises, a couple of broken hands and fingers, and things like that. One idiot nearly drowned when he tried to swim across the lake, even though he admitted he couldn't swim. One of our guards got a nasty cut that required 40 stitches. He told me that he appreciated our professionalism and caring.

Most of us dove into the work of ensuring our survival, but a few of the guys didn't—always the guys, it seemed, doing stupid things. They wanted to take and partake but not to work. As a group, we made it clear that they had to share equally with all of us or be excluded. From everything. And us women meant *everything*. It took a little while, but everyone came together in the end, and we functioned as a community.

Our first year's crops were not enough for us to survive the winter, all on our own anyway. The guards said that we'd done well, and they gave us M.R.E.s to tide us over. Those awful meals made us work harder our second year to grow more and better crops and make sure we had put aside enough for our winter survival—no more M.R.E.s for us. I still can't see how our military was supposed to survive eating those things even these many years later. "Warfighter Recommended, Warfighter Tested, Warfighter Approved"—crap advertising, for sure.

From Year 2 on, we were on our own. Though I struggled periodically with surviving 28 or more years of this, I was constantly busy. My hands were never idle, and so there was no time for devil's work in my head. I made a few good friends and even took several longer-term lovers in and outside of my gang and beyond my "stress relief" duties.

My work with the doctor went very well. He was a good man who'd made the mistake of getting caught up in an opioid prescription racket. Of course, he was the only one to go down when the operation collapsed. The bigwigs skated away, leaving him to take the fall. He took his failure badly and so worked doubly hard to make sure that we all stayed healthy. We had the only radio in the hospital to communicate with the outside if there was a significant issue and power for it and for some of our equipment. Before the guards left, they helped us to install several solar panels on the roof of the hospital that provided us with more than enough power for our operation. We never used the radio, except to order supplies for the clinic that we couldn't make ourselves and monthly family contacts for those of us who wanted them. Aside from that, we had little contact with the outside world. Everything could have gone bottom-up out there, and we'd never know that it did. Turns out that something like that occurred while we were behind the wall and isolated as we were.

With all of the great tech out there, I questioned why we couldn't do video conferences, but the guards, when they were with us, said we had to live with what we had. Anyway, I talked to my mother, father, and Jake every month until about year four, when communications got harder for some reason. We were never given a reason why, but family communications just stopped without warning right after that.

Years 3 through 10 were more of the same. It wasn't the daily grind like you'd heard about in other prisons. Living and surviving in our community was anything but routine and boring. We had the fifty-foot-tall wall all around us that dulled considerably and thankfully over the years and the ever-present drones circling overhead. Each year, we planned for that one and the next. We developed contingency plans for any catastrophe, which we, unfortunately, had to implement several times. It was my feeling that we were triggering these plans more and more as time went on. That worried me. The weather seemed to be getting more and more unpredictable and severe. As good as it was, the prison drainage system couldn't keep up with some of the more significant rainfalls—we measured several times more than a foot of rain in 24 hours, so we had several new bodies of water, which we interconnected with our lake. Back-breaking work to dig creeks and connect the lakes, but those clouds had silver linings as they helped grow our fish population and gave us more places for privacy and recreation.

We had a soccer and baseball league. Some people, like me, played in both. We alternated nights when the teams would play, and so some of us anyway rested between games. At the end of each season, we had a big celebration, and we gave the winners awards. Our blacksmith fashioned team awards and rings for the winners. Not as flashy as the World Series or Superbowl rings but treasured just as much by us winners. One guy had been a tattoo artist on the outside. A guard had brought him in his tools and lots of ink in exchange for some art that he wanted. He also gave the winning team the tattoos that they wanted at the end of each season. I quickly got covered by them. I thought that I looked pretty hot.

Our community was small enough that we all took part in governance. There were no Presidents, Officers, City Council. We just all got together and hammered out what needed to be done and then did it. I mention this here because we talked a lot about the weather and how it seemed to worsen each year and that the seasons had almost wholly disappeared. There was good and bad news there, of course. We had more and longer growing seasons, but we also had to watch our land use a lot closer to ensure that we weren't depleting the soil.

Early on, in Year 2, two guys tried to escape over the wall. It was comical—almost—to watch them try to toss grappling hooks up over the edge of the roof. They thought it would be easy to throw a hook over the wall and then haul themselves up. The hooks that would handle the weight of an average man were hefty, as were the ropes, and thus hard to throw. The few throws that made it to the top of the roof fell off the rounded edge designed to stop escapes like this. These guys didn't think about the fact that the roofs were designed to repel invaders or escapees from both sides. They were lucky that they didn't get crowned by the falling hooks. When they were trying to escape, the drones clustered where they were trying, and so, even if they had been successful, they would have landed on a guard detail waiting for them, or worse, got shot off the roof by the drones. After a few weeks of trying to be creative, they gave up, and life settled down. Our society formed and matured.

That is until one day, in Year 10, when several men arrived in a crazy-looking military attack helicopter. None of us had seen anything like it before. It had two primary rotor blades and a propellor in the rear. It entered the prison nose down—so cool, I thought—as it rotated and leveled out just before landing. It looked like it could really move. Later, we were to find out that it was one of only a few of this generation of choppers still in operation and was called "The Defiant." After it landed, we mobbed it. It wasn't metal; it was like plastic to the touch; composite the crew told us later so it could move faster and quieter. It had all kinds of armament and was built for stealth.

The pilots remained on board to watch over the craft. A tall, and I had to say, good-looking guy in fatigues came out of the ship with two heavily armed men. The guy walked like someone who was very sure of himself and came directly over to me. "Emma Hyde, correct?" he asked.

"Yes, Sir," I replied, totally surprised and concerned about what this could mean.

He smiled at me and said, "I need to talk to you privately. Can we use the hospital? This is not bad news. I can see you're nervous. Don't be."

"Sure," I said and led the way. Over the years, I'd learned to mistrust people who said things like that to me.

Once we were inside, he looked around and then plopped himself down on one of the exam room chairs. "Sit," he said. When I just stood there looking at him blankly, he said, "Please."

I grabbed a chair, spun it around, and sat on it, leaning over the back of it to look at him. I wanted to show him I was tough for some reason. "My name is Shay Sweeney. I'm an officer in the Army of the South. I'm sure you know nothing about us, right?"

"Correct, Sir. Not a thing," I said.

"Well, relax. I have got a story for you, and it'll take a little while for me to get through it. Stop me whenever you have a question. And stop this 'sir' stuff. I'm not your superior officer."

"Okay...just what's this about?" I asked.

"Well, I'm sure you remember Dash-Ed Hopes. Hopes was a psychopath who worked for several years here in the South. Unlike many of these folks who enjoyed bombing or murder or sex or something like that, he got his rocks off ruining lives. He didn't kill people outright, as some of these creeps do. Instead, he would target someone, usually a young woman, just starting on a career or life and then force her into breaking laws and getting thrown in jail, sometimes for decades. Like you."

I sat back at that and looked at him more closely. Was he going to tell me I was going to be released? Did I even want that? I'd spent nearly a third of my life here with people who I now considered kind of family. While I thought it might be good to get my record cleared and back to another life, I pretty much regarded day-to-day here to be normal now, though. Institutionalized, I guess. I wondered if I could stay if I were cleared. I also thought I might be getting way ahead of things and that I ought to listen again.

"Excuse me. I think you may have stopped listening to me," he said.

"Right. I *had* stopped listening. Sorry, Mr. Sweeney."

"Shay is fine. You're no longer a convict. Can I call you Emma?" he asked.

"Sure. Please start over from just after you told me what that bastard had done," I said.

"We caught him when he slipped up, and a person he'd targeted called us instead of folding under to him. He did the same thing he did to you and tried to get a young woman arrested for grand theft and assault with a deadly weapon, a car. She was the sister of one of my men, and so she called him. We walked with her through the entire process, and she wore a wire when she met with Hopes after her arrest and played stupid enough that he had to dictate to her what he wanted to have done. When he stepped out of the interview room, we were waiting," Sweeney explained.

"A lot of these types like to keep souvenirs of their conquests. So, when we searched his house, in a recess below the basement, we found a room full of his souvenirs, laid out like in a museum, under glass display cases. We've been trying to find as many of Hopes' victims as possible to let them know what we've found. You're one of the few still living or that we can reach."

"Does this mean I can go free?" I asked.

"Yes and no," he said.

"What's that mean?" I asked, sitting up.

"Settle down. Please. There are second and third parts to all of this that I need to talk to you about." I sat back in the chair but couldn't relax, as I had a feeling he had terrible news for me.

Here it came. "When you were in college, did you ever read anything by a guy named Malcolm Gladwell?" Sweeney asked.

"Yes. He wrote a book called *The Tipping Point*, right?"

"Correct, among other books, yes. That's what I need to talk to you about, and then I want to take you on a quick trip. A tipping point is a place in a process after which an unstoppable change takes place. For years, scientists have been talking about a climate change tipping point. Politicians have been talking about societal backlash reaching a tipping point. And there are several other types of tipping points that people have been talking about as well."

Figurehead

"What we never thought about," he resumed, "was that many of these things would reach a mega-tipping point simultaneously, and things would fall apart all around us more or less suddenly. A tipping point of tipping points, so to speak. That's what we're experiencing right now, outside these walls.... Now, come with me."

We walked out of the hospital and over to the helicopter. He helped me in and then buckled me into a seat. "Hold on. This thing moves like a bat out of hell." The chopper rose quickly into the air and above the walls. For the first time in ten years, I saw the outside, and it wasn't what I'd expected. They'd originally built the prison about fifteen miles from the Gulf Coast, near Summerdale, Alabama. The chopper oriented itself toward the south, and all I could see was water, starting less than a half a mile or so south of the prison. The water was almost lapping at the back wall of the prison. All that shoreline went where I asked myself.

"What happened?" I asked. All I could see was the coastline to the east and west into the distance.

The chopper headed off to the east at a high rate of speed. The ground below us was a blur. In thirty minutes, Shay said, "Look below. That's what's left of Tallahassee. Most all the rest of Florida's underwater, as are vast chunks of the east coast. Washington, D.C., and New York City are entirely gone. People live on the upper floors of buildings in New York City and get around with boats. Climate change hit all at once.

"Further west, in California and the northwest, it's almost all deserts. Fires that got larger and worse after 2018 wiped out most of the forests, and then wet weather washed almost all the topsoil there into rivers and the sea. Almost nothing grows there now."

The chopper returned west toward the prison but headed in a northerly direction. In the distance, I saw what looked like at least three more prisons like ours. One, though, looked like it was smoking. "They'd built four prisons like the one you're in. That first one, off in the distance, was successful like yours. That second one in the distance there failed. The third one over there that's smoking was also pretty successful until recently."

"What's that mean?"

"Let me go back a bit. Scientists had predicted that we would see a steep rise in sea levels starting around 2050. What they didn't count on was a collision of several effects. The damage we did to ourselves, huge solar flares, and a wobble in the moon, all of which caused sea levels to rise dangerously in the last several years. It appears to have stabilized for now, but researchers tell us that things will never go back to how they were. What you see is what you get. It's bad everywhere in the world. Bangladesh is gone; millions and millions died there or were killed when they tried to migrate to more hospitable surroundings that turned out not to be. The same thing happened here when people tried to migrate from Central America out of the water's path. A new administration here sealed the border, and a war started with Mexico."

"With D.C. flooded, they moved the Capitol to Denver where the new President. Jolly King Ronald, sits, holding court," he said with not a little sarcasm. "The rest of the country has descended into tribal warfare and anarchy. What you see out there," and he gestured toward the prison that was smoking, "are results of that. A raider army is heading toward you and could be here in a month, give or take. Even with that, you're in about the only safe place, it turns out."

He signaled to the pilot, and we headed back to the prison. The pilot looked at me in his rear-view mirror and seemed very sad. Also, something about him looked a little familiar, but I was so overcome by what Sweeney had told me I didn't stop to think about it. Plus, all I could see were his eyes. Bright green.

"So, Emma. You're free, but it turns out not so free. If I could, I'd apologize for what was done to you. But you're one of very few survivors. The U.S. is down to maybe 30 million people, and that number is shrinking every day. Again, you're one of the lucky ones."

I walked back into the hospital and sat down, crushed by what I'd seen and knew that was heading for us. A few minutes later, Shay came in.

"What about my brother and parents? Are they still around here so I can see them?" I asked.

"I knew you would ask about them. Your parents are in a camp in Georgia. They're well protected from marauders for the time being. Your brother is with me. He's the pilot on my helicopter," and he gestured toward the door.

"Hi, Emma," the man that I thought I might know stood in the doorway, looking like he wasn't sure of what to do next.

"Jake!" and I jumped up from my chair and ran to him. I went to hug him and rammed my head into the helmet he was taking off.

"Oops. Sorry," he said and swept me up. After a few minutes, he said, "I have to get back out to the chopper so that we can help the ramparts team get set up. I'll be back later so we can talk. Oh, and you look unbelievable, Emma. If you weren't my sister, I'd call you hot."

Sweeney stood back, looking at anything but us. He returned my brother's salute as he left the room.

"So, you said there were three things you wanted to talk to me about. So, what's the third?" I asked.

"Before I do that, I want to let you know I can get you back to your parents if you want to go there. But, as I said, this is maybe the safest place you could be for many reasons. There's another reason you might want to stay on, though." He hesitated before going on.

"What's that, Shay?"

"Remember that I told you we'd caught Hopes?" he said.

"Yes. I was going to ask where he was. I'd love to see him and maybe have a proper reason to be put back into prison."

Shay barked a laugh. "You and me both. Probably lots of people. Hopes was being held for transfer for trial in Birmingham when things up there lit up. Montgomery had fallen early in all of this, and the capital was moved to Birmingham about four years ago. You wouldn't have heard about that living out here," he said.

Figurehead

"Just when Hopes arrived in Birmingham, insurrectionists attacked and tried to take the capital like they tried in D.C. back in 2021. We beat them back. We shed lots of blood, and many good people were killed—and many of the insurrectionists. Hopes escaped in the fighting and has now weaseled himself into a leadership position with the raiders. He's heading here right now. Of course, he doesn't know that you're here and—don't get this wrong—wouldn't care, except maybe to see what you've turned out to be," he said.

He continued, "We're going to set a trap for them here. That's what your brother meant by the ramparts team. They're a special group of U.S. Army engineers who've worked through the plans used to build this place and are going to fortify it. All of you people here who want to stay are welcome to, but anyone who wants to leave can leave as well. We'll have some huge choppers coming in with our equipment and arms, and they can leave with them."

"Well," I said, "if there's going to be a battle, you'll need a nurse. I can't speak for the doctor, but I feel he'll want to stay as well. I wish there were more that I could do."

"Maybe there is. You and your brother are the only people here who're from around here. Things have changed a lot for sure, but it would be good to have someone who knew the land around here to go out with my group," he said. "Also, I'd like to give you a chance to get some closure with Hopes, if at all possible."

"Your group?"

"Yeah. I'm not in the formal U.S. Army, Emma. Neither is your brother."

"I was wondering what the Army of the South was."

"We're what used to be called a militia. Not formal military but allied with the U.S. military. We take on certain jobs for them. Things that need to be done, but the formal military is too, uh, hidebound to carry out on their own. We do the things they can't do. Here, we want to infiltrate and assassinate Hopes and his leadership team."

I sat back and looked again at this man. Good-looking to be sure, but now that I looked at him again, I saw the hard edges we had all developed here. I wouldn't kick him out of bed if it came to it, but I wouldn't mess with him either. "Where do I sign up?" I asked. He smiled and stuck out his hand. I shook it, though what I wanted to do was to shag him. Maybe there would be time for that. I'd gotten pretty bored with the pickings in prison, not to sound too much like a shameless harlot.

All sixty of us felt the same way. Most of us had little, if anything, to go back to, and this place had become our home. No one wanted to leave. When the large choppers started coming in with the ramparts team and equipment, the prison quickly became a military base. The military brought their stuff with them and had enough to share, giving us some variety in our diets. Yummy M.R.E.s. We melded quickly.

The Army engineers planned for and constructed what they called a rampart, like what you might find on a castle. Huge, prefab chunks of metal were airlifted into place and then hung and attached to the top of the prison. Once the engineers did this, they constructed a roof behind the rampart so that any projectiles would—hopefully—not enter our home. Next to last, enormous guns were mounted on the ramparts. These fired into the advancing army or could be angled to fire into any that got close to us. This wasn't to be our only protection. The U.S. Navy had dedicated a destroyer, the U.S.S. Fairhope and a Tomahawk missile submarine the U.S.S. Providence, to protect our backside and add offensive capability, though the raiders didn't have sea support and couldn't approach us from that direction given the alligator-filled waters behind us.

We sent combined teams of us prisoners and soldiers out of the prison to cut back the forest surrounding us, partly to create a "kill zone," as Shay called it with some relish, I thought, and partly to make some roadblocks. Last, several giant, what Jake called, King Stallion helicopters flew in with large cement mixers dangling from cables.

"Booby traps," said Jake. "Those things are filled with metal balls and explosives. One hell of an I.E.D." He had to explain improvised explosive devices to me. He'd a lot of experience with them in Afghanistan in the lead-up to the complete U.S. withdrawal while I'd been here. "We ignite those remotely if they get too close to us. We picked the oldest and rustiest wrecks to make them look less like the traps that they are. Make them think they're derelicts."

"Well, I wouldn't have known what they were if you hadn't told me," I said. "I just hope we don't need them. If we do, that'll probably mean that all of this impressive artillery hasn't worked too well."

When I had a few minutes alone with Jake, I asked him to tell me Shay's story. "Looking at him, Jake," I said, "he looks like he's been through some tough times. What can you tell me about him?"

"A lot. We were both in Afghanistan together. I was regular military at that point, and he was a contractor. He was unhappy with the decision to withdraw, though I wasn't. I knew all of us there were on borrowed time. The Taliban could never have beat us in a straight-up fight, and we both knew that. So, they and their friends just picked away at our allies and us. Even though the people there knew the results of our pulling out, they were tired of being caught in the crossfire. So, when they could've told us about things, they didn't, and men and women I knew very well got killed or maimed. I missed being like some of them quite a few times by just a few seconds and more than once was saved by Shay and his folks."

"Well, he was, I mean is, a brilliant soldier, and he had a few things to say about the impacts of the pull-out on our friends there. He tried to get some of his buddies out of the country and got caught. His company fired him, and Homeland Security prosecuted him for that. He got two years but was released when things fell apart on the condition that he organize local militias to support the government."

"One other thing, Emma: He likely wants Hopes as much as you do. His sister was caught up in one of Hopes' schemes and went to jail in Arkansas. She died there in a riot when a gang took it over, and the place literally burned down. I wouldn't get between him and Hopes. He may like you, but he wants to squeeze the life out of him himself."

"Well," I said, "I hope he doesn't have problems with another pair of hands on his throat. If he does, then we might have a problem."

"We should be okay as long as we work as a team and have each other's backs," said a voice from the doorway. Shay. Deadly serious, for a second anyway. Then he grinned. God, I wanted to have that man. Hussy.

"I'll leave the two of you to sort out the details of your relationship," said Jake. "I have some work to do on my chopper." He grinned at both of us and then left. Was I that transparent?

Our negotiations of roles went as I had hoped and imagined. He was every bit as good as I had thought he'd be. He said the same about me. Funny how that made me all happy inside. I had a rep here as an excellent lover, but no one had ever made me feel quite like Sweeney did.

The rest of Sweeney's detachment were men and women with whom he'd worked in Afghanistan and elsewhere and who, like Jake, had stuck with him before and after his troubles. Some had even felt as strongly as he did and helped him to get their friends out. The military caught none of them, and Shay didn't out them as I would have expected, even though he'd been offered incentives. They stuck together like they were brothers and sisters. I had a brother there and maybe even someone else. I told myself to wait to see what happened.

Over the last ten years, I'd developed physically, so that I was a match for most of the men in the prison. You had to be strong if you wanted to keep independent as I did. After a few skirmishes with several of the tougher guys, I got a rep as someone who wanted to be left alone, well, at least to pick who I did what with. The men and women in Shay's charge were many times stronger, faster, and better than me. I expected the better part. I'd no experience with the kinds of things they did and no time to learn other than the basics of that stuff. What I had was what Shay had said he wanted me for, my knowledge of the land around here, good strength and endurance, and being a medic. They already had one, but it was always a good idea to have a second one—redundancy. Plus, she, Michaela, said she'd much rather put bullets into these people than take them out. She was delighted to have me join the group, and we became friends.

I was going to be ground-based, along with most of the rest of the detachment. Jake would be in the air, giving us updates on the raiders' locations and assisting with his weaponry, of which there was a lot on the chopper. He wasn't happy about me being directly in harm's way but saw sense in his being above doing what he did and me being on the ground. I wasn't sure about what I would contribute, but Shay and Jake said to wait for combat and do what felt right at that point.

They outfitted me with what Shay called a C.Z. Scorpion, a Czech carbine that he said was simple and easy to operate and maintain. Michaela said, "Point and shoot, Emma. Keep it set at three-shot bursts; otherwise, you'll go through a mag in a few seconds—an excellent weapon for a beginner. Also, I have a few of these; take one. It's called a Glauca B1." She handed me a folding knife that was light and felt good in my hands. "The French developed it as an all-purpose tool for their special forces police. I've used it in many tight places. Not a throwing knife, but you don't have time to learn how to do that anyway. The blade can slice tomatoes as thin as you want them, and the serrated side of the blade will cut a zip tie if you need to do that. You can also club a guy over the head, and he'll likely not wake up. A gift."

Aside from that, they got me some camo clothes and an in-ear communicator that would pick up a whisper. Michaela gave me her med-kit, and I found it comparable to what we had in prison. I was ready to go. Shay said to stay near him, and I wasn't sure if that was because of my inexperience or that he didn't want me to get to Hopes before him. I'd made my deal. Even if I had caught him before Shay got there, I would have simply sat on him until we could both end him.

We were ready. And so just waited…

…For another week.

We'd done a little trailblazing over the weeks before and set out a few I.E.D.s in various places to move the raiders toward where we wanted them. Our drones and the surveillance choppers followed them as they meandered through the forests and bayous to get to us. They were cooperative, following the paths we had laid out. I was concerned about how easy it was to lead them. I gave my misgivings to Shay, but he said, "Hard to know what a psychopath is going to do. We just need to stay flexible."

The attacks, when they came, came on two fronts, one from the direction we expected and the other from the air, which was a surprise. Men on motorized parasails flew over our ramparts after the major force attacked from the ground. They dropped small bombs and Molotov cocktails on the rampart defenses, wounding us there before they were mostly all shot down by our ground forces and choppers, one of which, Jake's, took a hit from a ground-based R.P.G., forcing an emergency landing inside the prison. He and the rest of the crew were okay, but it would take some time to repair the Defiant if they even could. Parts were at a premium.

"I'm a little worried," said Shay, "that they don't seem to be too surprised about all of the military support here. They must have been watching us build the ramparts. Still, from what I can see they don't have any armament comparable to what we have. Their successes must have gone to their heads. We can only hope."

As soon as the attack started, we hurried into the forest to find Hopes and his leadership. They led us to themselves when Hopes moved to the front of his forces to offer a quick end to the hostilities if we simply gave up. Our side responded with a counterattack from the rampart defenses and the ships. A cruise missile from the destroyer and a Tomahawk from the submarine exploded in the ranks right behind Hopes, and they ran. Straight toward us.

Figurehead

They outnumbered us about five to one, but we had the advantage of surprise. Hopes' vehicle was disabled in the first few seconds. He was screaming into a microphone when we cut him short by blowing him out of it. He landed practically at my feet, looking battered and much less dashing than the last time I saw him.

"Mr. Hopes. It's been a long time," I said. He looked at me, bewildered.

"Do I know you?" he mumbled.

I smiled. "Maybe that's why you kept souvenirs. You're too full of yourself to remember the faces of your victims."

He looked like he was trying to remember me but couldn't.

"Oh, well," I said as I reached down to pick him up. "Come with me. I know someone who wants to see if you remember his family as well." I grabbed him by the collar of his shirt and hauled him to his feet. He weighed almost nothing, but then again, I could now press a utility hole cover, close to two hundred pounds, twenty times and barely break a sweat. He struggled a little, but I cuffed him on the side of his head, and he went limp. Maybe I hit him a little too hard, I thought, and then shrugged. I tossed him over my shoulder and carried him toward where Shay and the rest of the team were.

Several raiders surrounded them, but they were holding their own. "Shay, guess what I caught trying to escape?" I asked through my mic. "What if I were to send his head over toward them? Do you think that would help?" I watched Hopes, realizing that he was listening. I kicked him and pulled out the Glauca. "This edge of the blade is very sharp,

Dash-Ed. It would kill you way too fast. They designed this other side to saw things. Like maybe a finger or your throat. Would hurt like hell. Different from what you did to my family and me, but it would fulfill in a way." I sat down on his chest and watched and waited, looking for an opening of some kind.

Finally, it looked like the raiders had shot their wad and were running low on ammunition. I wasn't sure about Shay and the team but had to imagine that they were disciplined in using their supplies. I asked Shay about that, and he said they were fine and thought the same thing. He thought they might try to break out and lead the raiders away from Hopes and me. I was about to agree when I felt a change in the surrounding air. I turned, but it was a little too late, and I was gun butted.

When I woke up, they had tied me to a tree limb, spread eagle. Hopes was standing nearby, talking to another man. He saw me, smiled, and then walked toward me. "Glad you're back with us. I'm sorry, but you still have me at a disadvantage. Who are you? How do you know me?" he asked.

I shook my head and said, "I'm sad you don't remember me. Was I not your personal best, Dash-Ed?"

He stopped and looked at me more seriously. "Well, I'll be. Emma, uh, Hyde, right? I would've thought you'd have died by now. I lost touch with you once you went into that place," and he gestured behind me to the prison. "Well, it's good to see you, even if it's for only a few minutes. I've given my men a reason to finish this battle quickly.... I told them, if they do, they can have you. They're excited."

"Well, if you're the best that you have to offer, I'll outlast all of them. Then I'm coming for you, Dash-Ed. You see, one of the things you did to me by putting me here was that I don't care what's done to me as long as I get to cut out your heart," I said.

"I guess I'll have to make sure that the last man makes sure that can't happen, Emma," he said as he walked away.

The man with him walked over and ran his hands up and down my body. "If you cut me down, I'll give you pleasures you've never felt. My mouth is not the best part of my body, but others have said that it's right up there." I wagged my tongue at him.

He pulled out a large Bowie knife and walked over to me, slipping the blade into my shirt, and cutting upward, and slicing all its buttons away. He reached in and grabbed my breasts and began massaging them roughly. I moaned and kicked like I was in ecstasy. He smiled and cut my legs free. I pulled up on my arms and brought my legs up at the same time. He was so busy playing with my breasts he didn't see until too late that I hadn't stopped at his waist. Instead, I brought my legs up around his neck and twisted.

A guy in prison was a martial arts expert, and he'd taught us all basic moves. A few of us went on to more advanced techniques and exercises. My legs and hips were powerful, and this idiot saw that for maybe a fraction of a second before I snapped his neck. He fell. I grabbed his knife with my feet and jammed it into the tree limb near my wrist, where they tied it.

A few seconds later, I was on the ground and moving. None of my stuff was around, but my earpiece was still in place. "Shay, you there?"

"Yes, Emma. Where are you?"

"Near cement mixer number 3. I had and lost Hopes but am free again and will try to track him down."

"Can you wait for a couple of minutes? We're right behind you. I mean literally." He stepped out of the woods and walked toward me. "Looking pretty good, Emma," he said.

"Lucious," said Michaela, who threw me my medical bag and gun. "The Glauca is gone, sorry."

"That's okay. I took this Bowie knife off that guy. He won't be using it anymore."

We headed off in the direction that I'd seen Hopes go. There was still a lot of gunfire and explosions coming from the direction of the prison. "I think they may have more of those parasailers up in the air. We ought to find where they're coming from and put them out of business," said Shay.

Just after Shay said that I caught a reflection off a wing overhead and saw a parasailer returning from a bombing run. We followed and found a large contingent of men and equipment hiding behind what they thought was a good hiding place, a derelict cement mixer....

With them gone, we let the prison know what the explosion was and that they shouldn't have any more attacks from the air.

Figurehead

The explosion also brought several raiders over to check out what had happened. I think they initially thought that some malfunction had occurred with one of the fuel tanks, and while they poked through the wreckage, basically confirming that for themselves, we surrounded them. It only took us dropping a few of them for the rest to surrender. We laid them down on the ground and zip-tied their arms, ankles, and legs. Shay said that if they stayed out of the rest of this, they might survive. We left one of our team to watch over them, and the rest of us went after Hopes.

He wasn't hard to find. They'd set up a big top tent like you'd see at a circus a ways behind their front lines. Hopes' men guarded it. "I don't want to lose this chance to see those eyes go out," said Shay, "but I also don't want to put any of you at risk. Maybe I should just call in a cruise missile to flatten the place."

"I think we need eyes on Hopes before we do anything. I wouldn't want to find out afterward that he escaped," said Michaela. Everyone agreed.

"We need to get him out of that tent, then," said Shay.

"Simple," I said. Before anyone could say something, I stood up and walked into the torchlight with my hands up. "Tell Dash-Ed Hopes that Emma Hyde has returned from the dead," I said.

Two of the men moved toward me, and the other went into the tent. I saw several shadows move in behind the guards. Dash-Ed walked out of the tent a few minutes later, eyes fixed on me. "All the lives of a cat, Emma, but you're dead now." He pulled out a small gun and pointed it at me. When he was about to pull the trigger, the two guards next to him dropped to the ground. The two guards behind Dash-Ed also fell to the ground, throats cut by two of Shay's men.

Shay materialized behind Dash-Ed and clubbed him to the ground just as he pulled the trigger. I felt a burn along the side of my face and blood flowing. I walked over to Shay as the rest of the group entered the tent. We heard a few shots, but whatever action happened there was over quickly. Michaela, flashing a bloody sleeve, stepped out with several more bloody and zip-tied raiders. "All cleaned up in there. A few of them won't be going home to mom tonight, but we have the rest of them."

Shay and I looked down when we heard a groan from Dash-Ed. "Ah, he awakes."

"Just in time for us to turn off his lights for good," I said and kneeled next to him. "Look at us, Dash-Ed. We're the last faces you'll ever see." I looked up at Shay and nodded.

We showed off Dash-Ed's body to the rest of his leadership we captured and told the raiders who were still fighting that it was over. If they laid down their arms, we would commit that they'd be treated well—better than they had treated the people they'd attacked to date.

The answer to what to do with them was simple. We had an inescapable prison right on hand for them. There were about 80 raider survivors of the battle, and we switched them with our folks inside the ramparts. Some prisoners remained behind to serve as trainers like we had had ten years previous.

Figurehead

The rest, and a contingent of soldiers, remained outside the prison wall and guarded the ramparts, keeping watch.

There was still a lot to do to bring some peace back to the country. In all senses of that word, I joined with Shay, and he, Jake, Michaela, the rest of the detachment for that work. I even took some time to visit my parents in Georgia. They were happy to see Jake and me, especially in the Defiant, that Jake had gotten repaired. We go back a lot when we're not busy keeping the peace.

All things are relative, I believe. Peace, for instance. We're never going to have the peace that utopians envisioned. It's more like the Old West at the end of the 19th century. While there are still periodic outbursts from one separatist group or another, and we would need to intervene, Shay and I settled down.

As I look back on things now, some years later, if Hopes hadn't been the sadistic bastard that he was, I might not be alive today. Given where the world ended up, separate from me, I guess it was a good thing he was what he was.

I'm still glad we killed him, though.

The End

{ **9** }

Slipped Away

"Sold," announced the auctioneer. I breathed a sigh of relief.

My name doesn't matter, kind of like I didn't either except as revenue source; the powers that be erased my past as soon as the gavel struck. Since I was a child, I'd been prepped for this. But I'm dealing with many feelings right now—happy-sad, excited-apprehensive, and ready to get on with my life-wanting to go home.

I recently turned 15, the age when children were, what we have come to call "parceled out," auctioned off, trained in some job, or put to work in one or another state-run facility somewhere. Of the options, being auctioned was by far the best. Auction buyers had access to school and other records, and being selected at auction meant that the buyers thought you had some potential based on end-term exams you take when you're 15. In return for accepting indenture for 20 years, I would get an excellent education, be prepared for a top-end job in the future, and live in a home that would protect and inspire me. Still, I would be little better than a slave for that time; my training had conditioned me to accept this.

I was led away from the auction block and taken to the transfer tent, where the state Department of Indenture, otherwise known as DoI, representatives would complete my ownership transfer papers. I would become my new owner's property at that point. It was there I would meet them and be told what was next.

The Fairfield, Alabama Auction was held outdoors in the Spring and Fall, partly because the weather is nice and partly because the townspeople saw the auction as entertainment, especially to see young girls like me being sold off. So, they insisted on it being outside. Anyway, that meant a walk from the auction block to the transfer tent through a crowd of free people. I'd been told this was one of the worst parts of being sold; the freemen and women, many of whose ancestors were trafficked like me, jeered and threw insults.

I have to say I cried as they led me to the tent. All the preparations in the world that I got in school didn't ready me for the vile things they would say.

In the 2020s, the United States slipped from its preeminent position because it failed to keep up and we entered what my teachers called a "self-reinforcing" cycle of failures. We also had a series of governments that saw only to themselves—greedy bastards. The rest of the world watched as all this happened. Some with sadness, many with glee. Things failed at near the same time, likely because they were highly interrelated. Something no one saw, or if they did, denied the interrelationships. Most of these things you'd class as "infrastructure." Roads, power, fuel, transportation, water supplies, education, health care, banks, and so on and on and on.

Some of these failures were just because things were old and not maintained well. Then, because of so much stuff failing, people thought that the rich and powerful knew what they were doing elsewhere should run these things for all of us. So, the government "privatized" these services, and then their new owners, greedy bastards again, took all they could out of them while failing to maintain them. Also, being the huge "successes" they were in business, these same guys got appointments to government positions to take over the departments or areas where they had a competing financial interest. No surprise, they did more of the same: disassembled the things that protected us or delivered services. An early example of that was the U.S. Postal Service that was torn to pieces by a guy who ran a competitive service. It only made sense to put a fox in charge of the henhouse my teachers had said.

National actors or criminals caused some failures intentionally. Beginning in the early 2020s, we saw attempts by third parties, criminals, governments, thrill-seekers to infiltrate our infrastructure through the Internet. Many of these attacks failed, but a number succeeded. A radio ad then said that the bad guys had only to succeed once, but the good guys needed to be successful every time. Well, the bad guys succeeded here and there and dragged us down. Our failures had exposed almost our entire infrastructure. Nuclear and gas power, hydroelectric dams, and wind farms were weak because of crowd-sourced software in some cases and others because of just lousy maintenance or design. Back in the early 2020s, just before I was born, the State of Texas suffered power grid failures in the summer and winter because its government failed to exert sensible controls over the power grid companies and maintain services. Winters and summers saw massive "rolling" blackouts as people were made to suffer for their government's failures to live up to their obligations to their citizens. A study done back in 2001 also had said that a terrorist could cut off 65% of the nation's natural gas by taking only three sites nationally. That was tried a few times, once or twice successfully and catastrophically.

Think about what the entire city of Baytown, TX, would look like going up in smoke when hackers caused an explosion in a natural gas line. A line of dominoes fell after that obliterating the chemical plants in that area. A monstrous loss of life that made a large part of south Texas uninhabitable.

Hackers in the early 2020s also broke into several large companies and shut down oil pipelines, meat packing, and other things. In one case, they drowned an entire town when a hacker opened the floodgates for a dam upstream from them. That guy turned out to be from Tennessee and was living in his mother's basement. In another, all the hospitals on the West Coast shut down when a hacker entered their systems and took over medical records and hospital infrastructures like gas and air conditioning. Hundreds died because of that.

On what started as an unrelated thing, the State of Texas passed several laws that reinforced the right of citizens to bear arms. Well, their outraged—and now armed—citizens stormed the State Capital and shot it up. There was a lot of blood spilled for no reason. And, to add insult to that injury, nothing changed. The state continued to fall apart.

Our country had been a leader in many things, not all of them positive. For instance, we were one of the world's leading polluters. When the effects of pollution and what people called climate change rammed into what was happening, everything went down the toilet, or so they told us in school.

More than anything, what you saw was that people lost faith. Lost faith in everything that they'd taken for granted for years and years. They became angry, sometimes violent, and more and more isolated from each other. Neighbors would no longer talk to each other. People pulled their kids out of public schools and put them into private ones that created echo chambers of false information drummed into kids' heads.

I was fortunate because my school was one of the last public ones in our area and because so many kids had left it, we had small classes and got a quality education. Preparing us for, well, a life of what would have been called slavery in the past. But now was looked at as a way out. The alternative was a life in a state-run facility making license plates or, if you were lucky, working in state prison as a guard but being only slightly better than the prisoners. Used to be that prisoners made license plates. Now, they just vegetated in their cells.

Our teachers taught us that our leaders, government, companies all failed us. All were so danged focused on lining their pockets that they wouldn't do what was right. Protecting our infrastructure, maintaining it, paying people a meaningful wage, as it was called, protecting our environment, they did none of this, and we collapsed. More like a balloon, we popped.

Several of our supposed friends stepped up to help us when the end-times became apparent. They were strapped themselves and suffering from some of the same things, but most had made some decent investments and so could afford to help us a bit. But that was at a cost. I'm part of the payback for the help they provided. Guys like the buyers here made enormous investments in our country intending to siphon off goods, services, and eventually people. I didn't know where I was going, probably somewhere that we used to call a Third World Country, to be and do who-knows-what for the next twenty years. For the last four years, they had trained me in what was called "prep school" for this and anything. That was what the "prep" in school meant—prepared to give up myself.

In the tent, they placed me at the end of a line of maybe ten girls who'd been auctioned off ahead of me. The guard who brought me in chained me to the collar on the girl in front of me. He then attached another chain to a loop on the back of my collar. Before he walked away, he said, "You stand here with your mouth shut. No talkin' in the coffle. Understand?"

Being well-trained and polite, I said, "Yes, Sir."

He hit me in the back of my head with a leather strop he carried. "Didn't I say no talkin' in the coffle?"

I cried again. It looked like I'd failed my first test, so I nodded. He walked away, laughing at me.

I thought about my parents and brothers and sisters and the dark little shack that I'd called my home for the last fifteen years. They were likely on their way home right now. I'm sure my mom was crying, and my dad was stony-faced as he always had been. I never got one expression of love from him. Maybe the boys did because they were boys, but me and my sister, never. He looked at us as auction products in the making from our births. I wished my sister well when it came her turn in two years.

The U.S. government developed the Interstate highway system in the 1950s, almost 80 years before I was born. At one time, it was the pride of our country. Now, you took your life in your hands to drive as we did from our home to Fairfield, Alabama. Potholes in the road could eat a car. That wasn't the worse thing, though. There were mockingly called "toll booths" where the men there extracted a toll for passing up and down the highway. If they figured out that mom and dad had a lot of money in the truck, they'd be dead. Dad would go down fighting, though. I hope they make it home in one piece. I'll probably never know.

Figurehead

A man took, one by one, the girls in front of me to the head of the line where there were several sweaty DoI men in short-sleeved shirts and ties. They said some things and collected some information, made an announcement to the room, and a man would come up to lead the girl away. I guessed whoever that was, was their new owner and to hopefully a better life. Most of the girls were pretty like me. Ugly girls never made it to auction; they ended up in the state-run facility doing drudge work or something else.

The tent was boiling, and I sweated underneath the shift that they'd given me. The fabric was some kind of burlap not much different from a potato sack, and they had issued it to me when we went in for initial processing. They collected all my clothing and shoes and took them away. The shifts were not very comfortable in the first place and were even less so now with the heat in the tent. Mine was way too large for me, but I saw it was the same with all the girls as I looked down the line. One size fits all, I guessed.

One of the DoI men told me to stand in front of the table and not move forward of a brown line on the ground when it was my turn. I did as he told me. Not knowing what else to do, I stared ahead between the men.

The man on the right asked me my old name. I gave it to him.

"Do you think you're special? Uppity maybe?" he asked.

"No, Sir. I'm not special. I'm sorry if I seem to act uppity, Sir," I answered, now scared and confused.

"Well, you look at the ground until your betters tell you to do different. Understand?" he ordered.

"Yes, Sir," I answered, praying that this man hadn't bought me. I looked down at the ground and cried again.

The man in the middle spoke up, "Stop crying unless you want a strapping. You were sold at auction today and will be picked up shortly by a representative of your new owner. As of the moment of your sale, the DoI revoked your old identity. Sometimes, new owners will leave you with your old name. In most cases, that will not happen. Your parents are aware of this and that you no longer are their daughter. Your new last name will probably be your owner's last name. Not like you are a daughter or a family member, but to show who you belong to."

The third man began speaking, and I realized that they gave this little speech to every girl coming through here. They seemed to get some sadistic delight out of that, like the people outside. I was looking forward to my opportunities, and they looked at it only as debasement. Maybe I was wrong, and they were right. I shivered.

"You are," the third man recited, "from this moment on, property. A thing. Like this table and the chairs, we're sitting on. You will be marked accordingly." He picked a large stamp up and stamped the words "Chattel" on the papers, presumably mine, in front of him. "Owner of property 1618, please come collect your chattel."

A man stepped out of the crowd and led me out a side entrance, back into the open air, and then into another tent.

Figurehead

Where the first tent was an oven, this one was what I thought Hell might feel like. There was a large fire in the middle of the room in what I was to find out was called a forge, a place where a blacksmith worked. The man, the blacksmith, had stuck several tools around it and into the fire. There was also a table toward the rear of the tent to which the man led me. "Please, stand there and don't move," said the man who'd taken me from the other tent. He had a slightly accented voice. He had a kind look about him. This was the first time anyone had said "Please" anything to me and I relaxed a little.

Shirtless and coated in sweat and grime, a big man walked over to me. "Face me, Chattel," he said. I bridled at him calling me Chattel but thought it might get me into trouble, so I turned to face him. He unceremoniously pulled the bow I had tied at my waist so that the shift slipped from my shoulders. I reached up to keep it on, and he slapped me. "Let it fall. You'll get it back when we're done. Now, lay down on the table, face down. Place your hands behind your head."

I did. He reached across the table and picked up a thing that looked like a gun. My hair was bunched up, and he grabbed my wrists where they were behind my head. In the next second, I heard a pop and felt a searing pain on the back of my neck. "Stay still," he said. A few seconds later, I felt him grab my left leg, just above my knee. The other man put his hands on my hips—a second or two later, another pop and burning pain.

He stepped back. "You can put your hands down. Sit up, slowly. You've had a couple shocks, and you might be faint. Just sit there for a few minutes. He walked across the room, took a large ladle, and filled a cup hanging from the side of an old milk can. He walked over to me. "Drink," he said, "It'll help."

I did, gratefully. "Thank you, Sir."

He laughed and looked at the other man. "First time I had one of these, thank me for marking them as chattel." Both of them laughed.

"Sorry, honey. I didn't mean to make fun of you, but it don't happen often I get thanks for my work. Look here." He held a mirror down below my left thigh, and I could see a black and white bar code there. "That's your registration number." He looked over at the man and said, "Give me your phone." He did, and the man scanned the code on my leg. "See, it brings up your details when it's scanned. That way, if you wander away and someone finds you, they can return you to your owner. Okay. Come over here." Where the screen said "owner," all I saw was "R Enterprises." I wondered what that was. Now I was indeed tagged, like a dog. My teachers had told me that this would be a difficult part of the auction process, losing my identity as I had. Role-playing didn't capture what this was like in real life.

The blacksmith led me to what looked like one of those pommel horses I used in the gym at school. This one didn't have the pommels, though. "Lay yourself over the top of the horse," he said. When I'd complied, he took a pair of cuffs from the ground and then bound each wrist to the opposite ankle. They firmly held me on the horse. The blacksmith went to a cart and wheeled it over. I saw many things on it; I'd no idea what they were for but was pretty sure I would soon find out. He reached over and grabbed what looked like another gun, placed it against my shoulder, and a second later, I felt something shoot into me; it barely hurt. "That's your I.D. chip. The number recorded there and the other information on it would also get you back home. We do the same thing to cattle."

As if he needed to say that, and this wasn't hard enough. But I suppose he did.

"Now. I'm going to turn your left leg in and lock it down so you can't move. I'll tell you now, what I'm going to do will hurt like hell. This is my forge. I make things here, and I'm going to brand you with the last four digits of your I.D. number, 1618. That'll take a little time because after I brand you with the 1, I have to put it back into the coals to heat again. You then get a brand on your right hip showing that you are chattel for twenty years or until your owner frees you."

"Please, Sir. Why? Everything I read about the auctions never said that any of this happens," I sobbed.

"We'd never get kids to volunteer for this if they knew what processing was like. Kid, you need to understand that, despite this, where you're going is better than any of the things that would happen to you here. You're a lucky one."

"I don't feel so lucky," I said but steeled myself for what was coming.

"Until your owner names you or maybe lets you keep your old name, this number will be how we'll know you. 1618. Remember, 1618, you are an object now," the blacksmith reminded me. "Put on your shift." He let me rest for a few minutes and gave me another ladle of water.

The last thing they did was to replace the auction collar with my new owner's collar. The man who retrieved me from the transfer tent produced it from a man-bag he was carrying. It was a light blue-colored metal and felt good when he placed it around my neck. He spoke softly, "Belts and suspenders for the belts and suspenders. This has a GPS in it, too. It is a beautiful piece of jewelry, though. Right?"

"Yes, Sir." I fingered it. It was smooth all the way around.

"There's no lock or key on this collar. When I closed it, a small bottle of permanent glue broke, sealing the mechanism shut. You will wear it for 20 years. Only someone with the permission to do that can remove it," he said. He clipped a chain on the collar and said, "Come." We walked out of the tent and to a waiting limousine, me at the end of the leash. I felt like I should pant but thought that might get me a spanking. Or something worse.

- - - - - - -

I'd never been in a new car before, and this definitely was that. The leather smelled very good. I caressed it lightly with my hands. The man laughed. "We'll be in the car for a couple of hours until we get to the airport. Your roads here are awful, so we must take it slowly.... You need to know my name; it is Luis Hernandez. You may call me Luis when we are together

Figurehead

like this. Sir, otherwise. Do you want something to drink?" He opened a refrigerator I hadn't noticed between us. I gaped. There were things there I'd only read about.

"I've never had a Coke. Could I have one, please?" I asked.

He smiled sadly and said, "Certainly." He took the red can that I'd only seen in a couple of magazines we had in school, filled a glass with real ice from an ice bucket, opened the can, and then poured some of the bubbly drink into it. "Here," he said, with a repeat of the sad smile on his face.

"Thank you, Sir. Can I ask you a question?"

"Remember, Luis. Certainly, my dear. Ask away."

"Twice now, you looked sadly at me. Why's that?" I asked.

"You're observant. That will serve you well. Observe and learn how to behave, and you will be fine in your new home. I'm about 60 years old and was born elsewhere in a time before your country fell. It was one of the most successful countries that the world has ever known until people forgot what 'United' meant. You had a leader at the time. I was about ten who was an awful man." He paused and looked at me for a moment. "Do you know what the word misogynist means?"

"No, Sir."

"Luis. Well, among other things, it means a woman-hater. That was him, a misogynist. He was also all about himself, what was called an egotist. Everything he did was focused on self-aggrandizement, power, and money. He took everything he could get his hands on and sold your country out. By the time they swept him away in a landslide vote—that he never accepted—the country was already slipping away.

He did much damage in four years, and the good people who took over after he left had to fight his henchmen to repair the damage done to your country. But there was just too much to do. When things failed, it became an avalanche. No one could stop it, despite good intentions. And here you are today. A third-rate country that must sell off its beautiful and bright children to make ends meet. That's why I look sad. You should be doing something else other than to aspire to be a chattel. But here you are."

I was overwhelmed, and I guess he saw that. "You're going to a better life, my dear. Trust me on that," he said.

We rode on in silence, me looking out the window and drinking my Coke. It was wonderful; I could really get to like this. There were few sights along the road—primarily dark and ruined countryside. A little while later, we arrived at what I thought might be an airport. This had been a hell of a night for me. First, traveling so far away from home, then being sold at an auction, then having all these things done to my body to mark me, then a Coke with real ice, and now, it looked like I was going to go off on an airplane. I was weak-kneed when I stepped out of the limousine. "Are we going to fly in that thing?" I asked.

"Yes, my dear. Walk up those stairs," he said.

I did, and very quickly. I looked over my shoulder and saw him observing me, sadly smiling again and shaking his head to show I was doing well. Another man walked over to him from another vehicle that had pulled up, and the two of them talked, looking at me several times. Both men smiled at me. I took that to be a good sign.

A tall, beautiful woman dressed in a blue uniform met me at the top of the stairs. "Good evening, 1618. Welcome on board. Please follow me." As we walked down the aisle, I surveyed my surroundings and then the woman. More leather. Maybe ten large seats, each with what looked like a T.V. The plane smelled brand new. I ran my hand along the seats as we walked toward the rear of the aircraft. At the back, there were two doors.

Just before we got to one of them, I looked up at the woman and saw a glint of metal around her neck, just like mine. She was chattel too, but she looked very healthy and, well, beautiful. Poised was the word that I remembered from school. They had tried to teach us poise so we would be good chattel.

"Can I ask a question?" I asked.

We approached the door, and I saw a metal plate that said "Chattel Quarters" on it. "Certainly, my dear. What?" she responded.

"Uhm. Are you...?" and I fingered my collar.

"Chattel? Yes, I am. I've been with the Master since I was about your age. Now, almost 20 years. He is an honorable man to all of us. Come in here; you will clean up after we take off and then change."

She handed me a towel, some shampoos, and soaps and showed me a bathroom with an actual shower in it. We only had a bucket shower at home. She went to a closet, looked through several clothing items, and then handed me one of them. Another shift, but this one looked like it would fit very well. She handed me some brand new, still in the package underwear as well. "I think this will fit. Don't start your shower until that light there turns green. That'll mean we're in the air. If you need anything, let me know. You can sit over there. Remember to buckle your seat belt. Takeoff can disorient the first few times you do it."

"Ma'am? Can I watch us take off? There're no windows back here. Maybe a Coke too?" I asked. Also, I thought, "first few times?" Was I going to be flying a lot? I could get to like this too unless, of course, I got airsick and threw up.

She laughed, "Call me Elvira, 1618. That is not my birth name, but it is one our Master likes and gave to me. I have come to like it as well. Much better than my number." She lifted her skirt, and I saw a bar code and a brand there like mine. "Makes me feel like I have something of an identity. And, yes, to both your other questions. Come with me."

At the very rear of the passenger cabin was a service area. Elvira opened a refrigerator, and I again saw many things to drink. She took out a Coke, put ice in another glass, and then handed it to me. She put the rest of the Coke back into the refrigerator. "It needs to stay there until we take off. You can take it with you when you go to take a shower. Sit here." She later told me that what she had pulled down was called a jump seat; we sat next to each other. She showed me how to belt in, and then a voice from an overhead speaker announced we had been "Cleared for takeoff." In principle, I knew what that meant. But I tensed up anyway.

The ground dropped away, and I felt my stomach lurch. I reached out and grabbed Elvira's arm. She squeezed my hand. I made it through the takeoff without getting sick. I was proud of myself.

We were gone, and I had slipped away. I felt a weight lift from me, and a new one settled on my shoulders.

After a few minutes, the light turned green, and a bell dinged. Elvira retrieved my Coke and told me it was okay to take a shower. She told me to make sure that I used the special shampoo that she'd given me. I went into the Chattel Quarters and took off my old shift and my underpants, balled them up, and put them into a basket that said, "Dirty Laundry." I had to fiddle with the shower because I didn't understand how it worked. We had only sun-warmed water from the big, black plastic vat on the roof of our house that ran into a bucket we used as a shower. My father put it up there to capture our frequent rainfalls. I hoped that they had gotten home safely. They should be there by now.

I looked at the shampoo that Elvira had given me, "Mata Piojos." Lice shampoo. I was pretty sure that I didn't have lice as school checked us out monthly but shrugged my shoulders. Better safe than sorry, I guess. I lathered up my head and then rinsed it out. I then took a new bar of soap—another first for me—and washed off my body. My long hair always curled after a shower, and this would be no exception. I toweled off and then found a hairdryer under the counter and dried my hair, trying to brush out the tangles. This was something new as well. We didn't have electricity at our house.

I never heard the door open. "Let me help with that," said Elvira. She opened a cabinet, took out something she called a detangler, and sprayed it into my hair. The comb sailed through it. "You've beautiful hair, 1618." She helped me into my new clothes and looked at me critically. "That'll do, I suppose. You'll get real clothes for you after we get home. Here are some slippers. Come forward with me." I guess I looked confused because she said, "That means to the front of the airplane."

We walked out of the Chattel Quarters forward into the main cabin. Luis and the other man I had seen were sitting there, talking. We stopped in the aisle, and Elvira kneeled. She reached up and grabbed me, pulling me down next to her. "Master. It is excellent to see you again. This is your newest chattel, 1618."

I'd learned my lesson earlier, and I kept my eyes fixed on the ground. I felt him evaluating me.

"You've done very well, Luis. She will be a wonderful addition to our menagerie," said the man.

Out of the corner of my eye, I saw Elvira smile. I kept staring at the floor.

"1618," he whispered, "look at me." I did, and I saw a little shock on his face. "Beautiful. Your eyes are very unusual. Shocking. I've seen nothing like them."

Figurehead

"It's called heterochromia green, Sir. My eyes are both green and brown. The condition is very rare, and some people find it disturbing. I hope they don't bother you. There's not much I can do about them."

He laughed pleasantly. "My goodness, no, child. I love them. Now, some rules in my house. First, yes, you are my chattel; you'll learn more about that. We will select a good name for you, one as important to me as you are. I hope you come to like it as well. Second, I know some owners like their chattel to be meek. I expect you to show me respect, but I also will not tolerate your being meek when you see something that's important. Third, and so this means that I expect you will always look me in the eye. So, look me in the eye, please, as we are talking. Fourth, never, ever lie to me. I will never lie to you, and I expect the same from you. Fifth, I will assign you productive work to do, but I also expect you to keep yourself fit, regardless of the job you have. Sixth, you will have an overseer when you first arrive at my home. She or he will see to your education. You will treat her or him with the same deference that you show me. Is there anything unclear here?"

"No, Sir. I'll try my very best to please you," I said.

He smiled and said, "Elvira, it is only the four of us. Let's eat together. 1618, go with Elvira and help her. When we are ready to eat, call us, and we will dine." At the periphery of my vision, I saw Elvira give a little start.

"Sir, may I ask two questions? I hope that it's not too rude of me."

"Not at all, my dear. What are your questions? I expect you will have a lot of them. I see by your records and the way you carry yourself that you're not stupid. That doesn't mean, though, that you'll understand everything. If you had no questions, I'd worry."

"What's your name, Sir? Where are we going?"

He burst out laughing. "My apologies, 1618. I got lost in your eyes, and I forgot my opening speech. My name is Oliver Ramirez. I'm Chilean, as you now are, and we are going to my home outside of Valdivia, Chile. We will fly about 15 hours, with a few stops to fuel, to get there." So, the "R," in R Enterprises, I thought.

‑‑‑‑‑‑‑

Elvira handled most of the dinner. She told me how to set the table and how to open bottles of wine. She removed prepared dishes from a warming oven and transferred the contents of them to serving plates. "These are fine dishes, 1618. Break anything, and I will beat you myself," she said with a smile. While I didn't believe she would, I was extra careful. I put a tablecloth on a table that Elvira had me pull out of the plane's wall and then set out the dishware and silverware as instructed. As I worked, I saw the Master look at me periodically and then smile. He said something to Luis at one point, and he shook his head yes. Apparently, they had made some decisions about me. For my benefit, I hoped.

"You must have impressed Luis, 1618," said Elvira. "He's clearly talked to Master, and they have made up their minds about you. That's also something that I've not seen before. I have only rarely dined with Master and him when I fly with them. Whatever it is you're doing, keep it up, and you'll be fine. Why don't you get them? Walk up the aisle, kneel next to the Master, wait until he acknowledges you, and then tell them that dinner is ready. He will sit in that seat there. Walk behind him to the seat, turn it out toward him and then seat him. When seated, reach across him, attach his seatbelt, take his napkin, and put it in his lap. Then do the same with Luis. Then come back here, and we will serve the meal."

I did as she told me. When the men were seated, Elvira and I served. She poured the wine, and I was glad about that. There were four courses, and I observed as they ate to ensure that I wasn't making a fool of myself. Master watched me carefully as well. He asked many questions about my life, parents, brothers and sisters, schools, friends, things I liked to do. He made me the center of attention, and it was very tiring and scary.

Finally, he sat back and said, "That was an excellent meal. I've missed my fine Chilean wines this trip. Sena remains my favorite. Thanks, Elvira, for seeing that it was here."

"I live to serve you, Master," she said.

"And I, you," he said in return. Some kind of ritual, I thought.

He turned to me, "You, I want you to turn down my bed after you've cleared the table. When you have done that, wait there."

"Y-Y-Yes, Sir," I said. I knew something like this might happen, but I wasn't prepared. I didn't worry about sex. I'd gotten plenty of instruction on that and had been given birth control. The shot still hurt a little. I was more worried that I might fail to perform well, and that would doom me somehow.

I helped clear the table but was silent as we worked.

"1618, don't worry. Our Master is a very kind man. He will not hurt you or make you do things you don't want to do," said Elvira.

I looked at her and cried.

"Don't, my little girl. You'll be fine. Trust me."

We finished cleaning, and Elvira asked me to wait by the other door. She said that she would be right there. I saw her talking to the two men; I was hoping not about me. She met me at the unlabeled door and opened it. Lights came on automatically. It was an enormous bedroom, almost as large as my old house in Alabama. I was shocked. "When he says to turn down his bed, that means that you take the duvet at the top of the bed and roll it down."

"Duvet?" I asked.

"That quilt on top of the bed. He sleeps very hot and doesn't need it. Fold it back neatly. That's right. Now fluff the pillows. Good. I will lower the lights, and you should stand in the room's corner and wait for him. He's finishing with Luis and will not be long. I will probably not see you until the morning. Sleep well, 1618. Remember, this is an honorable man who has your interests at heart."

Figurehead

She smiled sadly, turned, and walked out after lowering the lights. I stood in the corner to wait. I was seeing those smiles a lot. I was scared to death.

I didn't have long to wait. The door opened, and Master walked in. When he closed the door, I jumped a little. He saw me and gave me the same sad smile as Luis and Elvira. "Are you frightened, 1618?"

"Yes, Sir. Scared to death, actually. I do not want to disappoint you."

"As I said before, I will always reward honesty. Come over here and sit on the edge of the bed while I change." He disappeared into what I saw was another bathroom, but much larger than the one in the Chattel Quarters. He came out a few minutes later wearing only pajama pants. Black hair curled on his chest, and he was very muscular.

"Now, go into the bathroom and take care of anything you need to. Behind the left-hand mirror over the sink, there are feminine products that will be yours. Let me know if I should be getting you anything more or different. In the bathroom is a chest, open it, and you will find several nightgowns. Take off your shift, hang it up, and then put on the nightdress. I will wait for you to come back out so we can talk."

I did what he told me to do, becoming increasingly panicked as I shed my clothes. When I got to my underpants, I stopped. If this was what I had expected it was going to be, I probably ought to be prepared. Then again, if it wasn't, I didn't want to appear too forward. Then I figured I was over-thinking things, and if nothing happened, he'd never know. I hung the panties with my dress.

He was sprawled on the bed, reading from a folder, when I returned. He patted a spot next to him on the bed. When I slid in, he put the folder aside and repositioned himself on the bed, facing me. "You should not be frightened of me. I won't take from you like some chattel owners do. For them, you are property to be used and then thrown aside for the next thing they own. With me, you will have to be willing and give yourself. This is way too early for that to happen. You're overloaded with everything that's happened to you today. You'd probably give yourself to me, but then you'd hate yourself and me. Whatever happens, will happen naturally between us. And, whatever happens then, will have no impact on your life with me. Understand? Finally, the only way you can disappoint me is to do something you don't want to do because I ask you to do it. That would disappoint me. Remember, I ask for honesty in all things."

"Yes, Sir, and thank you, Sir," I said.

"And stop this, Sir stuff. When we are alone like this, I'm Oliver to you. And you will be Layla. A name I've always loved. As with all my chattel and most others, you'll see, your last name is now Ramirez. That signifies you as part of a greater family and property. I hope that you come to like your new name and feel that as a Ramirez, you are now under my protection."

"Thank you... Oliver."

Figurehead

"Now, to your work. I want to develop you as my personal assistant. I've had no one to fill that role, and as my holdings are getting more and more complex, I need another head all the time. Luis cannot do that. People used to call what he does a Chief Operating Officer, but he has day-to-day responsibility for many very complicated things. I could never do what he does. But now, the array of what I do is getting to be too much. I want you to help me keep it all together. I talked to Luis about it, and he thinks it's a wonderful idea. You captured his heart, young lady. A hard thing to do with someone like Luis."

"I'm not sure I'm qualified, Oliver."

"No one is. This is a brand-new job, you will be a blank slate, and I will write on you as I want to. You're the best person for it. Your school report and all that I read about you," and he tapped the folder he was reading, "confirmed my feelings about you."

"What about Elvira, Master, I mean Oliver? She knows so much more about you, and you two seem to have a wonderful relationship," I asked.

"You're right, she would be ideal, but—and this is my first test for you—I will free her after we arrive back at my home. She's been with me for twenty years and deserves a life apart from service. While we have been traveling around, I've had a home built for her where she can live and come and go as she wants. She will have a Chilean passport and full citizenship. That differs from you. By the way, you are now Chilean, as I said before, but what we call a chattel slave. Twenty years from now, when you're 35, and I'm, well, older than that, you'll be free as well. Now, remember what I said about this being a secret."

"Yes, Sir."

"Good. Now to the jobs of my personal assistant. I'm still figuring them out, but you will travel with me all the time. Aside from your collar, no one will know your status. When we arrive home, I will have my seamstress make you clothes fitting for an assistant of your status. You will learn my businesses and give me insights and advice...."

"Sir, I know nothing about business. I can't give you any useful advice," I interrupted.

"I want someone like you. Innocent to the business who can give me honest input. I will tell you now, nothing you say will be stupid, maybe uninformed, but never stupid. Say what you think—respectfully—but say what you think. You will be at my shoulder at all events, work, or social. I know it will seem odd, you being only 15, but you have at least 20 years as my chattel, and you will age into the job like those fine wines I love so much. And, for right now, you will turn down my bed every night. Sleep where'd you like. There is another bed enclosed in the wall over there, and you will have your own room, adjoining mine, at home. See that handle? Pull it down, and the bed will come down. Or sleep here. Remember, you're safe with me."

I didn't know what to say or do.

Figurehead

I slept next to him. He was the gentleman he said that he would be. I was property but had a name, and he let me make choices. I was sure that was all intentional, to see how I'd handle things.

I awoke once during the night and left the room to get a drink. I knew he must have something in his room, but I wasn't about to root around and wake him—a question for another time. I stepped out into the service area and heard voices forward of me. I got myself a Coke and stepped out. Elvira was there with Luis and two other men, both in blue uniforms like what Elvira wore. She had her head on the shoulder of one man and seemed to be asleep.

"Ah," said Luis, "Layla, right? Cannot sleep?"

"Yes, Sir. Not really. It's been a heck of a day."

"That it has. This is the captain of our aircraft, Ismael Peña, and our Second Co-Pilot, Antonio Ascaso." Antonio was the man who Elvira slept against. "They're resting while the other two pilots are flying. We'll be landing in an hour in Belize to take on fuel for the next segment of our flight. We will make another stop in Iquique in northern Chile, and then from there, it's straight home after a stop in Santiago where I get off."

I said hello to the two pilots and Elvira, who'd woke and smiled at me with sleepy eyes. I excused myself and finished my drink in the service area before returning to bed. When I laid down next to Oliver, he rolled over and threw his arm over me. I didn't know what to do, but his rhythmic breathing soon had me fast asleep.

"Good morning, Chattel. Do you drink coffee? I own a plantation in Colombia that makes some of the best in the world. Here, try a cup."

"Thanks, Sir. Dammit. I mean Oliver. Sorry about all of that. I grew up in a house full of boys and men, and there was a lot of cursing."

"Don't worry. I've heard a lot that you've probably never heard," he said and ruffled my hair.

The coffee was excellent. He was right. When we had anything like coffee, it was chicory, so nothing like this. "Can I ask a question?"

"Sure. Why don't we agree on something? Ask your questions. You don't have to keep asking me if you can ask a question, and then I say yes, and then you ask your question. If I don't like the question, I'll just drop you off in the middle of a jungle somewhere, and you'll be on your own.... Seriously, ask away anytime."

"Did you make this yourself?" I asked.

"No, Elvira knows what I like in the morning, as you will, and the time that I get up. You will learn that as well. She gets up and prepares the coffee for me and brings it in here."

I must have turned white or something. "Oh, I see by the look on your face that I may have embarrassed you. I didn't think about that." He reached over and grabbed a telephone on the end table, hit a number, and said, "Elvira, could you please come in here? Thanks."

Figurehead

I jumped up out of bed and headed toward the bathroom, now even more mortified. "Come back here," he said. The command in his voice stopped me dead, and I came back onto the bed but sat on the corner of it away from him. He growled and grabbed me by my hair and the back of my nightgown and dragged me over to him. "Sit right there. Do. Not. Move. She's already seen you under the covers." I felt myself blush furiously.

There was a knock on the door, and Elvira came in. "Elvira, I think I may have embarrassed our friend here." And he gestured over to me. "You saw her sleeping in the bed this morning and maybe got the wrong idea about what happened here. Do you have any wrong ideas?"

"No, Sir. None at all. We are chattel and property for you to do with as you see fit. I don't think about anything other than how I can please you. Is that all, Sir?"

"Yes, but try. I know it will be hard; try to teach this chattel her place. She still thinks that she has another identity."

I looked back and forth at the two of them, and it then hit me they were playing with me. On the other hand, though, I was property and didn't act like I was. The lesson here that they were teaching me was that I should never be embarrassed. I was property, after all. Chairs don't get embarrassed.

"I get it," I said. "Apologies to both of you."

They both laughed, and then Elvira turned and left. He ruffled my hair again. "You're a good kid," he said, "and we will do very well together. Now, another one of your tasks will be to draw my bath and soap me down."

I did, and it was there that I gave in to him. It was the natural and right thing to do.

I had to admit; it was not the experience that I had expected. It was much, much better.

"Layla?"

"Yes, Sir."

"Stop that! Do I have to put you over my lap and give you a spanking? We just made love, and you call me Sir like that was a noxious chore. I truly hope it wasn't, and I know it wasn't for me. So, stop the Sir stuff."

"Okay. I'll try, but I'm just concerned about slipping up when we're in public," I said.

"All right. Do what you want. Just do not end a sweet little nothing you whisper into my ear with a 'Sir.'"

"Yes, Sir."

‒‒‒‒‒‒‒

We had been in bed through the plane's Iquique stop, and when we landed in Santiago, Customs agents came on board and processed me through as a new Chilean chattel slave. I never had time to say goodbye to Luis. The officers recorded my collar and chip, read my barcodes, took some pictures, and then said I'd get my internal passport in a few days. Oliver said that we would pick it up when we came to Santiago next. Then off to Valdivia, landing at the Pichoy Airport, about fifty miles from Master's home near the Riñihue Lake. Pichoy was a tiny airport, but it could handle Oliver's Gulfstream. Five SUVs were waiting for us when we arrived. It surprised Elvira when Oliver asked her to travel back to his home with us. We got into one of the SUVs, and three of them left, leaving the remaining two to take Oliver's belongings and some things that he had purchased for Elvira as freedom gifts.

We drove along in silence mostly, though Oliver took and made a few calls. I heard my name mentioned twice but could understand nothing else. "You will need to learn Spanish and German. I do a lot of business that will require you to be fluent in both," he said to me.

"Great," I thought, "Four years of French will be pretty much useless, I guess."

We drove for about fifty miles and then through a large gate that opened in front of us. I saw miles of fence in either direction. "The fences go to the mountains in the east and the mountains in the west. I have nearly 150,000 hectares of land here. Most of it is undeveloped. I plan to keep it as a nature preserve. You will need to familiarize yourself with it over the next two months while we're here. Do you ride horses?" he asked.

"I have a couple of times, but I'd say no, Sir," I said.

"You will have a lot to learn. I will challenge you, Layla. No rest for the weary, I always say."

Elvira smiled and then had a perplexed look on her face as we turned down a side road and drove up into the hills. "Where are we going, Sir? Home is that way," and she pointed in the opposite direction from where we were going.

"I need to look at the progress on a project here. We'll only be a minute." He picked up his phone again and lapsed into

French. I heard him say, "We will be there in about 10 minutes."

"Cela ne prendra que 10 minutes pour y arriver?" I asked.

Oliver's head snapped up, and he smiled at me. "Vous serez vraiment un trésor." I blushed.

In ten minutes, we pulled up in front of a large, modern home with miles of glass around it and terraces everywhere. "Let's take a walk through it. It's just finished today," Oliver said.

It had four bedrooms; maybe one was an office, a spacious kitchen, and a dining room that looked out over the lakes in the distance. The main living room was way larger than my old home in Alabama and had lovely, comfortable furniture throughout. The master bedroom, which was at the top level of the house, had windows on every wall, providing a panoramic view of the entire estate. In the distance, maybe two miles away, I could see an enormous home that this could have fit into a corner of. Oliver's house I was to find out. A few hundred feet away was what looked like a barn and a fenced-in paddock next to it. A man was leading a horse out of the barn.

"Now, wait a minute," said Elvira. "That horse looks just like my Gracie."

One of the other SUVs pulled up in front of the house, and a man ran in with Oliver's backpack. "Sit, Elvira," he ordered. She did but looked faint at his tone. "You were sold to me twenty years ago, correct?"

"Yes, Sir."

Figurehead

"Have they been a bad twenty years, aside from being a chattel slave? Did I ever ask you to do anything distasteful in all that time?"

"No, Sir." She kept getting whiter. I just stood back and watched as he fished through his pack for a file. Finally, getting frustrated, he turned to me. "Layla, come over here."

I did, and he handed me the pack, and as he did, he leaned in and said, "I'm more nervous than she is. See if you can find the file labeled 'Elizabeth Dillon.'" I flipped through several files, saw my old name on one, but flipped past that. I handed him the file he wanted. Maybe he was also testing me, I thought.

"Twenty years ago, when I took you in, I took much from you. I took your name; I took twenty years, and I took your life as an independent woman. You have served me very well over the years, and I know that I've done you a great wrong.... I want to give you four things." He handed her a Chilean passport with the name Elizabeth Dillon on it. "First, your identity back. You are now a Chilean citizen. Second, I want to give you this home. Third, I want to give you the freedom to do whatever you want. And fourth, I've been accumulating wages for you for the last twenty years and investing them for you. You will be very comfortable doing whatever it is you want to do. But I do hope you stay here. Oh, and I have known for years about the relationship between you and Antonio. Now you can consummate that however you want. I would love to give you away if you two decide to get married."

GEORGE CONKLIN

Elvira, Elizabeth, turned a bright red. I guess at that last revelation.

"Sir...",

"Oliver."

"Oliver, I don't know what to say."

"Just say yes to everything and get on with your life. By the way, I fully expect that you'll continue with your work on my plane, this time as a salaried employee. Not that you need the money." He handed her a bankbook. Her eyes jumped wide open when she read what it said.

Tears flooded out all around. She said, "Yes, and thank you so much for twenty of the best years of my life."

"And I hope we will have many more together. We will leave you to your new home." He got up, and we all walked out. As we did, Antonio came in from the SUV. He saluted Oliver and ran into the house.

"I love a happy ending. Don't you, Layla?" he asked.

"Yes, Sir."

We hopped into the SUV and rode to the biggest house I'd ever seen.

It had thirty-six bedrooms, many bathrooms, a large kitchen, and a staff/chattel dining room. Oliver made only minor distinctions between chattel and staff. There was a formal dining room and living area, an entire wing devoted to Oliver's offices and business center, a whole section of the second floor for his bedroom and gym, a small room, again the size of our house in Alabama, that the overseer told me was mine between the gym and Oliver's bedroom, a library with hundreds of books, a security center and what I was to find out was my classroom. Most slaves slept two to a room, and staff had their own rooms. I had my room because of my relationship with Oliver and his direct ownership of me.

Behind the house was a large barn and a bunkhouse where the farmhands and what Oliver called the huasos lived. Huasos are Chilean cowboys, like Gauchos. There were maybe 200 of them on the grounds. They filled the barn with all kinds of horses. My overseer, Julian Halconero, was a tall and imposing man; he managed the entire household. He'd once been a general in the Chilean Army and now pretty much ran things for Oliver here. I wasn't sure whether he liked me. "Mr. Ramirez wants you to ride the property with the huasos for a few weeks. We need to find you a horse and clothing. Also, while you're gone, we'll make you proper assistant's clothing. Mr. Ramirez's seamstress will come over later today to take measurements." He handed me some pants and a shirt and told me to put them on. I looked around for someplace to change. He huffed and said, "Layla. You understand what you are, correct?"

"Yes, Sir." I undressed. He regarded me clinically and then waved his hand in the air, a signal to hurry up.

"Another thing. Everyone knows you are Mr. Ramirez's, let us say, project. No one will touch you. And you should not try to entice anyone."

I colored bright red. "Why would you think I'd do that, Sir?" I asked.

"You chattel are always trying to ingratiate yourselves, that's why," he said.

"Not me, Sir. Never. I am as loyal as you are."

He took a step back and smiled. "I may have you wrong. Mr. Ramirez said you were unique, and it looks like he's right. As always." He reached out and ruffled the hair on the top of my head, then plopped a huaso cowboy hat on it. "There. Now you're ready for an adventure. Let's find you a horse." Ruffling the top of my head seemed to be a thing with these folks. I was beginning to like it.

An hour later, I'd been given a horse, a beautiful mustang, small enough for me. I'd ridden it around the corral getting help from the huasos I'd be traveling with; they trained me on how to take care of it, saddle up, curry it, and so forth. It turns out, none of the huasos spoke English. I was going to get Spanish immersion training, I guess. Julian handed me a set of saddlebags with some additional clothing and a bedroll. Enough for two weeks, he told me. I wasn't worried. At home, I wore the same clothes for two months.

Oliver came down on Leonado, a large Rocky Mountain Horse, with Elvira on her horse, Gracie, a beautiful Arabian, just before we departed. There was another woman with them. She turned out to be the seamstress, and she took me into a stall in the barn and made me strip so she could measure me. When she was done, she packed up her things and left. Oliver told me to have fun and learn as much as I could about my new home and his language. He gave me a peck on the cheek, and we left. Elvira rode along with us for a while as we headed back toward her home.

"So, what do you think?" she asked.

"I'm overwhelmed. A little over a day ago, I was on an auction block, and now I'm here. I can't believe it."

She smiled and said, "There's much more to come. Observe and learn. By the way, I saw what was on the passport, but I've decided among us to remain Elvira. I've been that far longer than I was, Elizabeth. Be safe, my little girl." She turned and rode away, back toward her new home.

The two-week trip ended up being more like three. We rode out along the fence line to the east into the lakes, stopping several times to repair sections of fence that had become damaged. I surprised the men by pitching in to help make the repairs. I became pretty good with a posthole digger and enjoyed the physical exercise. I went to sleep each night, in the middle of the huasos, sore and exhausted. They were very friendly to me and respectful. I slept well, enjoying being outdoors in an unfamiliar environment, different from boggy South Alabama. We made a circuit of the property's perimeter, spending several days along the shores of Riñihue Lake. The lake had a lot of history associated with it.

After the Great Chilean Earthquake in 1960, a large landslide threatened the dam on the lake. If it had collapsed, that would have flooded everything downstream, including the city of Valdivia. Brave workers opened a channel, and that lowered the lake to more normal levels. It is a beautiful area. Mountains, blue skies, and white, white clouds were dazzling.

We arrived back at home early in the morning after pressing day and night for two days on horseback. All our butts were sore, but this was an extraordinary experience—the best for me, ever.

"You look wonderful, little girl," said Oliver when I walked into our rooms.

"Thank you, Sir. I need a shower or a hot bath, though," I said.

"Let me draw one for you, and then I have a proposal to make to you."

He drew a bath and added some smelly salts to it he said would relax my muscles and heal my butt. He walked out as I climbed into the tub. I didn't know exactly what to feel about that. Equal measures of disappointment and relief. I thought about how much of each for a few seconds and then asked, "Are you busy?"

"Not really." He appeared in the doorway, naked. "I've actually missed you."

⌐⌐⌐⌐⌐⌐⌐

They could recycle the water in the tub to keep it hot, so we stayed there for a very long time. "So, my proposal," he said. "I need to do some business at a place called Termas Geometricas. I wanted to make that your first appearance as my personal assistant and take a little time to do some more soaking in the wonderful springs there."

Figurehead

"I'm not sure that I'm ready for that, Oliver. I just spent the last three weeks playing huaso. I'm getting the language, I think, but I'm pretty sure that it's not the same as what you use in business," I said.

"The good news is that this meeting is entirely in English. All the people there are from the U.S. or Great Britain. You'll be fine. Are you hesitant because of that?" He pointed to my collar.

"A little, yes," I said.

"Well, remember what you are, dear girl. That will help build confidence," he said.

I wasn't sure about that, but he was adamant, and I was his, so I knew there was no alternative but to go. I was also interested in seeing more of my new home country. We left the tub, looking like prunes despite the spices and soaps in the water, and went into the bedroom. "Look in your closet," he said, pointing to a closed door across the room. "There is a door in your apartment that opens into it as well."

"Oliver, is this for me?" I was startled by the clothing. There was everything from gym clothes and casual wear to formal outfits. I'd thought I would get a couple of business suits, but this was too much.

"Who else would it be for? I've never worn a dress. Do you like them? My seamstress has worked hard while you were gone. I told her I wanted to dress you appropriately as my assistant for whatever situation I'd put you in. You'll note that all the clothing is in the blue of my staff and shows off your collar, so everyone knows what you are. I expect that this will make some tongues wag."

I blushed and looked down at the floor.

"Did I offend you, my dear?"

"No, Oliver. This all is too much, and I'm still struggling with my status. On the one hand, you treat me like a lover and a friend and on the other like I'm a possession."

"Well, you are all three of those things. I'd say, 'Get over it,' but I don't want you to be hurt. I guess, on balance, what that means is that you are three-quarters friend and lover and one-quarter possession. Can you live with that?"

"Yes, Sir. I can. It'll be a struggle for a while, though."

He huffed at my use of the word Sir but smiled kindly and said, "Put on a T-shirt and a pair of shorts and come with me."

I did, and we left the bedroom. We walked for several minutes toward one of the service areas that I'd not explored, and that turned out to be a barbershop/beauty parlor. Two tiny women came over to me, took me over to one of the barber chairs, and sat me down. He said something to the women, and both giggled and replied. "What did you say to them?" I asked. "What language were you speaking?"

"It's called Mapudungun. It is the language of the Mapuche who live nearby," Oliver said.

"I told them I knew it would be hard to make a silk purse from this sow's ear but that they needed to try," and he pointed to me. "I will come back for you later. We have a drive and dinner at the springs tonight. Meetings start later and will likely run all night."

Figurehead

They worked on me for a couple of hours. I'd never had a manicure or pedicure before. The pedicure made me giggle and twist in the chair. I hated people touching my toes. Every time I wiggled, one woman would slap my leg and tell me to stop fidgeting. When they'd finished, they had painted my finger and toenails a lovely shade of red. I'd never had my nails done, much less been fussed over by two women like these.

But they weren't done with me.

I was led over to a large sink and made to sit down, so my head was over it. They shampooed my hair and then began doing some other things that smelled awful. I didn't know what they were doing and wished that Oliver could talk to them for me. I heard a noise at the door and saw Elvira standing there. "Thank God you're here," I said. "I don't know what they are doing to me. It smells awful."

"You've never had a perm before, have you?" she asked.

"No.... We didn't do that kind of thing at my house."

"Well, that's what they're doing."

She spoke to the women for a few minutes, said "Ah," and then turned back to me. "They're going to give you tight curls and then braid them together. It'll give you a bit of the native look to go along with the nice tan you got running around the property. I bet Oliver wants his visitors to think that you're some native girl he's shacking up with. Who knows what they might say to you?"

"A spy. Cool," I said.

She smiled and said that she'd be back in a while.

The women worked for another couple of hours on my hair, curling it, weaving it into many braids, and adding small shells and pieces of metal to make it sparkle. As I watched my transformation, it impressed me. I didn't look fifteen anymore. Still young, but definitely not fifteen.

Elvira came back and looked me over. She said something to the women. I told them they had made me look beautiful, and I thanked them very much. Elvira walked me back up to my apartment, where someone had laid out an evening gown. Two packed suitcases sat nearby. "Let's get you dressed," she said.

The dress was beautiful. A deep shade of blue and cut low in the front and back so that my collar was in full view, along with what Elvira called my other assets. As I looked at myself in the mirror, I thought there was much more to be concerned about here than the collar. The clothes left not much to the imagination. When Elvira finished, she put me in heels. I stumbled around on them, showing that I didn't know how to walk in them. Even in school, I struggled with this part of my poise education. "Okay. We don't want you falling flat on your face in your first outing." She opened the suitcases and poked around until she found a pair of dark blue flats. "Put these on. We'll get you some practice another time with the heels."

"Lovely," said a voice from the door. Oliver, looking handsome in a black suit. Elvira walked over to him and adjusted his tie. She gave him a peck on the cheek and then left us. "I could eat you," he said. "Heels a problem, country girl?"

Figurehead

"Yes, Sir. Elvira said we probably wouldn't want me to fall flat on my face. She said she'd teach me to wear them another time."

He smiled and held out his arm. I was way beyond my depth and comfort level, and he saw that. He came over and took my arm and placed it in his. Two men went into the apartment, took out my suitcases, and then got his as we walked away. They loaded us and our belongings into an SUV, and the usual party of three cars moved toward the northeast gate where we left the property.

He handed me a folder. "Read this as we're driving and ask any questions."

The file contained information about the two companies and the executives we were meeting. They were looking for Oliver to make a substantial investment in their operations. While most of the financial information was Greek to me, I sensed that both companies were in big financial trouble. Profits were down and going down further on a year-to-year basis. It looked like shareholders were selling their shares and leaving the companies as well. Bailing out as it was.

The men we were meeting were both the company CEOs and their CFOs. I wasn't a complete idiot; I knew what those letters meant. The British Company, Lancashire Electronics, based of course, in Lancashire, England, manufactured electronics used in the nuclear power industry to monitor the internal processes of the plants. They'd recently innovated a series of non-hackable control systems in partnership with the other company, "Powered Security, Inc." based in Cleveland. The bios of the executives were interesting. The Lancashire CEO was a technical nerd named Newell. He'd trained at Oxford and done a post-doctoral fellowship—whatever that was—at MIT. I'd heard of both schools and knew them to be pretty good. His CFO, Larry Ray, was American placed there by the backers of Powered Security. He, the Powered Security CEO, Lex Drannon, and CFO, James Lito, looked like bankers in another life, which meant, even to someone like me, that they were looking to make a killing and then cut and run. Much like what had happened in the U.S.: rape and pillage and then disappear with other peoples' money.

There also had been a harassment complaint against Drannon and rumors of several others. He looked like trouble. I told Oliver what I thought. "My conclusions as well. I would like to help Lancashire, but I'm not sure that we will do that. I want to get Newell apart from the others to see if we can work out something. Can you keep the others occupied?"

I had a feeling it might come to something like this. Just not this quickly. "What do you want me to do, Oliver?"

"Well, certainly not what you're thinking, and your face is showing. You're mine and mine alone. I do not turn my staff or chattel out like you're thinking. Just be nice to them and report back to me. I want to know if Drannon tries to make some moves on you. If he does, let me know immediately. I will deal with him."

"Okay. I will, Sir. But I can also take care of myself."

Figurehead

He smiled at me and put his hand around the nape of my neck, and cradled it. "I keep forgetting how strong you are, but it would be a criminal offense if you were even to defend yourself. Chattel must give themselves to freemen as they desire you. Your only protection from that is your status with me. Any person who'd scan you to see your availability would see you are not. If someone tries to force you, you cannot fight. Let me do that for you. I am there for you. And this is how," he said and reached into his pocket. He pulled out a small box and opened it. Inside rested a jeweled pendant. "This is for you to keep and to wear always, well, unless we're in bed or working out. The stone is called Alexandrite, and it is scarce. Like you. It goes nicely with the outfit and your eyes. The setting contains a panic alarm that will signal me and my security that you need help. Just press on the back, and I will come running. Remember. Do. Not. Fight. Even to defend yourself."

"Yes, Sir."

We talked off and on for the rest of the ride. One thing that struck me, and I mentioned it, was the condition of Chilean highways compared to ones in the U.S. "Yes. Again, it is sad what has happened to your country. I went to college in the U.S. before everything came apart, and things were so different. What happened to you was a lesson to all of us to protect what we have."

We finally arrived at the hotel at the springs. It was a nice place, the little of it I could see in the dark. The hotel staff took our things directly to our rooms, and others conducted us into a private dining area where the guests were already situated. The little bios in the folder in Oliver's pack that I had now slung over my shoulder must have been very recent as the photographs looked like we could have taken them today. Oliver greeted all of them warmly and introduced me around as his personal assistant, Layla Ramirez.

"You have a chattel as your personal assistant?" asked Drannon, looking at me like a wild dog might at some prey.

Oliver paused, letting the vulgarity of the statement sink in for a moment. "I bring on the best person for the work I need to be done, regardless of station. Layla is that. Shall we have some wine and sit down for dinner?" he said coldly.

I was seated between Oliver and Drannon. Oliver sat next to Newell. The two CFOs were next to their CEOs further down the table. They served wine to all but me.

"Drinking age here is 18," Oliver whispered to me. I smiled at him as they brought me a Coke. "It has real ice in it," he said with a quiet laugh.

The conversation was light and very pleasant, well, almost pleasant. Drannon kept asking me uncomfortable questions about my home and family, my schooling, other experiences, and so on. How old I was and how long I'd been chattel. He was especially interested in the process of acquiring and marking chattel. He didn't ask me how they did things. Instead, he asked questions like, "Is it true that you're branded with your chattel number? Is it true you've been bar-coded?"

Figurehead

He'd clearly read up on chattel-slavery. "I want you to show them to me right now."

I was honest with him but wondered what he was doing and leaned forward so he could see the barcode on my neck. Could it be, he thought, chattel liked to be debased and that he was giving me something I wanted? I thought this was all about showing how powerful and smart he was, most likely. Finally, the dinner was over. "Would you like to take a walk out to the hot spring, Layla?" he asked. I looked over to Oliver, and he tilted his head toward me and mouthed, "Please."

"Certainly. That would be very nice," I said.

We left the table and followed signs out of the building that led us to the springs. As we got closer, the man disrobed. "Would you like me to help you strip?" he asked.

"No, Sir. I will not be going into the water."

"My understanding is that chattel is supposed to do what a freeman tells them to do. I just gave you a command. If you refuse, I may beat you, I believe, here in Chile. There is nothing that Mr. Ramirez could do about that. I would be within my rights."

I reached up to my throat in a gesture that I hoped he interpreted as being fright. I pressed the back of the pendant, and I heard a soft click.

"Now, strip." He pulled his belt out of his pants.

I assumed he knew what he was talking about on the Chilean chattel law. I figured something else to learn. I bent down to loosen my shoes. I heard the whistle of the belt in the air and felt it slice across my back. "Stay bent down like that. I am going to whip the you-know-what out of you, chattel-whore." I heard the belt coming at me again, and I lowered my body so that it glanced off the tops of my shoulders. "You're supposed to take this. I'll report your disobedience, and you'll be lucky if I don't come away from this owning you." I raised my body back up and heard the belt come at me for the third time. It burned like the previous stroke. I readied myself for a fourth, but it never hit me. I heard a sound behind me, and there was Oliver, with Drannon's belt wrapped around his throat. The man's eyes bulged out as he struggled to get a breath. Oliver was staring right at me but didn't seem to be seeing me.

"Stop, Oliver. Please, stop," I said.

"I failed to protect you. I failed to protect you," he said but came out of the blackout or whatever it was that he was in. He released the man, who fell to the ground at his feet.

Drannon looked up at Oliver and said, "I'm going to get you for assault. Will own you... and her, that whore."

"Look up," Oliver said, and the man did. Hovering about ten feet over our heads was a small, black drone. "That cap-tured all that happened here tonight on video. Everything. I am sure my chattel's resistance will be deemed appropriate given that I have never given her permission to share herself with anyone else, and we can look, but I bet you never checked her barcode. No, I will own you, Drannon." He looked down at his watch and said, "No, I actually do. You're fired. Chilean security services will see that you never return to our country." Two black-suited men came out of the darkness and took Drannon away.

"He will not bother any woman ever again," Oliver said.

"Oliver, what are you doing?" I asked.

"Something that someone should have done with him years ago. You are not to think about that man again, ever. Now, turn around." He looked at my wounds and the welts that were forming. "I am so sorry, Layla. I failed to protect you."

"Oliver, you protected me. You protected me from me." I showed him the knife that I'd taken from the dinner table when Drannon invited me out with him. He took it from me and threw it into the undergrowth, and smiled at me. We walked back to the dining room. It was a hive of activity. The two CFOs were in discussion with Luis and several men that had come with him. When he saw me, he smiled, came over, and kissed both cheeks.

"It is so good to see you, Layla. You look wonderful. A month on horseback did you well." He walked back to the men, and Newell walked over. "Mr. Ramirez, I want to say that I had not expected what's happened tonight. I'd thought I was just going to end up further into these people. Your acquisitions of both of us will ensure that we survive. I couldn't be more thankful."

"I am happy to help Dr. Newell. You have wonderful technology and ideas that I want to see operationalized. We will do very well together. I'm afraid, though, that I'm going to have to prevail on you to take on the leadership of the new company we'll be forming here in the next day. Mr. Drannon had to leave the country for an emergency and won't be returning to the company. Will that be all right? You will report to Mr. Hernandez, and he will make sure that you have all the support you need. I want you to stay focused on the science. Leave the business to Luis."

When Newell walked away, Oliver turned to me and said, "Quite a night. You did well, young lady."

"I don't think I did anything, Oliver. Got whipped and almost raped, nothing else. Aside from maybe almost killing a man. All firsts for me."

"You'll get a lot of them with me. You helped a lot. What I needed was time for Luis to purchase the two companies, and you occupied that pervert so we could do it. I'm sure his partners will be glad that he's gone, too. You kept your head on your shoulders and did what I asked you to do. I failed to protect...."

"Okay. Stop that. I agree to stop being the way I am if you'll stop that. You're never going to be able to protect me from everything. So don't make yourself crazy."

"Okay. But are you still my chattel?"

"Of course. I kind of like it."

"Good. How about the springs, then? There are twenty-one of them, both hot and cold. The architect who designed this place is a family friend."

"Was that an order?" I asked. "I live to serve you."

He stopped and smiled at me. "And I, you. As much as I can order you to do anything, I think." He wrapped an arm around me, and I winced. "Sorry. Let's start with a cool pool." We walked up to our rooms, actually adjoining rooms, changed, and went down to bathe. Luis found us hours later at nearly 2 AM.

"Work's all done. The papers are being drawn up as we speak, and you should be able to sign them later today," Luis said. He looked over at me.

"Say anything you would say to me to Layla. She's a part of the family now."

"They found Drannon dead in his room at the hotel he was staying in nearby. The police are saying it was a suicide," said Luis.

"Very sad. He had no family, correct?"

"Correct, Sir."

"Then send a condolence to his former partners and tell them it aggrieves us we lost such a talent," Oliver said. "Care to join us?"

The three of us sat in the springs for the next two or three hours and then went in for breakfast. Oliver signed the documents, thanked all for their skilled work, and then we went up to our room. I wanted to ask about Drannon but decided that Oliver would tell me what I needed to know. Better not to poke around, I concluded. I'm glad I had him to protect me.

We returned to Oliver's home and settled into a routine. I got up very early every morning and made a pot of coffee for him and me; we drank in bed or on the terrace overlooking the paddock. After the coffee, we went over to the gym to work out for a couple of hours, spotting and pushing each other as we exercised. I built muscles I didn't know existed. We then took showers or bathed and then went to work. I had a small office right next to Oliver's. I managed his schedule and sat in on meetings and videoconferences. As my languages proficiency developed, Oliver allowed me to be equal in company business. I played wallflower during meetings with outsiders, at least initially. In the afternoons, I studied. We dined together every night and then went to bed. It was never dull.

We frequently traveled for business and now and then for pleasure. Oliver had an American friend who ran a sport fishing resort in Belize. I learned how to make chum—got the nickname of Chum Queen—and fish for bonefish and other large Caribbean fish. We spent a lot of time with Oliver's friend. Oliver was part owner of the resort. He told me once that when the U.S. collapsed, the man lost all his savings. That was when Oliver jumped in to help.

Traveling as a chattel slave was never dull. Most countries recognized us as property, and as long as we stayed with our owners, we could move about freely. Some countries didn't accept chattel-slavery, and I could only travel there with a special visa or to have a genuine passport. I could never leave Oliver's side while we were there, and I could not be out in public, even with the special visa. Interestingly, most of the countries that had outlawed chattel-slavery had been the most prominent promoters of it at one point. Hypocrites, I thought.

Figurehead

The last group of nations was the old Middle East countries. After the fall of the U.S., factions in the major powers had risen or taken firmer control and expanded into or annihilated their opponents. Without the U.S. looming over these countries, a nuclear war occurred, and vast swaths of the area would be uninhabitable for thousands of years. The Middle East had divided into three antagonistic units: an expanded Israel, a Shiite country called Pan-Arabia, and a Sunni country called Greater Syria. Because of my former status as an American and current status as a chattel, Oliver was concerned about my reception there, so when he had to travel there for business interests, he traveled with Luis and several members of his security. He asked me what I wanted to do while he was gone, and I said either to make chum or be a cowgirl. He generally left me making chum, saying that he loved the stench on me for the weeks after he returned. I didn't think I smelled too bad, either, honestly.

‑‑‑‑‑‑‑

Over the next few years, I took a series of remote classes at the Pontificia Universidad Católica de Chile, where I learned to speak Spanish, German, more French, a little Italian, and even Mapudungun. It turned out that I had a talent for languages and loved to learn. I learned about business and eventually got a bachelor's degree in language and international business and then a master's degree in International Business. I'm now studying computer sciences. Oliver wants me to get a doctorate in computer sciences and to eventually lead that division of his companies. I think about the opportunities I've had opened to me a lot and wonder what happened to my family. I've been tempted to inquire several times but always decided that was a door I didn't want to open.

More years passed. When I turned twenty-five, Oliver had a milestone birthday party, he called it, for me and a special gift. He wanted to take me on a European vacation. That meant something special. He took me to get a genuine passport in my old name.

"Oliver, I need a favor."

"What's that?"

"I want my passport to say, Layla Ramirez. Not my old name. I've thought a lot about this and talked to Elvira about it as well. I want to remain yours, even when I'm 35."

"That's a long time from now, Layla. Who knows what you might want then?" he said. "You might not want to stay with the old man that I will be by then."

"You're right, but right now, I want to remain yours. Maybe later, things would change. We can deal with that when it needs to be dealt with. I can't imagine that would happen, Oliver. You've given me so much I want nothing more than to be your possession for good," I said.

"Huh. Okay. I was going to do this when we were in Europe, but I guess I can do it now. Wait here. Do not move, Chattel."

He disappeared and returned a few minutes later. He had a small package in his hands.

Figurehead

"Another pendant?" I asked, fingering the one I had worn since that time at the springs—except in bed, of course.

"No. Open it."

I did. In it were two rings. One was a large diamond ring and the other a wedding ring. "The diamond was my mother's, and I had the wedding ring made in the same style. If you say yes, then I'll let you make a wedding ring for me. A style that you would like."

"Are you directing me to marry you, Oliver? If you are, then I don't have anything I can say other than yes," I said with a small smile and a tear running down my cheek. "I live to serve you."

"And, I, you. I'd hope you're saying yes because this is something that you want."

"Of course, it is. I can't think I want anything else I want to do more but to be with you for the rest of my life as chattel or your wife."

And so, we were married, and I went to Europe for my twenty-fifth birthday as Layla Ramirez, wife of Oliver Ramirez, and still wore my collar. Proudly. Jewelry now.

The End